MIST OPPORTUNITY

MARC BREMAN

BOOK THREE OF THE CRYPTIC CHRONICLES

Published by Lager Than Life Books.

Paperback ISBN: 978-1-9997337-8-0
Hardback ISBN: 978-1-7396650-0-5
eBook ISBN: 978-1-9997337-9-7

This book is a work of fiction. Names, characters, places, and incidents either are products of the author's imagination or are used fictitiously. Any resemblance to actual persons, living or dead, events, or locales is entirely coincidental.

To the Magnificent Seven guitarists who shaped my world,
in alphabetical order
(we must be democratic):
Allan Holdsworth
Steve Howe
Wilko Johnson
Leo Kottke
John McLaughlin
Jimmy Page
Stevie Ray Vaughan

YET MORE INTRODUCTORY WORDS

I'm not sure what made me set the beginning of these stories in December 2006, rather than the present day, currently January 2022, but I'm very glad I did.

That decision has exempted me from the dilemma facing many writers today, that of whether to acknowledge the all-pervading influence of COVID-19, or use the role of a purveyor of fantasy to justify pretending it never happened. I imagine I would have taken the latter path, avoiding the inconvenience of having Holly and his friends running around in masks. Social distancing would also have made most of the events in the book difficult, if not impossible. And having them all suddenly trot off to have their thirteenth booster shot would have played merry hell with the narrative. Fortunately for me, we'll never know.

If I sound unduly flippant, I can only apologise. I haven't lost anyone close to me to this dreadful virus, and the various lockdowns have meant this book has appeared a lot sooner than expected. But I am acutely aware, and appreciative, of how lucky I've been.

Anyway, a decidedly healthy Kia is tapping me impatiently on the shoulder – another tale, another song – so it must be time to get going.

THE GRID

CHAPTER ONE

'Heavens to Betsy! It's the end of the world!'

Captain Persona was standing in the same place Holly had been occupying a few weeks before when he'd caught sight of his friends busking. It was only at this close distance that the captain could believe the devastating information his eyes were giving him – surely some malicious fabrication on their part, a carefully crafted illusion that they would whisk away at the last moment for maximum comedic effect. But in the event, they were as blameless and helpless as the rest of him, the proximity merely showing in more detail the scratches and dents in the panels of second-hand plywood and the fraying around the screws that held them in place.

The pub was boarded up. The Luminous Steed was wearing plywood blinkers.

He turned open-mouthed to Baron Nonentity, keen to revel in a shared sense of outrage, but the baron merely looked up from the newspaper he was holding in front of him, surveyed the scene calmly, and located the sign he had expected to find.

'It's only closed for renovations,' he said, turning his attention back to his paper.

'Well, maybe so,' conceded the captain, his indignation

refusing to diminish, 'but it's closed now.'

'Well, it would be,' the baron said, absently. 'It's only nine o'clock in the morning.'

Their busking spot had been rather neglected lately. The plan for musical world domination was on hold. They both realised that, for their hostile takeover of the charts to be worth anything, their names would have to appear in brackets behind the song titles in the listings of any recordings they would make – on vinyl, in the captain's dreams. As he would say, 'You can't call the tunes if you don't write 'em.'

A feverish writing programme was initiated, more feverish in the captain's case as he would conscientiously discard anything that was veering dangerously into cheese territory. The only exceptions to this rule had been the songs "Soft, Hard Or Blue", and "Whichever Way You Slice It", both of which he considered sufficiently ambiguous.

The baron seemed to be taking a lot longer on his few, rather more off-the-wall contributions, but that was only because he was actually spending most of his time planning the concerto for two guitars and chamber orchestra he had mentioned to Holly. He had sorted out the instrumentation – discounting the kazoo, despite the captain's enthusiastic recommendation – and the two principal themes, one of which was the melody the captain had sung in St Paul's to such devastating effect. The baron couldn't resist using it, but out of fear had decided only to deploy it in a heavily disguised form whenever it appeared, only subjecting listeners to the briefest exposure to the complete version at the end of the piece.

On this particular day, it had been arranged that they would drop in on Kia and the uncles and exchange whatever news any of them may have had. But normally the two of them spent the mornings working through ideas on their own, with afternoons set aside for collaboration, which mostly involved the baron working out the chords that would best accompany the captain's lyrics. Then, by the time evening came and inspiration was running a little dry, the Steed would invariably come galloping to their rescue. It was the threat to this safety net that was now causing the captain such distress.

'How are we to keep the wheels of this production line turning smoothly without a squirt of Bentley's?' he wheezed, almost hyperventilating.

'They do sell it in bottles in the offie across the street,' the baron informed him, his eyes still firmly on his paper.

'Oh.' The captain visibly relaxed. 'Do they? Oh, good. Hah! Well, that's all right, then.'

In complete contrast, the baron's shoulders tensed. He slowly held up a silencing hand, peering ever more intently at the crossword clue he had been grappling with.

'No,' he said, very quietly. 'No, I'm afraid it's not. You may have been right the first time.'

*

At that very moment, seated just yards away, but in his own world, Colin Holly was having an identical shiver go down his spine.

His day already had an eerie feel to it. The variety of sky was his least favourite, a grey, featureless expanse. It was cold again, after a fortnight's warm spell – at least, warm for February – but he hadn't noticed that. What he had noticed, the moment he stepped out of his front door, was that the wind had taken the day off. The air seemed to be holding its breath. Holly was aware of his own breathing, which made it feel laboured.

As he made his way to the square, he remarked to

himself how typical a Sunday it was – few cars, fewer passers-by, everyone having a lie-in. He had to check with the date on the paper he then bought to confirm that it was actually a Wednesday.

It also told him that it was Valentine's Day. For the first time in sixteen years, the fact gave him a warm feeling, rather than the usual sadness and resentment. On two occasions in the past couple of months he had conjured up an image of his late wife Anna that was so vivid he was sure he could have reached out and touched her, even though he knew full well that he had been dreaming.

This had left him with a real feeling of her presence, which brought a comfort that was finally exorcising some of his demons, allowing him to lose himself in memories of the good times, rather than endlessly replay the nightmare of her death.

Valentine's Day had certainly provided some good times, as had anniversaries. He chuckled, as he remembered how he had at first scorned the contrived list of materials associated with anniversaries, lamenting the American influence, as he also had every Mother's Day and Hallowe'en. But in the end, he came to see the fun there was to be had, interpreting them in his own way. Paper became airline tickets to Venice. Wood became a DVD box set of a TV series featuring an actor that Anna liked but Holly didn't rate. And when copper hadn't conjured up any ideas, he found some silver jewellery instead and had his neighbour Gus's niece deliver it to the door in her WPC uniform.

The persistently uneasy atmosphere in the square wouldn't let him loiter in the warmth of these memories, diverting him instead to his usual table outside the pub, the venue for his daily conference meeting with his newspaper.

Aside from the quick glance to check the date, he wasted no time on the front page, turning straight to the all-important chequerboard and its accompanying clues. He had never been that involved in worldly events, particularly not the parochial issues this paper considered to be worthy of screaming headlines, but by now they had receded so far as to be almost invisible. The only events here that meant anything to him were all in the past, the rest of his thoughts inhabiting a different world, one of smoke and clouds.

Even the two noteworthy things that had happened to him recently were both related to this other world.

The first was when he had ventured out on one of his walks, an increasingly popular way of using up yet another day in a location where he didn't want to be. He had found himself on a street with an outdoor market he hadn't visited before, despite being only a saunter of fifteen minutes from his home.

Markets were things he had to be dragged to, on the whole, so it was no surprise that he had been drawn to an antiques shop that was lurking behind the stalls. As he'd approached it, he could see the proprietor through the window, a small man wearing a red-and-brown check, three-piece tweed suit – a throwback to the 1930s, Holly estimated. Reaching the door, he could make out that this flamboyance was capped off with a dark brown fedora, but it was only when he saw the feather jutting proudly out of the hatband that he froze, lingering just long enough for the dealer to look up before Holly turned and fled, congratulating himself on having extracted maximum awkwardness from yet another situation.

He'd turned the next available corner in case the man had stuck a curious head out of his door, then slowed to a halt. It took Holly a while to work out why that feather had tickled his memory. Then he located a description Kia had mentioned in passing of a previous Solver, a description that fitted this man like a suitably vintage glove.

This had presented him with a dilemma. Desperate as he was to be able to share these unique experiences, he couldn't really see how that would play out, marching into the man's shop, hand outstretched, proclaiming, 'Hi, I gather you too have been sucked into a parallel world that's governed by a cryptic crossword puzzle.' Besides, it was always possible that this wasn't another Solver at all, just a guy who liked to dress in clothes from a bygone era. There was no shortage of such people round there.

But that feather wouldn't let Holly rest. It was surely one coincidence too far. Nevertheless, he'd decided to file it away for another day when he had more courage. And, he had to admit, he was feeling way too possessive to want to discuss Kia and the team with a complete stranger. So he'd gone straight home. Since then, that courage had still not materialised.

The other event occurred when his curiosity as to the identity of the Compiler got so great that he finally had the brainwave of ringing the newspaper to find out who set their crosswords. The worst that could happen was that they might refuse to divulge such information.

This involved remembering that he had a phone. He couldn't think back to the last time he'd used it. After Anna's death, concerned colleagues, soon to be ex-colleagues after his departure, would call to check up on him. In time, this dwindled until it was only ever his mother at the other end of the line, always with the same admonishments to stop drinking. Even in his state, it hadn't taken him long to notice when these calls stopped as well. It turned out that his mother had been diagnosed with bowel cancer, had refused any treatment and hadn't mentioned it to him. After that, the phone had fallen into complete disuse, nothing in, nothing out.

But that day he had managed to find it, and the number

of the newspaper switchboard. He had agonised over which department to ask for, thinking it unlikely that puzzles would warrant their own. Then again, he thought, there were pages and pages of every sort of word game imaginable these days, and sure enough, the man there had put him straight through to the puzzles department, where he was informed that no-one there had ever met the compiler of the cryptic crossword and that the grids and their clues arrived by post, accompanied by an invoice that was paid directly into the man's bank.

But they had given him a name.

CHAPTER TWO

The excitement Holly had felt at gaining this information and the prospect of trying it out on his new friends was now draining away fast. The same two clues that had tensed the baron's shoulders were having the reverse effect on Holly's jaw.

'Ultimate force breaking nail (5)' and 'Cuts page out with blade that's now in view (9)' had looked harmless enough, both men spurred on to solve the harder second clue after breaking little sweat on the first. But the initial euphoria of finally cracking it was instantly swept away as the meaning implied by the combination of the two words sank in.

Holly stared at the clues, not daring to write in their solutions, going over them several times in the hope that he'd made a mistake. Then he considered tackling some others, just as a diversion, but there seemed little point.

The daily longing to find his house full of anyone but him now turned to desperation. He felt even more acutely the frustration of having no control over the crossing between his and Kia's worlds. He was frantically replaying his previous two transitions, even though he knew he couldn't pinpoint the moments exactly, trying to think of anything he had said or done that may have acted as a trigger, when something landed next to him on the table.

It was the size and shape of a small, fat chicken, but while the pale bottom half, especially the feet, were undeniably bird, the top was covered in a dark brown fur that suggested mammal. The head reminded Holly of an otter, except for the short beak. There were lighter spots in the fur that became dark against the chest and around the top of the short legs and, just before the fur petered out, Holly could see a set of horizontal creases or folds, but whether they concealed wings or anything else, he couldn't say. He had no idea whether this thing had landed on the table out of the sky or simply jumped up. What he did know was that, far from starting and recoiling from the creature's sudden appearance, he had barely flinched. Against all the odds, the word this confusion of nature conjured up was cute.

And he knew something else. As he stared at it, while it contentedly did that avian thing of turning its head from side to side as though it were listening, it silently told him exactly what he wanted to hear – that he was no longer in his own world.

Getting up slowly, so as not to cause alarm, he murmured his heartfelt thanks at this message. Far from showing any alarm, the bobbing head seemed not only to understand but even to acknowledge this gratitude, signing off on this conversation and turning its attention elsewhere.

Holly made straight for his house. Unknown to him, had he not spent so long staring first at the offending clues and then at his new informative friend, he would have shared this journey with the baron and the captain, but by now they had already arrived and been admitted.

On the way, Holly realised that, familiar as it was, this wasn't technically his house. Although he had the keys to it, he didn't actually live in this particular version. So he decided that, out of politeness, he would ring the bell, as any other visitor would.

But this decision soon became redundant. Just as he was approaching the gate, he heard a whistle, one he recognised as the referee's whistle that Uncle Jasper used to bring an unruly team to attention. Sure enough, there was the man himself, white boiler suit and red woollen hat as always, waving at Holly, but from the very unexpected location of Holly's neighbour Gus's front door. When Holly reached him, Uncle Jasper gestured to follow him and disappeared inside.

Holly had never set foot in Gus's house. A meeting was mentioned almost every time the two encountered each other but had still not been realised.

The layout was a mirror image of Holly's house. A staircase to the right led upstairs, and a bright hallway took a sharp left turn, past the kitchen door to the lounge.

Pausing to peer at the kitchen, Holly marvelled at the white, streamlined modern units and appliances, the pale grey granite worktop and the elaborate coffee machine perched on top of it. The only furniture was a small table and chair set that consisted of intersecting, brightly coloured wooden panels that reminded Holly of a Mondrian painting.

Making his way to the next doorway, he found the lounge equally surprising. To the left by the front window was a large, off-white leather sofa of a design Holly took to be Italian. It had short, straight, chrome legs, and one side was extended so that its occupant could stretch out while watching the large flat-screen television that was perched on the wide, minimalist unit against the opposite wall. Filling most of the intervening space was a low, square, wooden coffee table. It was supported by four blocks of wood, resembling short sections of a beam, which protruded slightly above the surface of the table, and were each positioned towards one end of its side, displaying the same rotational symmetry, Holly noticed, as a crossword grid.

Uncle Jasper was standing at the far end of the room, next to a large, round, glass dining table with a base of three intersecting wooden blocks, around which stood six angular dining chairs, also of bare wood. The pictures on the wall were all abstract swirling lines and geometric shapes.

The place could not have been more different from Holly's. The only things that seemed out of place were the numerous dilapidated bags of implements, power tools and building accessories that covered a large percentage of the floor space, both here and in the hallway. Holly assumed this had more to do with Uncle Jasper than with Gus.

He felt uneasy walking so freely through his neighbour's house. He was fairly sure Gus couldn't be at home, but he nevertheless expected the old man to pop out at any minute and ask them what they were doing there. So he had his excuses ready when he heard footsteps behind him, but it turned out to be the tall figure of Uncle Gordo, who was as surprised at the meeting as he was, and broke into a huge smile.

'E-W-E!' he cried in his falsetto voice. 'H-I-G-H!'

'Er, hi,' responded Holly, finding it irresistible not to smile back.

Uncle Gordo waved Holly into the lounge.

'P-L-E-A-S,' he pleaded.

Holly nodded and entered the room, amused at how at home Uncle Gordo obviously felt.

'T-E-E?'

The offer was politely declined. Uncle Gordo settled himself on the sofa.

'Isn't this Gus's place?' Holly couldn't help asking.

Uncle Gordo looked up and shook his head, amused and puzzled.

'K-N-O-W,' he said. 'H-O-U-R-S.'

'Parents' siblings,' Uncle Jasper agreed. 'Male relatives.' As was his habit, he gave the other party time to work it out for himself. 'Uncles,' he then finished off, beckoning Holly over.

A couple of objects on the table immediately drew Holly's attention, as Uncle Jasper clearly hoped they would. The first, as far as Holly could see, was a large twig from a tree, except that it appeared to be made of frosted glass. The other was an ornament, presumably for a mantelpiece, consisting of a shallow, square frame, with sides of around six inches, surrounding a round mirror, which was slightly curved, rather than flat.

Holly found himself drawn to this object first and picked it up.

'That's amazing,' he said, moving it around, watching the reflection. 'It's hollow.'

'Concave,' corrected Uncle Jasper.

'Concave, yes,' murmured Holly. 'Amazing.'

'Amazing,' Uncle Jasper echoed, with a sceptical expression. He gently took the item out of Holly's hands and put it into one of his many pockets. 'Astonishing. Staggering. Awe-inspiring.'

Uncle Jasper's gestures left Holly in no doubt that these synonyms were directed at the other object on the table, but, try as he might, he couldn't muster the same enthusiasm for it.

It was about ten inches long, a twisted main stem with smaller branches shooting off in all directions. It rested on a transparent, rectangular tray with straight sides with a height of roughly two inches.

Holly felt he should be showing more interest.

'What's it made of?'

'Master's letters,' came the response, but not from

Uncle Jasper.

Uncle Sid had just entered the room and was clearly just as enthralled by this object as his companion, approaching it with a reverence that overruled his normally gleeful reception of Holly's arrival. Only after he had stared at it for some time did he look up and give Holly a wink and a whack on the arm.

'Restless matter,' Uncle Jasper agreed, the wonder still audible in his voice. Holly was finally intrigued.

'How does it work?' he asked.

'Domes,' explained Uncle Sid.

Holly knew this was nothing architectural.

'Modes?' was the best he could do.

The other two men nodded. Uncle Sid turned to him.

'Foiled mud,' he said, squinting at Holly as though he'd just set him a test. Holly was aware that Uncle Jasper was giving the branchlike thing on the table the same look.

Holly assumed that 'mode' was part of the answer, so tried to remove those four letters and see what was left. Uncle Sid's constant attention didn't make it any easier, especially when it acquired a degree of impatience.

'Fluid mode,' Holly suggested, eventually.

The effect was instant and audible. The previously solid object suddenly turned into a liquid, the pale grey drops falling lightly into the tray. After a few splashes against the side when it seemed to be trying to get out, the liquid settled and came to rest.

Holly joined the others in marvelling at this miracle. But Uncle Sid wasn't finished.

'Same dog,' was his next challenge, this time not able to tear his gaze away from the tray. Holly had less trouble with this solution, particularly knowing he had the right procedure.

'Gas mode.'

The liquid immediately started rising as a cloud, one that was being constantly reshaped by the currents in the air but never dissipated, remaining just inches above the table.

The trio watched the display of ever-changing forms in a trance, until Uncle Sid snapped out of it enough to finish the cycle.

'Dodo slime,' he whispered, having to nudge Holly in the ribs to make him concentrate. Holly soon arrived at the answer, as much out of logic as by rearranging letters.

'Solid mode.'

Maintaining its final shape, the contorted mass of gas instantly froze and clattered back on to the tray, looking again for all the world like a twig.

They continued staring at it, barely breathing.

'Solver, then. Only ones who can do that. Solvers.'

Holly turned at this new voice to see a man in the doorway, a man who must have been the same age as Great Uncle Sid but looked less frail. His unkempt, shoulder-length hair was an even mixture of white and dark grey. His head hung forwards, but whether from old age or because he was fixing Holly with a sad look over his half-glasses, Holly couldn't tell. Holly's deductive faculty had in fact ground to a halt on seeing that the man was wearing striped, fleecy pyjamas and navy slippers.

Before Holly could think of an appropriate response, or indeed any response, the man grunted, turned and shuffled into the kitchen.

Holly turned an enquiring look at the others, but they just shrugged their shoulders.

Forcing himself to focus on the matter at hand reminded Holly that there were bigger issues, one in particular. Giving the occupant of the tray one last admiring look, he decided to address it.

'We need to go next door,' he said, taking his paper out

of his pocket and waving it about. 'We need to work out what to do – if there even is anything we can do – or if it's too late.'

Blank looks passed between Uncle Jasper and Uncle Sid, then all the way over to Uncle Gordo still sitting on the sofa, and back again.

Holly stared at each of them in turn in disbelief.

'You don't know, do you?'

CHAPTER THREE

Kia knew and was locked in a staring contest with the barmaid at the Folies Bergère.

Great Uncle Sid had entered the room some time before, white as a sheet and, in answer to Kia's concern for him, had filled in the top line of her crossword as fast as his concern for her would allow, adding the explanatory breakdown of the clues on an empty part of the page to confirm the worst. They had then both wandered aimlessly around, unable to settle, until Kia eventually came to rest in front of Manet's painting. If she was looking for reassurance in the girl's eyes, she didn't find any.

Conceding defeat, she went and sat down on the sofa. Great waited for some sort of pronouncement, but Kia had withdrawn into herself, so he took his place next to her, making her jump.

'I'm sorry,' she smiled. 'My mind's been going places without me lately.'

He took her hand, and for a while they sat in silence.

'I knew it was going to be a niggly day,' she said at last. 'I woke up with a head full of really stupid questions. Why are there always bits of monkey nut shells on the floor by the fireplace? Why does the woman across the road always drive past her house and park in the side road? Is the

Compiler a real person or just an idea?' She looked round the room. 'And where on earth are my keys? I haven't seen them in three days.'

The doorbell rang. Kia looked anxiously at the old man.

'That'll be the uncles. Do you think they know? What if they don't? What do I tell them?'

He gave her a calming look that said yes, they would have to be told, but they would be able to cope with it and everything would be all right. She nodded her agreement, took a deep breath and went to open the door.

In the event, the breaking of bad news was postponed. The bell-ringers turned out to be the baron and the captain, and Kia could tell immediately from their expressions that they already had all the information they needed.

The three of them stood in the doorway, not knowing what to say. Unusually, it was the baron who broke the silence.

'One Across?'

Kia just raised and lowered her eyebrows in acknowledgement, turned and went back inside. The others followed her into the lounge.

'Old king?' the baron asked Great, knowing the old man's role in the team to be codes and abbreviations, both 'old' and 'king' appearing in cryptic clues to represent their initial letters, combined now to make sure he was OK. Great Uncle Sid snorted, smiled, and gave the baron a weary nod.

'So – what do we do?' the captain wanted to know.

There followed a lengthy, drawn-out discussion. The only thing to come out of it was that the captain was alone in being convinced that anything could be done, the others arguing that it was all there in black and white. Eventually, Great had enough and went off for a lie-down, waving away Kia's offer of assistance. Helplessly, she watched him leave the room, then sat back down heavily.

‘That’s all he needs,’ she sighed. ‘It’ll take a miracle to get him through this.’

Before the captain could support his positive message by describing a miracle that had actually happened to him, one that involved an underground train, a maypole and a pair of braces, the doorbell went again, the baron echoing Kia’s previous reaction.

‘Oh, dear. Do they know?’

‘Well, one thing’s for sure,’ said Kia, as she made her way out of the room. ‘We won’t be getting a Solver today.’

Unaware he’d been dismissed before he’d even arrived, but realising he wouldn’t be expected, Holly had anticipated Kia’s look of surprise on finding him at the door, but not the squeal and the lung-busting hug that followed, much to the amusement of the three uncles behind him.

‘But you shouldn’t be here!’ Kia suddenly insisted, finally stepping back and allowing him to breathe. ‘You’ll have to go back. Haven’t you…?’

‘Well, I can’t,’ Holly replied, ‘and yes, I have. But they haven’t. Maybe because they were in there. Why were they in Gus’s house, by the way?’

‘They live there,’ was Kia’s reply. ‘You didn’t think they all lived over here, did you?’

Holly hadn’t really thought about it before, but had to concede it would be a little impractical.

‘Anyway, it’s not Gus’s house here,’ she went on. ‘They’ve never even seen Gus. They can’t see your world. It started as a sort of halfway house for new arrivals, one of quite a number. They commandeered it early on. It’s very convenient, being next door. But it does mean they occasionally have to share it for a while.’

‘With that old guy in his pyjamas, for instance?’

‘Yes,’ Kia frowned. ‘We haven’t figured him out yet. He arrived not long after you were here last. Anyway, we’d better go in, if you're staying. It looks like that may all be irrelevant.'

They all trooped inside, the uncles exchanging mystified glances.

The baron and the captain were as surprised as Kia had been, but confined themselves to smiles and slaps on the shoulder. Great Uncle Sid had reappeared at the sound of the bell, and when Holly went over to greet him, the old man seemed genuinely moved, grasping his hand and nodding sadly. Holly had trouble freeing himself, and did so with reluctance, but felt the day's business needed addressing.

'We should establish,' he began, 'that we all agree on that first line in the grid, starting with "Ultimate force breaking nail", five letters. Have we all got "final" for that, "force" being an F, followed by an anagram of "nail", meaning "ultimate"?'

The only ones looking at the paper were the uncles, huddled around Uncle Jasper's copy. After a moment, they joined in the general agreement.

'The next one was a lot harder,' Holly continued, 'but not too hard for most, apparently. A nine-letter word, "Cuts page out with blade that's now in view". Nothing leaps out, especially not from the definition side, whatever that is, so start from the beginning. Coming up with a synonym for "cuts" took a while, but I figured that "page out" meant removing a P, so I was looking for a word that already contained a P, eventually deciding that "crops" would fit the bill, leaving us with "cros". After that, it didn't take long to arrive at "sword" as an example of a "blade", giving "crossword", which, while you're reading the clue, is indeed "now in view".'

He paused for the uncles to catch up. The smiles, as they followed this logic to its conclusion, vanished as they joined the two solutions together.

'Yes,' Holly confirmed. 'Final Crossword.'

The ensuing silence was too much for Great Uncle Sid, who got up and left the room again, this time at a speed that belied his age. Kia restrained herself this time and made no effort to help him.

'So, is this the end?' she asked quietly when the door had closed.

Holly shrugged.

'Does it have to mean that?' he demanded. 'Couldn't it signify something else? Or have no significance at all? And I haven't filled it in yet. Would it make any difference if I left it blank?'

Kia shook her head.

'No, fill it in. A solution like this won't be affected. And it always means something,' she confirmed. 'I would say this is pretty unequivocal.'

'Isn't that a sort of triangle?' the captain whispered to the baron.

'No,' the baron replied. 'It means there's no room for doubt.'

'Well, of course there is,' protested the captain. He addressed the others. 'We can't base a conclusion like that on just one pair of words. What if the next pair across reads "Not Really" or "Only Kidding"? Some obscure, multisyllabic way of saying "Had You There!". I wouldn't put it past this Compiler character. He's clearly about as out there as you can get.'

The light relief spread like wildfire. Uncle Sid had to stop himself breaking into applause.

'All right,' Holly smiled. 'We would seem to have absolutely nothing to lose. So here goes.' He consulted his paper. 'The next line down starts "Saw, hardly chilled", seven letters.'

'Why would a saw be chilled?' Kia asked, wearily.

'Cold saw?' suggested the captain. 'I used to get those…'

Uncle Jasper shook his head.

'Saw – witnessed – observed – noticed,' he rattled off, glad to be doing something constructive. 'Hardly chilled – barely refrigerated – not iced.'

'Neon ice,' muttered Uncle Sid, slapping his companion on the back.

'OK, "noticed" it is,' smiled Holly. 'On to the next, which is "Twice, old object turned around – interesting stuff". Also seven letters. Anything?'

Uncle Jasper shook his head. Uncle Sid just frowned. After a moment, Uncle Gordo looked up, smiling, as ever.

'G-R-A-T-E?' he suggested.

The baron had come to the same conclusion.

'Yes,' he said. 'I think this one's for Great Uncle Sid. It looks like abbreviations.'

'I think you're right,' agreed Holly. 'In his absence, we'll have to do the best we can. Let's see. "Old" can be an O, "twice" would then be "OO"? Not many words beginning "OO". Or it can be "ex".'

There was silence as they all mulled this over, until the baron made them all jump.

'Both! How about both? "Ex" and O? That's "twice, old". "Object" is usually "it", and "around" can be "ca", short for "circa", meaning "approximately", or "around". And when "it" is "turned", you get "Ex-o-ti-ca". Which is "interesting stuff".'

'If you say so,' said the captain, doubtfully. 'Oh! Hah! I see. It means "interesting stuff". Exotica.' He looked pleased, but only for a second. 'That's not the contradiction of the first line I was hoping for. Noticed Exotica. Not remotely helpful. On to the next pair?'

'No,' said Holly. 'This was the only line that was likely to refer to the first one. I'm afraid that particular glimmer of hope has gone.'

But he only entered alternate letters into the grid, just in case.

'Lots,' echoed Uncle Sid, in a faraway voice.

'Lost? Gone? Extinct? Defunct?' Uncle Jasper's tone revealed that he strongly disagreed with each word.

'I would say so,' murmured the baron.

'No, I'm with Uncle Jasper,' declared the captain. 'Why does everyone assume that no more crosswords means no more world? What if the crosswords are the only thing that is coming to an end? That would mean everything can carry on as it is, except that you lot aren't tied to sorting the world out for everyone else. You might actually – I don't know – get a life.'

This new idea circulated in silence.

'I like that,' said Kia, at last. 'I'm going with that, whether it's right or wrong. I'm not ready to join the dodos in that museum. Why should the puzzle's last day be our last day?'

At that moment the door burst open to reveal Great Uncle Sid, holding a transistor radio that could be heard mumbling to itself.

'Tritium, vanadium,' he announced, reverting, as he always did in times of stress, to his beloved chemical symbols.

Uncle Sid dutifully grabbed the TV handset from the coffee table and turned it on. The episode of *The Professionals* that appeared betrayed Uncle Jasper as having had most recent command of the remote. Uncle Sid changed over to one of the 24-hour news channels.

The presenter was standing outside, pointing at the sky as he spoke, despite the unbroken blanket of grey cloud making this utterly pointless.

'...hearing from NASA,' he was almost shouting, 'is that the comet, which seems only recently to have come into view, is travelling at around 3,000 mph and has a nucleus with a diameter of 60 miles, making it bigger than the asteroid that wiped out the dinosaurs. But we are assured that the comet is on a course that will miss the earth by 300,000 miles, which is further away from us than the moon, but only just.'

Coverage switched to a couple sitting on a sofa in a studio.

'Well, thank goodness for that,' the man chirped, staring straight into the camera. 'I don't think I'd like to be a dinosaur.' He turned to his co-presenter with a grin. 'Gail, if you were a dinosaur, which one would you be?'

Gail's answer may as well have been 300,000 miles away, for all the attention it received from the occupants of the room, who were trying hard to assimilate this new information with a combination of open mouths, wide eyes and raised eyebrows. Kia started laughing, some of the others following suit.

'This day really couldn't get any weirder,' she decided. 'But at least all we're going to get is a spectacular light show, assuming the cloud ever breaks. It would be just our luck…'

The strident tones of the roving reporter interrupted her.

'I'm just hearing from astronomers in Cambridge that the US team neglected to take the moon into consideration. It seems the comet will pass quite near it, and slingshot around it, increasing its speed considerably and…' He put his finger to his earpiece. '…and changing its course. It will now hit the earth head-on at – 00:15 tonight.' He let his arm fall by his side. 'I'm sorry, Justin. Looks like you're a dinosaur after all.'

1 F	I	2 N	A	3 L	■	4 C	R	5 O	S	6 S	W	7 O	R	8 D
	■		■		■		■		■		■		■	
9 N		T		C		D	■	10 E		O		I		A
	■		■		■		■		■		■		■	
11							■	12						
	■		■		■		■	■	■		■		■	■
13					■	14		15						16
	■	■	■	■	■		■		■	■	■	■	■	
17		18		19					■	20		21		
■	■		■		■	■	■		■		■		■	
22						23	■	24						
	■		■		■		■		■		■		■	
25							■	26						
	■		■		■		■		■		■		■	
27									■	28				

CHAPTER FOUR

'Clean slate. That's what he's going for. He's wiping the slate clean.'

Kia's assessment of the Compiler's intentions received no contradictions from anyone. They were all still mesmerised by the silent, scrolling headlines on the television screen, Uncle Sid having long since pressed the mute button. The images being broadcast were hastily assembled, graphic simulations of the comet's path, complete with its deadly deviation around the moon.

Reactions around the room were variations on a sad theme. Holly and the baron just looked stunned.

The captain's face showed his struggle to think of a way of making light of the situation, other than mumbling, 'Where's an Altitude Censor when you need one?'

The uncles generally looked dejected. Even Uncle Gordo's smile was affected, accompanied as it was by a furrowed brow. Uncle Jasper took the concave mirrored ornament out of his pocket and placed it carefully on the mantelpiece, next to piece of Intuitive Coral, in a vain attempt to provide some cheer.

Only Kia had shunned the downward spiral. She preferred anger.

'I'm not going that way,' she thundered. 'Swept away in

a wave of fire. That's not for me.'

'Fire?' queried Holly.

'There's a sodding great fireball heading straight for us, in case you hadn't noticed.'

'Fireball?' Holly echoed again, more frostily than he had intended. 'What are you – a Moomin? Comets are made of ice and dust. Most originate in the Oort cloud, a disc of – well – rubble that surrounds our solar system.' He shuddered as he heard himself say that events were once again being dictated by a cloud. 'They're dry and cold.'

'Takes one to know one,' Kia countered, petulantly. 'Either way, I imagine the result is much the same.'

After staring dejectedly at the carpet for a moment, she looked up at Holly, then round at her companions. Satisfied that they were all preoccupied by their own thoughts, she took a deep breath.

'Holly,' she began. 'There really is something you should know.'

Holly tensed, as he always did when things started turning serious.

'You've said that before,' he said.

'Yes, I know. Things looked bleak enough then, but they look a lot bleaker now, and if this really is to be our fate…'

Three loud, deliberate knocks on the front door made them all snap out of their collective torpor and look up. It was uncomfortably similar to when they had been in St Paul's, particularly for the captain, who had been the architect of them on that occasion so was on the receiving end for the first time. They were all relieved when, after a pause, the door started taking a more frenzied hammering.

'I'll get that, then, shall I?' Kia muttered.

The woman standing at the door wore a grey, plastic raincoat and faded green wellington boots. She was holding a furled umbrella, not by the handle, but in the middle, like a javelin. Framing her face was a headscarf that may once have been white.

She was looking at Kia in expectation, but of what, Kia had no idea.

'Er, no, thank you,' Kia managed at last. 'We don't need…'

'Kia,' the woman barked. 'Not having an assemblage of books under my arm does not make me any less of a librarian, child.'

Kia leaned forward and peered at her visitor more intently.

'Cordelia?'

The librarian raised her eyes to the sky.

'Great merciful heavens,' she lamented. 'The slightest adjustment in apparel and suddenly I'm the cat's mother. Are you going to leave me standing here, today of all days? You do know, I suppose, what day it is? And how little time there is left?'

Flustered, Kia stood aside and ushered the woman in. She couldn't help smiling at this supposedly subtle change of wardrobe, remembering the finery Cordelia had been swathed in at their last meeting.

Cordelia stopped in the hallway to remove her scarf and tidy her hair in the mirror on the wall. Kia was pleased to be able to pass her and enter the lounge first, as she felt some form of introduction was demanded, Holly and Uncle Sid being the only other members of the team to have set eyes on her. She cleared her throat loudly.

'The Record Holder, the keeper of the archives – Cordelia,' she announced.

All eyes turned in expectation, Uncle Sid getting a dig in the ribs from Uncle Jasper. They had all heard a detailed description of the robed matriarch astride her equine throne, so when a woman in a plastic mac poked her head round the door, confusion set in as to whether this was the genuine article.

The woman herself, though, recognised most of them, if only from hearsay, and gasped.

'Oh! You're all here, and you're really… real.'

Her eyes scanned the room like radar, resting long enough on Uncle Sid for an exchange of nods, before finishing her sweep and settling on Great.

'No,' she murmured, 'not quite all here. There's a Lady missing.'

Great Uncle Sid smiled faintly in acknowledgement, as Cordelia's attention turned to Holly, who had seated himself on the sofa next to the old man. Her eyes narrowed.

'You owe me a chair.'

'Yes, well, at least I can offer you a seat for now,' said Holly, getting up and going to stand by the fireplace next to Kia.

'Sweet of you, Kia, to give me such a grand entrance,' Cordelia said, wasting no gratitude on taking what she clearly saw to be her rightful place on the sofa and at the centre of the team, 'but unless you do something, I fear that position will soon become obsolete.'

'She's got some of her plums back, then,' Kia said to Holly, under her breath. The librarian's tone had indeed recovered some of the imperious quality it had when they'd first met her.

'Don't whisper, child,' that tone admonished. 'Most unbecoming.'

'Unless we do something,' Holly picked up on. 'You do think there's something we can do, then?'

Cordelia registered surprise, but without looking at Holly.

'Of course there is. There's always a way out. That's the bottom line.'

'I'm sorry,' faltered Holly. 'What's the bottom line?'

'I've no idea.'

'But you said it's the bottom line.'

'That's right.'

'So, what is it?'

'I've no idea.'

Holly searched for some support, but everyone looked as perplexed as he was, apart from Uncle Sid, who had a big grin on his face.

'I can manage anagrams,' the woman continued, by way of an explanation, 'but I don't do cryptic. That's your department. And I take it, from the air of unmitigated gloom, that you haven't solved it yet.'

'Solved what?'

Cordelia stood up to look Holly full in the face.

'The bottom line! The one beginning 27 Across!'

Pleased as Holly was by this revelation, he was equally intrigued to see that the Record Holder was still restricted to her horizontal vision, having to stand up to make eye contact with him. Point made, she sank back on to the sofa.

'Nigel,' she continued, 'who deals with statistics, told me that, if there's an overall remedy to something drastic in the grid, it's most likely to be found in the bottom line. Statistically speaking.'

Holly thought back to the minions in Cordelia's library and wondered again whether Nigel was the name of an individual or just a generic name for them all. This musing was cut short by the captain.

'Hah!' he erupted. 'I knew it! They both had to be in there. Top and bottom. The highs and the lows. Problem and solution. Thesis and – you know – parenthesis.'

'Antithesis,' corrected the baron.

'Exactly. Always together.' The captain folded his arms in triumph. 'Statistically speaking.'

‘Well, all right,’ said Holly, not entirely convinced. ‘If that’s the prevailing theory, then we have to give it a go.’

No-one in the room could argue with that, so he consulted his paper.

‘Let’s see, the first clue on the bottom line reads “Total twist, here in Paris, a couple of Poles becoming players”. That’s nine letters.’

There was silence, as everyone approached the clue from their own particular angle. Cordelia looked from one to another, excited to be part of this fabled process.

‘There are a lot of Poles in France, apparently,’ she commented, when the lack of obvious progress got too much for her. ‘So that’s not really much of a twist, is it?’

Disappointed at the lack of response this got, she continued.

‘Whereabouts in Paris do we think they mean? The Tuileries? Montmartre? Never been, myself. Always wanted to. Just too busy.’

Kia was enjoying having someone present who was worse at solving these clues than she was, and would normally have given the librarian free rein for the sake of the entertainment it provided, but felt now that the seriousness of the situation demanded that she step in and bring these ramblings to a halt before someone else did, probably with much less tact. She squatted to attract the woman’s attention, smiled, and patted the air while jerking her head at the others, hoping to convey that they needed quiet to work their magic. Cordelia seemed a little crestfallen, but nodded earnestly, and fell silent. It wasn’t too long before her self-control was rewarded.

‘Total.’ Uncle Jasper had decided that, definition part or not, this word was isolated enough to require a synonym or two. ‘Entire – complete – whole – full.’ There were no takers for any of these, so he started again on another tack.

'Total – sum – aggregate – whole…' Still nothing. 'Wreck – crash?'

' "Here in Paris"', Kia mused. 'Could that just be the French word for "here"?'

'Yes, it could,' Holly was happy to say. 'Which is "ici". So – Poles?'

He consulted Great Uncle Sid, who nodded solemnly.

'Knight, son,' he confirmed.

This reassured Kia that Great was back in the game, as he hadn't resorted to the chemical symbols for nitrogen and sulphur to convey the letters N and S.

'So, "a" and "couple of Poles" gives us "ans", following "ici". That would imply that "sum" was the word for "total" we were looking for, which, when given a "twist", gives us a synonym for "players", which is…'

'Musicians,' completed Uncle Jasper.

Cordelia could not contain her excitement.

'Bravo!' she shouted, breaking into applause. Kia politely calmed her down.

'We're only halfway through,' she explained. 'Each line has two words.'

Fighting his urge to laugh, Holly forced himself to concentrate on the next word.

'OK,' he announced, 'a five-letter word, "Saying German measles start first"'.

'Typical,' said the captain.

'What do you mean?' Kia asked.

'The Germans. Getting in there first.'

'Looking at the clue,' Holly ventured, ignoring the captain, 'the word "saying" looks the most likely candidate for the definition, but does that mean we're looking for a present particle, because there aren't that many of only five letters – going, being, er, vying…'

'It does look that way,' agreed the baron. 'If "measles

start first" means that the word begins with an M, being the "start" of "measles", then we're looking for a four-letter German.'

'Ending in "-ing"?' said Holly, quickly, in case the captain had any choice four-letter words in mind. 'That doesn't seem likely. All I'm getting is Kurt and Rolf.'

The room went quiet. Even the captain was struggling to find something humorous in the situation. Cordelia had lost her enthusiasm, Kia noticed, to the point of appearing quite downcast.

'You all right?' Kia asked.

'Oh, I'm sorry, my dear,' the woman answered. 'I'm not very good with illnesses, I get very sentimental, and the idea of poor little Otto here having German measles...'

Everyone turned to her, a few smiles developing.

'Well, I'm sorry if that amuses you,' she said, defensively, 'but I've not always been in the most robust health myself, and...'

Holly bent down, joining Kia on Cordelia's eye level.

'You've solved the clue,' he said, gently. 'The name is indeed "Otto", preceded by the letter M.'

After a nod from Kia, he wrote the two words in the grid.

'It's not "saying" as in "speaking" or "declaring",' the baron explained. 'It's *a* saying, as in a maxim or a proverb. Or in this case, a motto.'

Cordelia still seemed perplexed, until Holly started clapping, followed by everyone else, after which she was all too happy to abandon her attempt to understand the details and just revel in this well-deserved adulation.

'I don't want to be the one to rain on this particular parade,' said the baron, as the applause died away, 'but what does "Musicians Motto" have to do with anything?'

'Oh, you'll figure it out,' declared Cordelia, refusing to

be brought back down. 'You're resourceful. You'll find a way round it. Like you did with bringing that Robin fellow back.'

This last remark was directed at Kia, who suddenly looked mortified.

'What? Did you think I wouldn't notice?' the Record Holder went on. 'I know those archives like the back of my hand. I know when entries have been tampered with.'

She spotted Holly's puzzled expression.

'You didn't even tell him, did you? Him, of all people.'

This made Holly more intrigued, and he gave Kia a questioning look.

'No. Well,' said Kia, squirming. 'There was this boy – young man. He was really nice. His name was Robin. It was a year ago, the same day as the cloud first appeared. We got on really well. But he was part of the grid, only we didn't know that, and before we realised, the Solver wrote the relevant words in,' she looked down at her feet, 'and that was that.'

She looked round, hoping that would be accepted as the end of the story, but the expectant faces, not to mention the tutting coming from the uncles, told her otherwise.

'Anyway,' she addressed Holly, but without looking at him, 'that last time you were here, as you know, we decided we had to go and repeal some of the archives. And it was when we were in Cordelia's library and I saw the page – and I swear it hadn't occurred to me before or made me push anyone in that direction – it was only then that I realised I could repeal him as well.'

No-one said anything to break the silence she'd been dreading.

'So I did,' she said at last.

The distraction she'd been praying for came in the form of the doorbell, and she wasted no time in going to answer it.

'Speak of the devil,' said the baron, as Kia ushered the new arrival into the room.

He was a young man with fair, tousled hair, wearing jeans and a fawn leather jacket. He smiled and nodded at each member of the team in turn, clearly on good terms with them all.

Until, that is, he caught sight of Holly. His expression instantly changed to one of rage and hatred. With a snarl and a roar, he launched himself at his astonished target, grabbing him by the throat and knocking him backwards.

'Robin!' Kia called, running towards the tangled mass of limbs on the floor, just as Holly managed to raise a foot to his assailant's chest and kick him away. The attack was about to be renewed when Holly remembered his voice and his first visit.

'One Down!' he shouted.

1 F	I	2 N	A	3 L	■	4 C	R	5 O	S	6 S	W	7 O	R	8 D
	■		■		■		■		■		■		■	
9 N		T		C		D	■	10 E		O		I		A
	■		■		■		■		■		■		■	
11							■	12						
	■		■		■		■	■	■		■		■	■
13					■	14		15						16
	■	■	■	■	■		■		■	■	■	■	■	
17		18		19					■	20		21		
■	■		■		■	■	■		■		■		■	
22						23	■	24						
	■		■		■		■		■		■		■	
25							■	26						
	■		■		■		■		■		■		■	
27 M	U	S	I	C	I	A	N	S	■	28 M	O	T	T	O

CHAPTER FIVE

There was a breeze. It was cold but not freezing. There was a winter sun, feeble but comforting. And there was a view down on to a wide, green valley that snaked into the distance. Captivating as this view was, its most attractive feature was that it didn't contain a fast-approaching, homicidal young man.

Still on his back, Holly propped himself up on his elbows to find himself lying in some long grass next to a narrow footpath near the top of a steep hill that formed one side of the valley. The irregular, vertical folds in the opposite side reminded him of a barcode. Between the two sides, a couple of large, solitary shadows of clouds slithered over the undulating terrain. The way the dale narrowed, turned and vanished from sight in both directions reminded him of his own street.

Holly didn't bother standing up. For the moment, he was happy to let his eyes take everything in. The setting was just as relaxing as that ship had been in his first 1 Down – possibly more so. He wondered if that clue number always fulfilled this function, before he remembered that last time it had read 'Residual Flambé', leading them to a charred remnant of a song. He immediately heard that tune in his head, but still couldn't bring himself to hum it out loud in case the ground started dissolving beneath him.

In any case, the silence was reassuring. Pressing though matters clearly were back in the house, he was glad of the opportunity to be completely alone, however briefly. It was briefer than he expected.

'Are you all right?'

Holly simultaneously ducked to dodge some imaginary blow and spun his head round painfully, annoyed at himself as he did so, knowing full well it was Kia's voice. And there she was, crouching not two feet away from him. She must have grabbed his coat just as he'd said the clue number and hitched a ride.

'Apart from the heart attack you just gave me,' he muttered in bad grace, 'just fine.'

She smiled at him, nevertheless.

'It's good to see you again,' she said.

'Not a sentiment shared by your... friend, unfortunately,' Holly commented.

'No, apparently not. I'm sorry about that. I've never seen him behave like that. I can only assume that, as an inspiration of the grid, he's hardwired for self-preservation, having an innate desire to eliminate the biggest threat to his existence, even a year later, even when that threat no longer exists. And I suppose that must be the Solver. I can't remember him meeting one before. And he's never done that with any member of the team.' She looked coyly at the grass. 'Certainly not with me.'

This was a side to Kia that Holly hadn't seen before, and it wasn't one he felt comfortable inquiring about. But given that someone obviously important to her had just tried to kill him, his curiosity won out.

'You repealed him?' The question granted the grass a silent smile. 'Why?'

She looked at him, her eyes shining, then turned them

to the sky.

'When I first saw him, that day, over a year ago,' she began, 'it was instant. And I knew he felt it, too. There was a spark there; I could see it in his eyes.' She sighed. 'There was that damn cloud on the horizon, all set to wipe us all out, and yet, in spite of that, all I could think about was the very future that it wanted to deprive us of.'

She paused, staring off into the distance.

'We arranged to meet up the following day, and he went back to work.' She shook her head. 'And then that idiot Solver went and ruined everything by solving him. No wonder he hates Solvers. Not always their biggest fan myself.'

Holly was too keen to follow up on something she'd said before to react to that.

'He went back to work?' he asked. 'I thought he'd only just arrived.'

'Sometimes new arrivals just slot into some preordained role,' she explained. 'Like that sailor at the pub last time you were here. He knew what his profession was, even which ship he was serving on. Well, Robin's like that. He's a policeman – a detective constable.' She exaggerated every syllable of the last two words. 'What's funny about that?' she asked, sharply, seeing a grin appear across Holly's face.

'No, nothing, just a bad joke,' he apologised. 'You repealed a peeler.'

Her expression was one of disappointment.

'I knew you wouldn't understand.'

'Oh, for heaven's sake,' he protested. 'Why do teenagers always think they've invented these emotions? You think I was born this age? You think I didn't go through all this nonsense at the start of an infatuation? Sorry,' he held up a defensive hand at the angry look she was giving him. 'Relationship. But most of them do begin as an infatuation, you know, however deep and meaningful they may eventually become.'

'And how many infatuations were there for you?' Kia demanded.

'Oh, no, I started late on that particular road. I wasn't even sure I'd ever find that road until I met Anna, and then it hit me like a sledgehammer. But however right and inevitable it all seemed to me, it wasn't plain sailing. I was pretty sure I wasn't top of Anna's list. I had to pull out all the stops. And I don't have many stops, as I'm sure you'll have noticed.'

Kia held her glare for as long as she could, and then burst out laughing.

'I'm sorry,' she managed, when she'd calmed down a bit.

'No, that's fine. Honours even. But hilarity aside, I'm afraid there are more pressing matters we need to attend to. Important though your bobby undoubtedly is, for the moment, I'm far more curious to find out where we are.'

'You mean, other than in the path of a comet?'

Holly snorted.

'You know, I'd actually forgotten about that. It must be down to the charm of this location. Which makes it all the more intriguing to find out where it is.'

Kia allowed herself to survey her surroundings for the first time.

'Do you recognise it?' she asked.

'No, but the sun is as low as it ought to be for this time of day, so I don't think we're too far from home.'

Kia gave him a quizzical look.

'Were you a Boy Scout? Orienteering badge?'

Holly ignored her and took his newspaper out of his jacket's inside pocket.

'I suppose these clues might give us a clue. Let's see,

first one going down. Nine letters. "Cooler cat with its convertible is dazzling".' He looked up at the landscape in front of him. 'Well, it's not hard to see where they got the dazzling part from.'

'Robin's got a convertible,' Kia suggested. 'Do you think it's anything to do with him?'

'Unlikely, however much of a cool cat you may find him. And he's clearly dazzled you. But then it would have said "his", rather than "its".'

'What, then?'

Holly thought for a moment, studying the grid.

'We already have an F and an N, first and third,' he said. 'So, I think that's your cooler.'

'Fan,' said Kia, sooner than Holly expected. But she still looked disappointed. 'And I thought "cooler" was going to be "jail" or "prison".'

'Shame it wasn't,' Holly agreed, pulling a commiserating face. 'That would have been impressive.'

He held this expression for so long that Kia felt the need to chivvy him along.

'So? What's the answer?'

'Oh, it's "fantastic". "Fan" followed by a "convertible" anagram of "cat" with "its". Fantastic.'

'So it is about Robin, then,' Kia smirked.

'As you wish,' Holly conceded, hurrying on to the companion clue. 'Next we have "Imagine shot has some point", five letters,' he read out.

'Seems obvious,' Kia remarked. 'The sentiment, I mean. Why shoot someone if there's no point? No, I'm sorry,' she continued, seeing Holly's mouth open to correct her. 'That's frivolous, I know that's too literal, and that "point" is going to be one of the points of the compass, stuffed forcibly into a word for "shot", making a word for "imagine".'

Holly's mouth stayed open for a while before snapping

shut. Then they each found a different location on the horizon to stare at while they thought.

'I suppose,' Kia mused, 'a "shot" doesn't have to be made by a gun. It could be a camera. So "shot" could be "photo" or "snap".'

Holly heard her muttering, captain-like, testing some possible permutations.

'SnNap. SnaWp. SnEap.'

'No,' Holly hesitated to interrupt. 'It's not that kind of shot either, but only because I found the answer first, going through synonyms for "imagine". It's "dream". "Shot" is a "dram", a shot of whisky. So, as you say, forcibly stuff an E for "east" in, you get "dream".'

'Fantastic Dream,' Kia intoned. 'That pretty much sums it up for me. "Fantastic" in the sense of "surreal", rather than "wonderful". Although, of course, it can be that as well.'

'It may describe it,' Holly complained, 'but it doesn't explain it. As you say, at least two senses to the word "fantastic", and if it is just a dream, whose dream is it? The Compiler's not giving anything away, as usual.'

The beauty of the view drew them both in again, making them less interested in who its creator might be, if it was just an illusion.

Kia was about to do her duty as the team leader and rally the troop, when that troop spotted something.

'You see that big shadow moving along the centre of the valley?' he asked.

'Yes,' Kia confirmed. 'There were quite a few earlier. They're just shadows of the clouds floating by.'

'Of course,' agreed Holly. 'But the thing is, if you look up now, there are no clouds.'

CHAPTER SIX

Having found the presence of a cloud so oppressive on his previous visit, Holly was now surprised to find the absence of a cloud so disconcerting.

The disembodied shadow approached them from a distance, moving at quite a pace, and sticking to the middle of the valley. As the far end came into view, it became apparent that the ground it had vacated, previously a vivid patchwork of greens separated by a haphazard pattern of hedges, had become a uniformly flat plain of a dull beige, as though scorched. Even the occasional clump of trees had been eradicated.

'Ooh,' said Kia, and not in a good way, to Holly's mind. 'That's not a cloud.'

She left Holly dangling for what seemed to him an age, unable to tear her eyes from this scene of desolation. Eventually, she forced herself to blink several times to break visual contact.

'I'm sorry,' she said, 'but I haven't seen that before. Not for real. On telly, yes, and always in some reassuringly remote part of the world. But not with my own eyes. Or so close to home.'

She paused, long enough for Holly's impatience at this lack of useful information to reach bursting point.

'It's the Pitch-Black Army,' she said, just in time. 'One of our unsolved things. It appears occasionally, wreaks its havoc and then disperses until the next time it's needed. And that's as much as anyone knows about it. We don't know where it hides, what it's made of, what summons it. We just know…' she stared at its growing, lifeless wake, '… what it does.'

'We also know,' said Holly, 'if you'll allow me another bit of scouting, again judging by the position of the sun, and assuming that we are still in England, that it's heading south.' He glanced sharply at Kia. 'Should I be worried?'

'Oh, it's been around far too long to be bothered about a Solver,' she assured him.

She was nevertheless relieved to see the malevolent, dark shape start to sweep past them without so much as a sideways glance.

'Yes, well, on today's experience,' Holly decided, 'forgive me if I don't put too much faith in the notion of distance lending enchantment. It's more a question of familiarity breeding contempt. Speaking of which, do you think we've given your Robin long enough to remember he's a man of the law, or will he still be singing "The Self-Preservation Society"?'

'My Robin, as you call him,' Kia bristled, 'will doubtless be back on his best behaviour. All the same,' she conceded, 'I'd better stand in front of you when we go back. Just in case.'

'That's not going to happen,' Holly asserted. 'Use you as shield? I don't think so.'

She turned her back to him anyway, holding out a hand behind her. He was about to argue the point, when he noticed that she was now facing the other way from how they had arrived, so would be behind him. He turned as well, so that they were back-to-back, and grabbed her hand, confident, as he brought them home with the word 'grid', that he would be the one in the firing line.

Back in the living room, he was perplexed to find that the only hostility facing him was the disillusioned expression of the barmaid in the painting on the wall.

Spinning round, he was relieved to see his attacker sitting calmly in an armchair, nodding meekly in greeting without showing any sign of wanting to renew the assault. The detective constable was using a tissue Uncle Jasper had just given him to wipe some blood off his upper lip.

'I slipped,' he explained, in a lighter voice than his previous roar had implied, but Holly was sure Uncle Sid was nursing his right hand. Indeed, it seemed that everyone bar Uncle Jasper was showing more concern at the unexpectedly aggressive turn of events than for the young man himself. Even Cordelia had sprung to attention, umbrella at the ready.

'I'm really very sorry, Mr Holly, sir,' he went on, letting a concerned Kia take over the nursing duties. 'I don't know what came over me. I just lost it. It won't happen again.'

Before Holly could remember the last time he had been called 'sir', let alone reply, Great Uncle Sid interrupted.

'Time, velocity,' he barked, pointing at the article in question and simultaneously unmuting it.

'...seen for a long time, but the Pitch-Black Army is on the move again,' the voice-over was saying, accompanying shaky helicopter images of the same dark smudge, now crossing a flatter landscape. 'And for the first time, it's here in the UK. It was seen leaving the Peak District, preferring open countryside to roads, as usual, and seems to be heading towards London, on a course parallel to the M1.'

The reporter fell silent for a moment, before adopting a more jovial tone.

'Fortunately, despite this pincer movement of comet

and army, salvation is at hand, and this lady knows what our saviour looks like.'

The picture cut to a young woman standing in the street, a big, furry microphone held in front of her.

'Yeah, I've seen him,' she confirmed, in a soft Yorkshire accent. 'He saved us from the cloud, and he'll save us again.'

'I see. And you've come down here to London to find him.'

'Yeah. Finding him won't make any difference to what he does. I just want to be here when he does it. And I know I'll find him. I saw him on the day he made the cloud disappear – only briefly, just before he flew off, but I'd recognise that boiler suit anywhere.'

'Thank you, Camille.'

Great turned the sound off again. All eyes turned to Uncle Jasper, who looked very uncomfortable and could only shrug his shoulders.

Meanwhile, the footage returned to the marauding army, the shakiness now explained as the camera zoomed out, revealing just how high the helicopter was. It was keeping a very respectful distance. The overall effect from this altitude was a long, winding, grey line, freshly cut through the terrain, with a black dot at its head.

Kia and Holly exchanged glances.

'We've just seen that,' Kia announced.

'What?' the captain marvelled. 'Where you went just now? There was a television there as well?'

'No,' she said, calmly. 'We were – in a Fantastic Dream. That was the line starting 1 Down that took us there. Fantastic Dream.'

The uncles pored over their shared copy of the paper, eventually nodding their agreement.

'What happens,' Holly almost whispered, 'if I write that in? I mean, if this whole thing is someone's dream, and we solve it, does it all just vanish?'

'Shouldn't do,' said Kia, uncertainly. 'It's just a description of something that was already here, rather than something that only appeared this morning.'

Nervous looks bounced around the room.

'Do it,' Kia commanded.

Holly hesitated and then complied. He wasn't alone in flinching as he wrote in the last letter, only opening his eyes fully when, as Kia had predicted, nothing happened.

'So, anyway,' Kia hurried on, 'we found ourselves on a hill, overlooking the most amazing valley. Presumably that was the Peak District. It was idyllic. Until that thing suddenly marched right by us.'

'But what's it doing here?' the baron asked, almost to himself. 'It's heading in our direction, but it can't be after either of you,' he nodded at Holly and Kia in turn, 'because it had you there on a plate.'

They both agreed, relieved to have their previous reasoning confirmed.

'So what, then?' the baron continued. 'It can only be that it has something important to do today.'

'Or,' Kia suggested, 'that it's coming to prevent us from doing something important today.'

'Which would mean that there is something important we can do!' cried the captain in triumph. 'It's coming here with a purpose, and that purpose gives us purpose. It's telling us there has to be a way out!' He nodded vigorously in agreement with his own logic. 'Pitch-Black Army, thank you very much!'

'Well, of course there's a way out,' Cordelia said in exasperation. 'That's what I've been trying to tell you. That's why I'm here.'

'You mentioned the bottom line,' Holly said, 'which turned out to be Musicians Motto, which didn't tell us anything.'

'No, not that. You'd have solved that eventually, wouldn't you? Assuming you ever snapped out of this self-indulgent bout of defeatist despondency, and I'd hope you wouldn't need me for that. No, I'm here as the keeper of the archives, to bring you the solution.'

'Well?' prompted Kia. 'What is it?'

'I've no idea.'

The stunned silence that followed was only broken by Uncle Sid's unsuccessful attempts to stifle his amusement.

'What I mean,' Cordelia continued, to everyone's relief, 'is that I don't understand it. It's something Nigel came up with. He found it in the Good Book.'

'He found it in the Bible?' Holly asked.

'In a manner of speaking, I suppose. He found it in our bible, the *Principia Cruciverborum*, the book that sets out the rules of this place. Most of which,' she frowned at Kia, 'you've managed to break at some time or other.'

'Only out of necessity,' Kia assured her, winking at Robin. 'So, what is it?'

'What is what?'

'The solution you don't understand.'

'Oh, yes! I've got it here somewhere.' She rummaged through numerous pockets, muttering to herself, her umbrella changing hands several times before she found a folded, dog-eared piece of tracing paper that she flourished above her head. 'Here it is!'

She handed it gingerly to Kia, who inspected it dubiously.

'This is our salvation?'

'Yes. Well, a copy of it, anyway. Couldn't bring you the real thing. Even I'm not allowed to take that out of the library. According to Nigel, it's the ultimate "break glass in case of emergency" item, a sort of reset button, although hopefully not actually a reset button, or half of you would disappear.'

The captain and the baron had indeed already registered some alarm at the prospect.

'No,' she continued, 'it's more like restoring things to how they should be. Putting them back to normal – whatever that is.'

Something that restored normality sounded good to Kia, but she still couldn't bring herself to unfold it. She looked around the room for some encouragement. The only one to give it was Uncle Gordo.

'W-Y-E K-N-O-T?' he asked, shrugging his shoulders with a smile.

'Why not indeed,' she agreed.

She took a deep breath, opened out the semi-opaque sheet of paper and stared at it intently. No-one moved. Even Holly was rooted to the spot.

Eventually, Kia looked up at the librarian.

'And what does this mean?' she asked.

'I told you,' was Cordelia's cheerful reply. 'I haven't the foggiest notion.'

'Hah hah!' The captain could contain himself no longer. 'This keeper of the archives,' he directed at a beaming Uncle Sid. 'She's definitely a keeper!'

1 F	I	2 N	A	3 L	■	4 C	R	5 O	S	6 S	W	7 O	R	8 D
A	■		■		■		■		■		■		■	
9 N		T		C		D	■	10 E		O		I		A
T	■		■		■		■		■		■		■	
11 A							■	12						
S	■		■		■		■	■	■		■		■	■
13 T					■	14		15						16
I	■	■	■	■	■		■		■	■	■	■	■	
17 C		18		19					■	20		21		
■	■		■		■	■	■		■		■		■	
22 D						23	■	24						
R	■		■		■		■		■		■		■	
25 E							■	26						
A	■		■		■		■		■		■		■	
27 M	U	S	I	C	I	A	N	S	■	28 M	O	T	T	O

CHAPTER SEVEN

'Decibels, frequencies and a poem.'

Kia's summing up of the contents of this supposed lifeline couldn't hide her disappointment. She even turned the sheet of paper over, hoping to see something on the other side that would make it all fall into place, but it was blank.

She offered it to any takers. The baron reached her side first and took it from her. He studied it for a while, then turned to his expectant audience.

'It's a graph,' he revealed. 'Frequency along the bottom, measured in hertz, from zero to five thousand. Apart from a generally fuzzy line along the bottom, there are several definite spikes at different frequencies. The left-hand side is labelled "Loudness", and is in decibels, with zero set at the top of the highest spike.'

The captain was puzzled and went and stood next to the baron, looking over his shoulder.

'Zero at the top?'

'Mm.'

'But, doesn't that mean that anything lower than that is inaudible?'

'Mm?' The baron looked up. 'Oh. No. It's all relative. They've taken the loudest frequency as the standard, and then they've measured everything against it to show exactly how much quieter they are. Than it.'

'Oh. Oh, I see. So this one,' the captain said, pointing at one of the smaller spikes, 'is half as high so is only half as loud.'

'Yeah, no. The decibel scale is really weird. If you double something's sound level, it only goes up three decibels. That spike there, it says it's minus twenty decibels, which actually means it's one hundred times quieter.'

The captain looked around the room for an explanation, but got only sympathetic looks.

'And you know that, how?' he demanded. 'Oh yes, never mind. Past life.'

'And along the top,' the baron continued, 'is the verse "All through this hour, Lord be my guide, That by thy power, No foot shall slide". Whatever that means.'

Everyone could be heard murmuring their own versions of this rhyme, Cordelia being the most prominent.

'No foot shall slide,' she declaimed.

'Handle is lost, fool,' echoed Uncle Sid.

'You remember the Inoperable Hero from your first visit?' the baron asked Holly, as he handed the conundrum over.

Holly remembered, all too well, and what had happened to him. It was an image that had woken him up in the middle of more than one night.

'Didn't he mention something about frequencies?' the baron went on. 'Everyone connected to the grid could be identified by their frequency, or some such thing? Wasn't that what the Culprit's contraption homed in on?' Here he ran out of steam. 'Just an idea. Maybe it's connected in some way.'

'No, sure,' Holly agreed. 'That's as good a hypothesis as any other. Certainly sounds consistent with this Compiler's way of thinking. Oh, which reminds me,' he addressed the room. 'I know his name.'

He allowed this revelation to sink in, but didn't get the dramatic response he'd expected, given that they all just stared at him in silent disbelief.

'The Compiler?' Kia wanted confirming. 'You know the name of the Compiler?'

'Yes. I just rang the paper and asked who sent this puzzle in every day.' He let them dangle for a few more seconds. 'Apparently, his name's Smith. Sylvester Smith.' He regretted building this up, as he could see the feeling of anticlimax spreading from person to person. 'No, I'd never heard of him either.' In a last ditch effort to spice it up, he added, 'Sylvester W Smith.'

This generated a loud snort from Robin, which he immediately felt he had to justify.

'I'm sorry, but what's the betting the W stands for "word"?'

He searched for any evidence of a penny dropping, but in vain.

'It's my line of work,' he explained. 'I've lost count of the number of individuals we've arrested who gave their name as Joe King, or Justin Case, or Adam Sapple. Or my favourite, for obvious reasons, Robin Banks.' He shook his head at Holly. 'Sly Wordsmith? Really?'

Holly frowned, mulled it over, and had to concede to the logic.

'Fair enough,' he said. 'Well done. Sly indeed. Well, that takes us right back to square one.'

'Oh, no, it doesn't,' countered Kia. 'Half an hour ago, we were all ready to throw in the towel – all but Mr Positive Thinking over there,' she added to prevent the protest that the captain was clearly about to lodge. 'But things have changed. We've been sent a comet, which may have been intended to finish us all off, but has actually sorted out the Final Crossword question. As in, why bother wiping us all off the face of the earth if Final Crossword had already done that. So, we can assume that, without the comet, everything will go on as normal, just without the puzzles, just as the captain suggested.'

She paused, long enough for everyone to catch up.

'But even this comet, it would seem, may have a solution. It may even be in the grid. That's unlikely. It's probably more like that awful cloud. In any case, we have a lifeline in the shape of this diagram, whatever it means, thanks to Cordelia.'

The librarian, who had been glazing over a little, started and sat up.

'That's right, dear,' she said. 'And I wouldn't hang about making pretty speeches. There isn't much time. I would strenuously recommend going to the location of that Musicians Motto. My little Otto,' she added, proudly. 'Oh, and do be careful. There's something about cataclysmic events that always brings out the maniacs.'

Kia smiled and took her hand.

'We will,' she assured her. 'And thank you for that graph. We'll let you know how we get on.'

'Oh, but I'll know, won't I? If I wake up tomorrow and I don't exist?'

Nobody could argue with that logic.

'Well, my job done, then,' she concluded. 'Over to you. But before I go.' She leant forward and whispered to Kia, but loud enough for everyone to hear. 'Could I just watch you solve another line?' She gave a sheepish grin. 'I may never get another chance.'

Her childlike enthusiasm was irresistible, and contagious. Kia gestured to Holly to take the lead.

'You never know,' she said. 'It might be the one that

knocks a comet out of the sky.'

'Indeed,' said Holly. 'Well, let's see.' He skimmed through some of the clues. 'The line beginning 13 has the word "puzzles" in it, so maybe it's going to say it's not the final crossword at all.'

He raised his eyebrows at the captain, who sent an 'I told you so' look back.

'Five letters, then. "Small youngster meets sticky end." That's…'

He was interrupted by a cry from Cordelia.

'It's poor little Otto!' she cried. 'He didn't make it!'

Before Kia could go and console her, Great Uncle Sid, still sitting next to Cordelia on the sofa, gently took her hand.

'Sticky end,' he said, by way of an explanation. 'Your head. Loyal heart.'

This could easily have gone the wrong way and tipped the woman over the edge, but she stared into his sad eyes and calmed down immediately. Despite not having the faintest idea what he was talking about, she found the words comforting, even complimentary.

'That's right,' Holly joined in. 'They're all ways of depicting the letter Y – the end of "sticky", the start of "your", the middle of "loyal". Which means we're looking for a four-letter word beginning with T for "youngster" preceding that Y, and the overall meaning will be "small"?'

'Teen,' said Uncle Jasper, to the annoyance of Uncle Sid, who had wanted to impress. 'Teeny.'

'OK, "teeny" it is,' said Holly. 'Which leaves "Puzzles this writer's programme? About time". Nine letters.'

Kia looked hopefully at Robin, who just shook his head, indifferently. Cordelia had nothing to contribute to this, but wouldn't have anyway, still embarrassed by her last outburst. It was Great, still holding her hand, who made the first contribution.

'Time,' he said to her, as though imparting some age-old wisdom.

'There's a T in there, somewhere,' the baron elaborated. 'And "this writer". Isn't that the same as "yours truly", meaning "I", or "me"?'

'Are you sure it doesn't mean "Sylvester", or "Smith"?' Kia directed at Holly in a mocking tone, getting a laugh from Robin.

'All right, very good,' admitted Holly. 'No, in this case, I think "this writer's" does indeed mean "my". So, "my", then another word for "programme", containing a T, meaning "puzzles"?'

'Series,' said Uncle Jasper immediately, getting an even bigger glare from his comrade.

'My series, with a T,' Holly nodded in admiration. 'Mysteries. Puzzles. Nice.'

Uncle Sid scowled, got up, and went and stood next to the fireplace.

'So, Teeny Mysteries,' Kia said, with obvious disdain. 'That hardly seems to cover an astronomical disaster. Yeah, write it in, whatever,' she replied to Holly's tentative waving of his pen.

No sooner had he finished than she spotted something under the sofa next to Cordelia's foot. Reaching down to pick it up, she exclaimed in surprise.

'My keys! So that's where they were. Why didn't I see them before? And what are you doing?' she directed at Uncle Sid, having heard some cracking noises coming from his direction.

Like a naughty schoolchild, he held open his hand to reveal some peanuts and the remnants of their shells. He quickly threw the nuts into his mouth as though they were in danger of being confiscated, showering bits of shell on the floor as he did so.

'That same patch by the fireplace,' Kia marvelled.

'Verminous,' said Uncle Sid in his defence.

'Well, you must be nervous all the time, judging by how often I find that stuff on the carpet.' She gave Great a look of disbelief. 'That's another of my morning's niggles sorted. He'll be telling me next he knows why that woman across the road always drives past her house and parks in the side street.'

'Oh, I know that.' This revelation came from the captain. 'Yes, she was walking past the Steed one day just as me and the baron were finishing our set, and we got chatting. We got on to the subject of foibles, strange personal characteristics, often embarrassing. She said she never turned right when she was driving. Too scared. And the one-way system around here meant that she couldn't park outside her own house because then she couldn't turn left. So she has to leave the car round the corner.'

There was a stunned silence as everyone tried to accept this reasoning.

'OK,' said Kia, finally. 'That's all my Teeny Mysteries solved. Except, of course, what your contribution to this edifying conversation could have been.'

'Oh,' said the captain, cheerfully. 'I told her about that particular dance I always do when I've had too much tequila.'

1 F	I	2 N	A	3 L	■	4 C	R	5 O	S	6 S	W	7 O	R	8 D
A	■		■		■		■		■		■		■	
9 N		T		C		D	■	10 E		O		I		A
T	■		■		■		■		■		■		■	
11 A							■	12						
S	■		■		■		■	■	■		■		■	■
13 T	E	E	N	Y	■	14 M	Y	15 S	T	E	R	I	E	16 S
I	■	■	■	■	■		■		■	■	■	■	■	
17 C		18		19					■	20		21		
■	■		■		■	■	■		■		■		■	
22 D						23	■	24						
R	■		■		■		■		■		■		■	
25 E							■	26						
A	■		■		■		■		■		■		■	
27 M	U	S	I	C	I	A	N	S	■	28 M	O	T	T	O

CHAPTER EIGHT

'Otter-birds?'

Holly had gone over to the window. Everyone's apprehensive expressions had followed him, as had Kia's question.

'Yes,' he said, peering left and right, then up and down. 'That's the best description I can come up with. You haven't seen them? Plump little things, wings and all, as far as I could tell, with furry, little heads? No, well, they must be one of today's things, then. I was wondering whether they were one of your Teeny Mysteries. I can't see any now.'

'No,' Kia faltered. 'I'm pretty sure I'd have remembered them. They don't sound like they're in the same league as a missing set of keys.'

She raised her eyebrows at Cordelia, who was frowning.

'Is he all right?' she asked in her customary, strident whisper.

Kia laughed.

'Never a dull moment when he shows up,' she confirmed, in a hushed but equally audible tone. 'But the fact that he's here at all today is a good sign. He must be here for a reason. Surely the Compiler wouldn't have sent him out of the goodness of his heart just to say goodbye?'

'Well, I'm afraid that's what I have to say now,' said

Robin, getting up. 'Not that this hasn't been fun, but I'll be needed back at the station.'

He went over to the mantelpiece, where he turned and addressed the room.

'The lady's right. The maniacs will be coming out of the woodwork today. No-one's going to be worried about tomorrow, if this huge lump of rock heading for us means there isn't going to be one. We'll try and keep them at bay. In the meantime, see if you can come up with a solution. I wish you all the best of luck.'

With a cursory nod at all present and a fleeting squeeze of Kia's hand, he left the room, closing the door behind him to ensure there were no prolonged farewells.

Cordelia also made her excuses.

'Time to get the old glad rags on,' she said, 'especially if it's for the last time.'

No-one pursued the point. They all realised that, whatever the next day had in store, if there was no crossword, there would be no need for any archives, other than as a matter of historic record.

Once she was gone, they turned their attention to the graph she had left, which still meant nothing to any of them. They decided, as it consisted of frequencies and decibels, that their recently acquired music expert would be the best person to consult.

Claire was living on the other side of the square, beyond the station, opposite the entrance to the park. It was decided that the baron and the captain would go and see if she was at home, and to take her to her local café if she was, to meet up with the others who would follow shortly, after they had solved a few more clues.

Once outside, the pair looked up, hoping for a sighting of the fateful asteroid, but there was still no break in the cloud to show anything looming over them.

As soon as they were out of sight of the house, the baron stopped and turned to his companion.

'Cap, this – "reset button" thing...'

'I know,' the captain reassured him. 'If it works, it may well reset everything to a version from a time before we appeared here. In which case, we're actively working towards our own annihilation.'

'And you're OK with that?'

'Well, let's see.' The captain looked up at the sky, squinting. 'I wouldn't want to be in a world where there isn't a me. But if that reset button does get activated, and we're still here, having done nothing to help make that happen, then that's not a world I'd want to be in, either. So, on balance...'

'We go on.'

'To oblivion! And beyond!'

They set off with renewed purpose.

'Who would have thought librarians would be looming so large?' chortled the captain, effortlessly changing the subject. 'I'd rather face a comet than Cordelia, any day, even in a plastic mac. I can't imagine what she'd be like all togged up. I don't envy that Nigel. Mind you, I don't think I've ever envied a Nigel... Heavens to Betsy!'

They were approaching the Luminous Steed, still looking dark and forlorn.

'Yes, I know,' sighed the baron. 'It's still boarded up.'

'No, look, strutting about on that table!'

The baron squinted. What he had assumed to be a pigeon turned out to be larger, fatter, and decidedly hairier.

'There's a few of them!' enthused the captain. 'They must be what Holly was talking about. They really do exist. I owe him an apology. Not that he would have guessed what I was thinking.'

The baron stared at them in some awe. They, in contrast,

were oblivious to any human presence, absently pecking at whatever surface they happened to be on.

'Considering what's going on today,' the baron whispered, 'they have the appearance of some dreadful omen.'

'You're right,' replied the captain. 'They're like the Four Otter-Birds of the Apocalypse.'

Finding the creatures suddenly more sinister than cute, they made their way on to the square and past a row of parked buses, then over the railway bridge. As they passed the overground station with its flower stall outside, the captain waved at the woman busily making up bouquets.

'How do you know a florist?' asked the baron with a smile. 'I bet you've never bought a bunch of flowers in your life.'

'I talk to people,' was the captain's simple reply.

At the point where a dark, tree-lined path led off into the park, they crossed the road to the final parade before the buildings became residential. In the middle was a bookshop. To its left was a door with two bells. The one for the first-floor flat had no name, sporting instead a sticker with two connected quavers that its occupant thought was sufficiently informative for anyone who knew her.

Despite finding some suitable part-time work, Claire was still kicking her heels after readily abandoning the burnt-out shell that had been her music library. To her amazement, she had immediately acquired a small flat, one of a network that seemed to be provided for such new arrivals, but was aware that she was spending far too much time in it. She was enjoying the bustle of city life, but sometimes the contrast between that and her previous, solitary existence proved too great, and she had to hide herself away for a while.

It was into this reclusive state that the captain and

the baron intruded by ringing the anonymous bell. They exchanged concerned looks at the tearful voice that came over the intercom.

'Yes?'

'It's Cap 'n Baron,' said the captain.

'Oh, hi, guys. Come in.'

The buzzer sounded, and the pair climbed the dark, narrow staircase to the first floor, where they found the door open. They entered and made their way to the lounge, where they found Claire sitting on the sofa, staring disconsolately out of the window.

The baron was, as always, struck by how different Claire looked in urban clothes, in this case jeans and a jumper. The floaty, white dress they had found her in was all she had, so for a while she had borrowed things from Kia, being roughly the same size.

The big day had arrived when she could go on a spending spree and buy things for herself, and Kia and the baron had gone along with her – not so much invited as press-ganged, Kia for help making the choices, and the baron for his approval once the choices had been tried on. Since then, she had acquired the confidence to go alone and had developed a style of her own. This veered occasionally into hippy territory, which everyone agreed suited her very well.

Today's colourful jumper was rather at odds with her expression, but did match the red around her eyes.

The two men stood awkwardly next to her, not knowing what to say.

'You know, then,' the baron said at last.

She nodded, weakly.

'I'm not normally bothered with the news,' she said, an audible tremolo in her voice, 'especially not first thing in the morning. I prefer to get a head of steam up before I confront reality. But today, something told me to turn the radio on.'

Claire had seen a television at Kia's and found it alarming. This reaction had surprised the baron, as it didn't fit in with his theory of them all having had a previous existence. Surely she would have come across a television set before.

But he had already established that she knew about rain, French and crossword puzzles, even though none of them were to be found on the cloud that housed her ill-fated library, so maybe she had always found television alarming.

She preferred the radio. Although it was still a disembodied voice coming out of a box, there was at least the added option of music and in a variety she hadn't dreamt of.

'Sure enough,' she went on, 'there was reality with a vengeance. Within twenty-four hours, it seems, we're to be wiped out by a comet colliding with the earth. And it was all going so well; fun job, great friends, nice flat – above a bookshop, for heaven's sake. I've only just started living.' She covered her face and burst into tears. 'And it's all coming to an end. It's just not fair.'

The captain bent down and put a hand on her shoulder.

'Come on, Claire,' he said, gently. 'Granted, it's neither just, nor fair, but – it's not like it's the end of the world.'

Claire's sobbing stopped. She uncovered her face and looked up at the captain for a moment before snorting with laughter.

'That's not funny,' she insisted, against all the evidence.

'But it may be true,' said the baron, sitting down next to her.

'You mean, keep a stiff upper lip, because miracles happen?' she said, taking a tissue out of her pocket and blowing her nose loudly.

'That's not quite how I would have put it, no. Miracles

can be made to happen. After all, the day we met you, we were all about to be destroyed by a weather phenomenon that contained a military onslaught, and yet…'

'Yes, all right,' she admitted, 'we all contributed to that in our own small way, but it was mainly down to Mr Holly, bless him, so unless…'

Something about the baron's expression made her stop, and her eyes widened.

'He isn't!'

The baron nodded solemnly.

'He is.'

Claire uttered a shrill cry, and then seemed to forget how to inhale.

'And there's something else,' the baron went on, hoping to distract her into breathing again. 'We had a visit this morning from the keeper of the archives herself, no less. And she brought a clue as to how we could restore normality, whatever normality is around here. Presumably that does at least cover the removal of troublesome comets.'

'Cordelia, paying you a personal visit,' Claire breathed, having had a full account of the trip to the archives library. 'I bet she looked amazing in her ceremonial robes.'

'Oh, unforgettable,' the captain assured her.

'The point is,' the baron said, 'this clue is in the form of a graph, decibels against frequencies.'

Claire's eyes widened still further.

'Decibels?' she squeaked. 'Frequencies?'

She leant forward. The baron could feel her breath on his face.

'Is there a series of spikes?' she asked, slowly.

When he nodded, she jumped off the sofa like a jack-in-the-box.

'Show me!'

CHAPTER NINE

'B-E-E, F-O-U-R, A-T-E.'

Kia translated, for Holly's benefit.

'That's Uncle Gordo-speak for seven,' she explained, 'because it comes before eight.'

Holly could see the logic of that, so accepted it without question. He checked the grid and located 7 Down.

'Interesting,' he muttered. 'It ends in an I. That should narrow it down. "Old equipment soldiers said is an art form", seven letters.' He looked over at the homonym expert. 'Is it the "said" that spoke to you?'

Uncle Gordo nodded.

'I,' he said.

'OK.' Holly returned to the grid. 'We have…'

'Old,' offered Great.

'Right,' agreed Holly, now knowing that had to be an abbreviation, confirmed by the letter already in the grid. 'It does indeed start with an O, for old. Then we have "equipment", which is…'

'Rig,' from Uncle Jasper.

'Sounds good,' said Holly. 'Which leaves "soldiers said", which is…'

'A-R-M-Y,' concluded Uncle Gordo.

'Sounds like another word for "soldiers", which is

"army", which then becomes "-ami", giving us O-rig-ami, which is an art form.'

Smiles all round, particularly from Kia, who knew all too well that having a team didn't always guarantee such teamwork.

'On to the next,' ordered Holly, 'which is "City diplomacy provides severe reprimand", four and three letters.'

He consulted the others. Uncle Gordo shook his head. Uncle Sid was making a point of surveying the walls with a look of disinterest. Two clues in succession without a hint of an anagram was trying his patience.

'Isn't "city" usually an abbreviation,' Kia suggested, 'like LA for Los Angeles?'

Great Uncle Sid shrugged in agreement. 'New York…'

'Or NY for New York,' Kia conceded.

'I can't think of any four-letter words beginning NY,' said Holly. 'But LA's a possibility…'

'Tact!' Uncle Jasper had been looking for a word meaning 'diplomacy', that ended in the T already in the grid, and had found one.

'I like that,' said Holly. 'That gives the three-letter word as "act", which sounds promising, and it follows a four-letter word that's a three-letter city followed by a T.'

After a moment of intense concentration, they all jumped when Kia smacked her hand down on the coffee table.

'Rio!' she said, triumphantly.

'Which gives us "Riot Act", a severe reprimand.' Holly was audibly impressed. 'You're getting the hang of this.'

'Bit late, as it turns out,' she commented.

'On the other hand,' said Holly, determined not to allow any downturn in the prevailing mood, 'if there is a vacancy for a Compiler, maybe you should all offer your services.'

'Thanks,' she said. 'But if this is the last one, then good

riddance. I mean, look at it. Origami Riot Act? Who needs that? Yes, by all means, write it in. What does it even mean?'

'No idea,' admitted Holly, when he'd added it to the grid. 'So let's go straight on and do another. "Woman has flipped lid, and not in an ambiguous way", seven letters, seems to leap out. Can't think why.'

Kia snorted in mock indignation.

'Actually,' Holly continued, 'we've got enough letters to see this one off. It ends in a Y, which implies an adverb, as in "not in an ambiguous way". Chances are, the preceding letter would be an L, common adverb ending, LY, so that L is probably part of "lid" that's got flipped…'

'Idl!' shouted Uncle Sid, grabbing what may well turn out to be his only opportunity to play his part.

'Exactly. So "-idly". The woman's name would then be L blank CY, which would be "Lucy", so – Lucidly.'

'Of course it is,' asserted Kia. 'I wouldn't flip my lid any other way.'

'And that leads on to "Without thinking of ears, fellow takes the lead". That's another seven.'

Kia's shoulders dropped.

'You know,' she sighed, 'I think I would actually welcome this being the last one.'

'And I wouldn't blame you,' said Holly. 'Let's try and fast-track this one. I'm going to assume the definition is "without thinking" and just set Uncle Jasper off.'

The man in the boiler suit sat straight up and closed his eyes.

'Automatic,' he began, even more deliberately than usual. 'Mechanical – automated – unmanned – push-button – robotic…'

Holly held up his hand and thought for a moment.

'Yes,' he said, at last. 'That's it. "Otic" means "relating to ears", and the fellow taking the lead is Rob.'

Uncle Jasper relaxed and got a slap on the back from Uncle Sid.

'Super,' said Kia, rubbing her eyes while waving her permission for Holly to enter the relevant letters. 'Lucidly Robotic. That'll come in handy.'

'That's just the thing,' Holly couldn't help enthusing. 'They always do. Eventually. At the right juncture.'

'Junction.'

Holly was puzzled as to why Great should be correcting him, until the old man continued.

'Very.'

That, and the shaky finger pointing again at the television, reminded Holly that 'junction' was used in clues to imply a letter T, as in T-junction, rather like 'turn' for U, and 'Very' was abbreviated to V. Holly marvelled at how many ways Great could arrive at the letters TV.

Kia reached for the handset and turned the sound back on.

It was a progress report on the Pitch-Black Army. It had just passed directly between Derby and Nottingham, and was proceeding in its usual relentless manner.

As if that wasn't disconcerting enough, the continuation of the story had everyone in the room leaning forward for a better look.

The prevailing opinion was that the Pitch-Black Army was heading for London to act as reinforcements for its more regular counterpart, which was entrenching itself in great numbers in and around Parliament Square, supposedly to safeguard the Houses of Parliament.

Kia was the first to voice what they were all thinking.

'How on earth is the army going to protect the Palace of Westminster from a comet?'

Giving the item a final twist, the reporter informed them that the prime minister had denied all knowledge of the army's motives – in fact had denied having given them any orders whatsoever.

Again, Kia was the group's spokesperson.

'So, who's a higher authority here than the prime minister?'

Both questions being rhetorical, Holly turned the television off.

'I'm sorry,' he said, in reply to the looks of surprise, 'but given the amount of hardware out there, I feel we need as much ammunition of our own as we can get. So we'll do one more line before we go and consult Claire.'

'Fair enough,' said Kia, wearily surveying her newspaper. 'How about 17 Across? It's got the word "shot" in it, just like the clue for Dream. Maybe it's also about whisky.'

This got a wistful sigh from all the uncles.

'Fine,' said Holly, feeling a little left out, having sworn off the stuff. 'We have "Turned up and spots variable, not wanting to be shot", six, three, hyphenated.'

They all pondered this for a while in silence, apart from a quiet 'Well, who would?' from Kia.

Eventually, out of desperation, Holly tried to get some sort of ball rolling.

'It's got a C at the beginning and an R in the middle,' he said. 'So it can't start PU, as in "up", "turned". So the whole thing could just mean "turned up". The variable is usually an X, a Y, or a Z. But that doesn't conjure anything up.'

Another tortuous minute dragged by.

'Leave it,' Holly commanded. 'We'll come back to that one. The next one is only five letters, "Fight for what pig hasn't left on plate". There's an R from Riot Act in the middle.'

Kia pulled a face.

'Aren't pigs famous for eating in the same place they… you know… do their business? God knows what he'd leave on his plate.'

Holly laughed, as did Uncle Jasper, who had arrived at the solution at the same time.

'The word is precisely,' explained Holly, pen at the ready, 'what a pig, as in a greedy person, would not leave on his plate – as well as being a word for "fight". And you're almost right, only there's an S in front of it.'

'Scrap,' confirmed Uncle Jasper.

CHAPTER TEN

'Camera-shy!'

The only person to make any sense out of this was Kia, who now understood why Holly had hardly said a word since leaving the house, even when they'd encountered several of the furry, birdlike creatures. The brain had been far too preoccupied to allow for the distraction of conversation. Which clue had just been solved, she had no idea, but she was happy enough that progress was being made.

The timing, though, was undeniably unfortunate. Holly, Kia and Uncle Jasper had made their way to Claire's place, where they had been spared the effort of ringing the bell by the timely emergence of Claire, the captain and the baron. Holly's exclamation had come just at the point when he would normally have greeted their new musical ally.

'Er – no, not especially,' was Claire's hesitant response.

'I'm so sorry,' Holly said. 'I was miles away. That clue was really bugging me. "Turned up" was "came", spots turned out to be "rash", and the variable was indeed a "y". Came-rash-y. Not wanting to be shot.'

'Well, who would?' asked Claire with a smile, which was mirrored by Kia, who always found it reassuring when others reacted to clues in the same way she had.

'Introverted!' shouted the captain, pointing at Holly.

'Oh, I thought mentioning people's shortcomings was the new way of greeting them.'

'No,' said Holly, 'I still prefer Hello. Hello,' he addressed to Claire. 'It's lovely to see you again. How are you settling in?'

'Well, the change in the air quality takes some getting used to,' she said. 'But apart from that, it's all good. I've got a job in a small, local library, I live above a bookshop, and I couldn't wish for better company. Ooh, and I've made some new friends. I'd love you all to meet them. They'll be in the café over there.'

Kia and Claire led the way. There was no hint of any impending doom in their excited chatter. Holly's mere presence had been enough to dispel Claire's previous melancholy.

Holly and the baron brought up the rear of the group, synchronising their copies of the crossword.

Coffee-Nosed was the café at the end of the parade, just before a side street. There was a small table outside, with two more around the corner, hidden from the main road. All six of their accompanying chairs were occupied.

The couple at the first table spotted Claire. The man stood up, his full-length leather coat making him look tall. He took his cigarette out of his mouth and waved.

'There's Hugo!' shouted Claire, waving back.

'Hugo?' questioned the captain. 'You don't get many of those to the pound.'

'Not here, maybe,' said Claire, proudly, 'but he's French.'

She ran up to Hugo and kissed him on both cheeks, then did the same with his companion, a woman in a floral dress under a brown woollen coat. There followed a brief interchange in French, with some embarrassment on Claire's side, but with much encouragement from the other.

'They're teaching me French,' Claire explained, as the

others caught up. 'I saw a card in the newsagent's. Hugo does the conversational stuff. But I also wanted to know the nuts and bolts. I love grammar and syntax, must be the librarian in me, and Andrea here is brilliant at the academic side, so she's teaching me that.'

Andrea smiled proudly at her student, and the couple were then introduced to the five members of the team.

'Ah,' said Hugo, shaking Holly's hand. 'So, you are the famous Holly.'

The baron knew, as soon as that name was said in that French accent, missing the initial H, that the captain would make some remark about Laurel and Hardy. He tapped the captain on the shoulder and shook his head, getting a rueful smile in return.

'And these are our compatriots and good friends,' Hugo went on, indicating the couple at the next table. 'This is Gilbert,' a serious-looking man in a bomber jacket, 'and Odile,' a woman dressed all in black, who looked the youngest of the party, despite having long, bright white hair with a beret perched on top. She waved a hand without looking round.

'This gentleman,' Hugo said in conclusion, referring to the stockier of the two men on the last table, both of whom were wearing sunglasses, 'is another one of us pesky émigrés. We've only just met.'

'Talleyrand,' the man introduced himself in a nasal voice. 'And this is a work colleague.'

He indicated the man next to him, who was wearing a green greatcoat.

'Marlowe,' the last man said, without a trace of an accent. 'Awfully pleased to meet you.'

'I'm guessing you've been here longer than the others, Marlowe,' remarked Holly.

'Since the year dot, actually, old man. Born here.

British as the flag. The only bloomer among these baguettes, you might say. But Randy here…' Talleyrand snorted and shook his head. '…He's been doing his cultural attaché bit, promoting the Gallic way of life, and I must say, if this coffee's anything to go by…'

'And does that stretch to the clothes?' the captain wanted to know. 'Because France is either decades behind, or there's a '40s convention in town.'

Uncle Jasper spluttered, taking a moment to get his obvious mirth under control.

'Captain!' Kia forced out between clenched teeth. 'I expect their boiler suits are in the wash,' she directed at Uncle Jasper.

'No, he's quite right,' said Hugo, laughing. 'We just like this style; it's one of the things that binds us together. And then Monsieur Talleyrand here turns up, and it seems he has the same good taste we do. That's how we got talking. And then to find out he was also from la belle France…'

'La belle France,' Claire echoed. 'I think those were the first words you taught me.'

Hugo shrugged his shoulders happily in a show of non-surprise.

'I can't wait to go,' Claire went on. 'The food, the wine, the way of life – it sounds idyllic. The first chance I get…'

Her expression clouded over as she remembered what little chance she was going to get. Andrea took her hand and squeezed it.

'Never give up hope, ma chérie,' she said. 'There's always a way.'

Kia was so absorbed in Claire's anguish that it took her a while to notice Holly nodding his head vehemently at the object in her hand.

'Oh! Of course!' She unfolded the piece of paper and held it out to Claire. 'We brought you this, courtesy of the keeper of the archives. We were hoping you could make some sense out of it. It means nothing to any of us.'

Claire stared at it for a moment, not daring to take it, until suddenly she snatched it out of Kia's hand.

'I've seen this,' she muttered. 'I know this. Where have I seen it before?'

Hugo held out a hand, and she passed it to him without looking. When he drew a blank, it did the rounds of all three tables. Andrea shook her head sadly, Odile barely glanced at it before handing it to Gilbert, who frowned at it, as he did at almost everything. Talleyrand held it like it was an item of dirty laundry, and Marlowe just uttered a mystified 'I say!' before handing it back to Claire. She in turn glared at it, challenging it to reveal its secrets, but it didn't respond.

'No foot shall slide,' she murmured, shaking her head. 'That means nothing. But the frequencies…' She looked up, frustrated. 'It's no good. I'll need to look it up in the library, but until I work out what it is, I won't even know where to look.'

'Well, come along with us, if you like,' Kia said. 'We can do some brainstorming. Something usually comes out of that.' She turned to their new friends. 'Au revoir, hopefully. This has been wonderfully sociable, but time is running out, and we have work to do.'

'Ah,' came Talleyrand's pinched voice. 'You too are carrying on as normal. You too do not believe in this comet.'

'Quite right,' agreed Marlowe. 'Load of rot. Probably an April Fool's joke, or some such.'

'In February?' queried Gilbert, generously providing the month with four syllables.

'Wouldn't work on the day itself, would it? You have to catch people off guard.'

'Real or not,' said Kia, rounding up her team, 'we all have to deal with it, in our own way.'

Andrea stood up.

'We're going in the same direction,' she said. 'May we walk with you?'

'Of course,' said Kia. 'The more the merrier.'

'I'm going that way, too,' said Talleyrand.

He and Gilbert got to their feet. Hugo put his cigarettes and matches away, but not before lighting up again. Andrea looked over at the only member of her original foursome still sitting down.

'Odile?'

'I stay here,' Odile said in a husky voice, revealing for the first time not only that she had a voice, but also the thickest accent of the group.

'Spot of business,' explained Marlowe, now the only other person seated. 'Randy and I work for the local rag, for our sins, and I've managed to persuade the powers that be to run an article about what London's like for resident aliens, you know, foreign expats, or ex-Odiles. This lady has kindly agreed to give me an interview. For a fee, of course.'

Odile, who hadn't taken kindly to being called an alien, now made a big show of being indifferent to the idea of financial reward.

'OK,' said Andrea. 'Well, see you later.'

Odile waved without looking at her. The two groups set off together round the corner and were soon out of sight, although they were still audible for a good while.

Marlowe took out a notebook and pen.

'Now, my dear...' he got as far as, before his mobile phone started ringing. 'I'm terribly sorry...'

He answered the call, spending most of the time listening, apart from the occasional 'Really?', 'So soon?', and 'Seems a shame.' Eventually he hung up, sighed, and put the phone down on the table.

'It appears,' he said, with exaggerated sadness, 'that the

expat is of more use as an ex-Odile after all.'

He slowly removed his sunglasses. Odile could only stare at him. She couldn't move. She couldn't scream. She couldn't breathe.

She couldn't even see his eyes. All she could see were flames.

1 F	I	2 N	A	3 L	■	4 C	R	5 O	S	6 S	W	7 O	R	8 D
A	■		■	U	■		■		■		■	R	■	
9 N		T		C		D	■	10 E		O		I		A
T	■		■	I	■		■		■		■	G	■	
11 A				D			■	12				A		
S	■		■	L	■		■	■	■		■	M	■	■
13 T	E	E	N	Y	■	14 M	Y	15 S	T	E	R	I	E	16 S
I	■	■	■	■	■		■		■	■	■	■	■	
17 C	A	18 M	E	19 R	A	S	H	Y	■	20 S	C	21 R	A	P
■	■		■	O	■	■	■		■		■	I	■	
22 D				B		23	■	24				O		
R	■		■	O	■		■		■		■	T	■	
25 E				T			■	26				A		
A	■		■	I	■		■		■		■	C	■	
27 M	U	S	I	C	I	A	N	S	■	28 M	O	T	T	O

CHAPTER ELEVEN

'How long have you all been here?' Kia asked Hugo.

'Oh, not long.'

'You must miss home terribly,' sighed Claire.

'Of course.'

'And what was it that dragged you away from your paradise on earth?' the captain wanted to know, rolling his eyes.

'The weather,' said Gilbert, drily.

'Oh, Hugo!' Andrea grabbed her companion's arm. 'Odile has the keys. I'll go back and get them.'

She turned and made her way back to the café.

'The landlady only allows us one set of keys,' Hugo explained.

'Seriously?' Kia commiserated.

'Why?' said Gilbert. 'Does it sound like a joke?'

'Ooh! Ooh! I know a French joke,' cried the captain, getting them all to stop.

'Seriously?' Kia repeated. 'Hardly the time...'

'No, no, it's really good. There's this French admiral.'

The baron winced. Uncle Jasper smiled, but shook his head.

'The punchline had better not include the word "surrender",' muttered Talleyrand.

'And this admiral,' the captain ploughed on, 'was so impressed by Nelson's rallying cry to his navy, "England expects every man shall do his duty", that he thinks, *I'm going to have to get me one of those.* So he racks his brain and, finally, he has it. "Ready the flags, men," he goes. "The message is…" '

The captain raised an arm, as though declaiming some epic poetry.

'…"To the water! It is time!" '

Kia's team and its French counterpart were easily distinguishable – one was staring at its collective feet, the other was giving the captain a mystified look.

'Which is, in French…' the captain prompted.

'Á l'eau, c'est l'heure,' said Gilbert, hesitantly.

Uncle Jasper's mirth was only outdone by that of a euphoric captain.

'Hello, sailor!' he blasted, laughing enough for the whole group.

Talleyrand gave him a particularly sour look.

'You really think that's…' was as far as he got, when they heard a loud scream.

'That's Andrea!' shouted Hugo, launching himself in the direction of the café.

In seconds, they were near enough to see Andrea standing on the corner outside the café with her hands over her mouth. She was next to the one table that was visible to them, and there was an otter-bird strutting nervously about on it. It was only when they rounded the corner and could see the next table that they realised what the real cause of alarm was.

Odile was on her own, slumped across the table. She was facing away from them, one hand resting next to her head. It was this hand that caught Hugo's attention. On closer inspection, to his horror, he found that it was wrinkled and covered in liver spots. Gathering all his courage, he went round the table. What he saw made him recoil like he'd touched a live wire. The others joined him. There followed a chorus of gasps and shrieks.

The face that had shown such youth had aged by almost a century. The hair had done nothing to minimise the shock, being already white. Odile's eyes were closed, and her mouth was open. It would clearly never draw breath again. And, despite all the wrinkles, the anguish in her expression shone through.

Hugo looked around, just in time to see Marlowe disappearing around the corner at the far end of the side street. He caught Gilbert's eye and nodded in that direction. The earnest, young man set off at a pace.

'Odile,' Andrea moaned. She had gone up to the table and was gently stroking the stricken woman's hand.

By now, a crowd had gathered, keeping a respectful distance. The owner of the café was among them, wringing his tea towel, not knowing what to do.

'It's OK,' Hugo announced, getting his cigarettes out again. 'There's nothing to see here. It's all under control.'

As if on cue, an ambulance suddenly appeared and pulled up next to them, although the only thing that told them it was an ambulance was the large white square with a red cross painted on the side.

The vehicle was dark green, essentially a box with a cab welded to the front. The high bonnet tapered to the front, with wide mudguards over the wheels lower down on both sides. The windscreen consisted of two, flat pieces of glass, and the doors were absent on both the driver and the passenger side.

Two men emerged, one out of the back and one from the front. They were wearing dark uniforms and tin helmets with flattened brims, bearing the letters FAU. The man from the back was unfolding a rudimentary stretcher.

Pushing anyone in their path brusquely out of the way, they put the stretcher on the ground next to their patient and dumped her unceremoniously on to it. They then picked it up and conveyed it to the back of the ambulance.

Odile's beret had fallen on to the pavement. Andrea retrieved it, only to have it snatched from her hand by the ambulance driver, who then climbed into the cab and drove off, causing the tyres to squeal.

The crowd quickly dispersed. The café owner gave the remaining French group a distrustful look and disappeared back inside. The baron, the captain, Uncle Jasper and Claire stood in a stunned circle. Kia looked imploringly at Holly for some sort of explanation.

'What on earth were the Friends' Ambulance Unit doing here?' was all he could say. 'And why were they driving a World War II ambulance?'

Hugo had more pressing questions, and he turned on Talleyrand.

'Who the hell is this Marlowe?' he demanded. 'What did he do to Odile?'

The little man had been expecting this onslaught, but still wasn't ready for it.

'I don't know him,' he snivelled through his nose. 'He's just a guy I work with. How could he do that? What sort of person could do that?'

Hugo held him in a glare for a moment, and then let him go. Kia was staring dejectedly into space.

'We haven't had any warning about people who can do that,' she protested. 'We don't have a clue.'

'Yes,' said Andrea, 'we do.'

She held out her hand and showed everyone a mobile phone, but when she spoke, it was only to Hugo.

'Odile had her hand over it. But it's not hers.'

This was too much for Claire. She had started off fighting back the tears, but having watched the friends she thought she knew behaving so oddly, sadness had turned to anger.

'This may be the weirdest place,' she began, 'but there's the world of difference between weird and wrong, and something is very wrong.'

She rounded on her language teachers.

'You're hiding something. Sending Gilbert after Marlowe, taking what happened to Odile so calmly. And why are you all suddenly wearing these ridiculous clothes? And why did you say you'd heard about Holly? I never mentioned him to you.'

She went up to Hugo and got right in his face.

'What the hell is going on?'

CHAPTER TWELVE

When the doorbell went, Camille was still in her pyjamas. She'd never had any feel for punctuality. If she overslept, as she had now, she just assumed everyone else had.

She'd missed two trains down to London, the first due to her customary late start, the second because she'd had to go back for the purse she'd left in the pocket of her other coat.

It was the *Bridlington News* that had sponsored her trip. The seaside town was still buzzing, having been designated Ground Zero of the Cloud of Death, largely by itself. It had only been a few weeks since the world's media had descended on it, eager to cover the biggest story in ages – or ever, in the minds of the inhabitants. The international reporters soon faded away, particularly as there was a distinct absence of actual eyewitnesses, everyone having vacated the danger zone at the earliest opportunity.

So, when a young woman suddenly appeared, claiming that she had seen not only the demise of the cloud close up, but even the person or persons she believed to be responsible, the local paper became very possessive, getting Camille to sign an exclusive contract. The possibility of her being able to identify a particular individual as what she insisted on calling a 'saviour' proved irresistible.

They packed her off to the capital – where she insisted the man was to be found, because she had 'a nose for these things' – but in secret, deciding not to go public just yet in case the woman's story turned out to be as preposterous as it sounded. Seeing her being interviewed on the national news was a shock, but as she hadn't mentioned the paper, they decided to sit back and see what happened. Until, that is, the comet story broke, after which they gave her no thought whatsoever.

The employee who had found her the small garden flat on a short-term lease must have had an equally efficient nose, as, unknown to them all, it put Camille within half a mile of Kia's house.

Having arrived the previous day, early in the afternoon, she had gone straight out to explore the surrounding area, spending a pleasant hour rummaging around an antiques shop, owned by a lovely man wearing an old-fashioned suit and a fedora with a feather sticking out of it, before remembering what she was there for. She had then trudged the streets for hours, getting some suspicious looks as she squinted at everyone she passed, before returning to the flat, dead on her feet. She was therefore in no way surprised when she awoke a mere quarter of an hour before the man said he would be calling round.

He had rung her the day before and introduced himself as a reporter from the *Ham & High*, without bothering to explain that they were short for Hampstead and Highgate. She wasn't curious anyway, any more than she was about why a man with such a heavy foreign accent would be working for a local London weekly. He said that he'd seen her on the television and got her number from their sister paper in Bridlington. If this saviour was indeed on his patch, he had explained, he wanted to be the first to know about it. He may even be able to help her find him.

‘Mr Puttynectar?’ Camille asked the man waiting patiently on the doorstep.

‘Puttanesca,’ the man said, smiling. ‘But that’s close enough for me. Call me Arfa.’

He was wearing a dark blue suit with a matching tie, which suddenly made her aware of her casual attire.

‘Sorry I’m not dressed,’ she said, waving him in. ‘Bit of a late night.’

‘Not at all. A very charming outfit. Green, white, and red. Reminds me of home.’

‘Wow. You live in a very colourful house.’

‘No, the flag of my country.’

‘Oh, right. Where’s that, then?’

‘Italy. The land of my fathers.’

‘Wow,’ she said again. ‘How many fathers have you got?’

‘Forefathers,’ he corrected her.

‘That many? That must be confusing. Can I get you a tea?’

This talent for avidly and unerringly grabbing the wrong end of any stick could have been infuriating, but such was Camille’s personality that people generally found it endearing, and Arfa was no exception.

‘No, thank you,’ he replied. ‘I’ve just had a coffee.’

‘That’s probably just as well. I’m not sure I’ve got any. Do you mind if we pop outside? It’s a smoke-free apartment.’

He shrugged, and she slid open the patio doors that led on to the small area that gave them their name.

She still wasn’t sure if she liked smoking, which she had taken up quite recently, but it forced her to go outdoors on a regular basis, an excursion she enjoyed but otherwise wouldn’t have bothered making. She knew her mother didn’t like the smell of tobacco around the house, so she made a point of going into the garden, especially as she knew her mother wouldn’t dream of asking her to. Following this routine here in London made her feel more at home.

Once outside, cigarette in hand, she looked up. The sun was straining to shine through the layer of cloud, casting a feeble light through the glass doors and on to the table inside, but other than that, there was still nothing to see.

'I wasn't sure you were going to turn up,' she said.

Arfa cocked his head to one side by way of a question.

'I mean, because of this comet. I thought you might have more important things to do.'

He laughed.

'No, that's not real,' he assured her. 'That's just a media invention to spice things up a bit. I even know the guy who dreamt it up.'

'Oh.' Camille wasn't sure whether to be pleased or disappointed.

'Of course,' he continued, 'it doesn't matter much to you, one way or the other.'

'What do you mean?'

'Well, if this saviour is as good as you say he is, you have nothing to worry about. Have you found him yet?'

'No, not yet. But I will.'

'I was wondering – do you have an actual picture of him?'

'Oh, it's all in my head,' she said, at which he pulled a rueful expression. 'But I can draw him for you.'

'That would be most helpful, thank you.'

'Let's go in. That low sun is giving me a headache. I can see now why you're wearing sunglasses. I thought it was a bit weird, you know, indoors.'

He smiled.

'I'm photosensitive.'

'Ah, right.' She nodded, thoughtfully. 'I don't much like having my picture taken either.'

She stubbed her half-smoked cigarette out and led

them inside, leaving the door open for the fresh air, the heating being on full blast. She went and sat at the table, habit making her sit where the sun that had driven her inside was still shining in her face. He sat down opposite her. She had a pad of plain paper already open in front of her, full of sketches made through a train window.

'I draw all the time,' she explained. 'I'm a draw-oholic.'

She began to translate the image in her mind into a physical representation on the page. Occasionally, she would raise her eyes to her guest and then turn her head to look behind her. After a while, he asked her what the matter was.

'It's really strange,' she replied. 'I keep catching a flicker of flames, reflecting in your shades. But there's nothing back there.'

'That is odd,' he commented. 'Although I have been told there's a fire in my eyes.'

'Oh, right. That'll be it, then.' She put the finishing touches to her sketch and slid it across the table. 'There, that's close enough,' she said. 'I had to guess what the sideburns would look like when he wasn't falling from the sky.'

The man held the picture out in front of him and studied the likeness, taking in the distinctive eyes, the facial hair, and the all-important boiler suit.

'Oh, yes. It shouldn't take too long to draw him out,' he said, obviously pleased at his pun. 'But then you'll need to find a new saviour.'

He put the drawing down on the table.

'And there's never one around when you need one,' he said, taking off his sunglasses.

CHAPTER THIRTEEN

Holly heard himself sniggering and immediately stopped. Not only was it singularly inappropriate, given the circumstances, but it would have been childish at the best of times, given what had triggered it.

After the antique ambulance had driven off, he had gone to sit at the furthest of the café tables, making his way through several otter-birds, while Claire remonstrated with her two instructors. In a reversal of roles, she was teaching them a whole new vocabulary.

Talleyrand was standing some way off, nervously shifting his weight from one foot to the other. Kia and Uncle Jasper were also keeping their distance, along with the captain, who was enjoying the librarian's performance hugely.

Unable to assimilate everything that was happening, Holly sought refuge in the familiarity of his crossword. He felt fully justified in this, knowing that any solutions he may find would only expand their arsenal. The baron came and sat next to him, just in time to hear his childish outburst.

Holly had gone straight to 8 Down, for no reason other than it was the only one of the four sides not yet completed. 'Depicts underwear, unhesitatingly' met his eyes, a five-letter word of which the first D and the middle A were already present. Striking it lucky by working backwards, he determined that 'depicts' could be 'draws', confirming this answer by taking the 'underwear' to be 'drawers', 'unhesitatingly' meaning that the common hesitation 'er' was missing. He decided that his involuntary show of mirth was caused more by relief at finding his feet back on the ground than by any amusement the word itself may have generated, although he was pleased to get a chuckle from the baron when he shared his findings.

They moved on to the second clue, 'For one, daredevil policeman doomed priestess', nine letters, the first of which was an S, the third a P, and the last an O.

'Who was a doomed priestess?' Holly asked, not falling into the trap of taking 'doomed' to be a verb, but an adjective.

'Hero,' was the baron's instant reply.

'Really? That was quick.'

'Well, we have the O at the end, which helps. And although you'd assume Hero was a bloke, she was actually a priestess who lived on one side of the Hellespont, while her chap Leander lived on the other. He would swim over each day to see her. But one day there was a storm, which blew out the lamp she used to guide him over, and he got lost in the waves and drowned. And she couldn't live without him, so she didn't. Sounds pretty doomed to me.'

Holly gave a matter-of-fact nod.

'Well, you lose the love of your life, that's what happens.' He gave the baron a faint smile. 'Some people just deal with it by hallucinating to bring that person back. That means our policeman must be super.'

It took the baron a moment of confusion to realise they were back on the clue.

'Super! Yes. Short for superintendent. So – "super-hero".'

Holly frowned.

'It's giving "Daredevil" as an example of a superhero. Is

there one? Other than, they all are?'

'Oh, yes,' the baron confirmed. 'Blind guy, I believe. Not one of the big guns.'

'I see. Well, that gives us Draws Superhero,' Holly said, entering the letters. He stared at the completed entry. 'Can't see why anyone would make a sketch of some mythical saviour. How on earth is that relevant?'

'All right!'

Hugo had finally lost patience with Claire's questioning.

'All right. Yes, there are strange things going on, even stranger than these furry flying things that seem to be everywhere. But you're all used to strange things, it would seem. There's something far more bizarre playing out in the background here than us wearing these "ridiculous" clothes.'

He went and sat at the corner table. Everyone was still standing round in a huddle, no-one willing to sit at the middle table – Odile's table. Hugo waited until he had their attention.

'We woke up this morning,' he began, 'and something was different. We all had – certain information, in our heads. Then we met up here, and we were all wearing the same style of clothing. So, yes, Claire, there is something "going on", but although I know what it is, I have no idea why it is. And I have a feeling that's tied up with you people. Particularly you.' He looked pointedly at Holly. 'On top of everything else, there are these idiotic, spotty, feathery things wandering about, there's a comet on its way to wipe us all, one of our colleagues has been killed – and you sit there doing silly word puzzles. Defence mechanism?'

'Quite the reverse,' Holly told him. He tapped his paper. 'This is the best, actually the only, form of attack we have.'

Holly wasn't sure what to do next, and consulted Kia, who slowly nodded her consent. He still had no idea where to start.

'Don't worry.' Hugo seemed to have read Holly's thoughts. 'Whatever you say will not shock us. Yesterday, maybe. But not after this morning.'

'OK, then,' Holly started. 'This silly puzzle governs what happens on any given day. If it appears in here, it will become real, and if we manage to solve it, and write it in, it will disappear, as long as we write it into this copy, my copy, because I'm the Solver.'

He waited for this to sink in, which took less time that he had expected.

'Nothing about a comet in there, then?' Andrea said, calmly.

'Not so far, no,' said Holly, relieved that his explanation had been so readily accepted, although he could see Hugo eyeing the newspaper on the table with some disdain.

'I would be happy to demonstrate,' he said, 'but we haven't…'

'Noticed.'

This struck Holly as an odd way to finish the sentence, and even odder, given that it came from Uncle Jasper.

'Noticed?' Holly asked. 'You mean the solution line Noticed Exotica? But we had no idea what that…'

'Noticed,' the handyman repeated. 'Espied.' He pointed at one of the otter-birds that was pecking at one of Talleyrand's shoes. 'Spotted.'

'Spotted,' Holly echoed. 'You think these are Noticed Exotica, because "noticed" is a synonym for "spotted"?'

Uncle Jasper shrugged.

'Wow,' said the baron. 'That takes it to a whole new level.'

As if sensing that it had become the centre of attention, one of these creatures flapped its way up to Holly's table and took a couple of bites out of his paper.

'I'd be happy to give it a go,' Holly said, snatching the

vital document away.

'Oh, you can't!' cooed Kia. 'They're so cute.'

She bent down to stroke one on the head. It promptly bit her hand.

'Fine,' she said, straightening up. 'Get rid of them.'

Holly didn't need to be told twice. He filled in the missing letters. The otter-birds were instantly no more than a memory.

'Shame,' muttered the captain.

The bewildered French trio blinked at each other. Hugo held out his hand for the puzzle so he could examine it more closely. The baron passed it over with some reluctance, and only after Holly had given his agreement. Hugo scanned it for a moment.

'But how do you get from these words to those solutions?' he wanted to know. 'It's just nonsense.'

He handed it back.

'I see number 24 mentions a "good time in Paris". I've had a few of those, and I certainly wouldn't want them solved away. But how would you approach that?'

'By not asking for too many details, I expect,' suggested the captain.

Holly located the relevant clue.

'So, it's "Hello – good time in Paris?",' he read out, 'and it's seven letters. It looks like the "hello" is the overall meaning. "In Paris" isn't usually anything geographical, it just means something is in French. And if the time is a day, then "good time" in French would be…'

'Bonjour!' Claire exclaimed, proudly.

'…bonjour, exactly, which means "hello". So that's the answer.'

Hugo looked less than impressed.

'And how does that affect anything?' he asked. 'You fill that in, and we disappear?'

'No, no,' Kia assured him. 'In the first place, you were already French before today. And in the second place, it's the pairs of words that form the overall solutions. So, we need the word before, for which the clue is…' She consulted her copy. '…"Badly wrong about ancient city, in a tough way". Also seven letters, first is a D, fifth a B.'

Having confirmed that French blank looks were much the same as English ones, the former teacher resumed control of the class.

'Well, "badly" and "wrong" are both anagram indicators, but as we already have a D and a B, we can guess which is which. And if it's an anagram of "badly", then we need a two-letter ancient city in the middle.'

'That's usually Ur, isn't it?' suggested the baron.

'Er – what's an Ur, when it's at home?' asked the captain.

'An ancient Sumerian city,' the baron explained. 'Its ruin is currently at home in Iraq.'

'And an anagram of "badly",' Holly continued, 'that's "about" "Ur", would give us – "durably", which means "in a tough way".'

The sense of achievement left as fast as an untied balloon being let go, as everyone could be seen silently mouthing the words Durably Bonjour. Holly could see no reason not to write them in, so did.

It was Talleyrand's turn to want to inspect the puzzling article. Again, the baron, who was standing between the Frenchman and Holly, turned and passed it to him.

'That was… very interesting,' said Andrea. 'But what does it mean? Is something going to happen?'

'Oh, it's going to happen, all right. Don't you worry about that.'

As he spoke, Talleyrand lifted the paper and waved it in the air.

Everyone stared at him, not so much for the inexplicable

gesture, but for the fact that his nasal tones had switched from urban French to deepest Essex.

At that moment, an old motorcycle loudly announced its presence. Its rider was wearing a black-and-white, leather motorcycle suit but no safety helmet, just a black mask that covered the entire head, apart from two holes for the eyes. The bike came to an abrupt stop at the corner.

'Good luck sorting it all out,' Talleyrand shouted, as he ran towards his getaway vehicle, still waving the paper, 'coz you're stuffed without this, incha?'

Several members of the team had set off in pursuit, but hadn't taken three steps when the masked figure on the bike waved an open, gloved palm at them.

Before his arm was back down by his side, the sky had turned a deep red. The pursuers immediately stopped to look up in alarm. What they saw made them all cower.

Half the red sky was taken up by an even darker red, almost black, cloud. Colour aside, history seemed to be repeating itself, so vividly did it echo the events of just a few weeks ago. Like last time, it was flashing and ejecting fireballs and their smoky trails in every direction, many of which must already have landed, as the horizon was pulsating in bright shades of orange. London was ablaze.

Before anyone had time to take in this apocalyptic scenario, the cloud spat out a huge, fiery mass directly above them. It came straight out, pausing momentarily before it plunged, spinning, in their direction. In seconds it was close enough to see the sparks flying off it like a Catherine wheel.

And then it disappeared, and the sky reverted to its previous blue.

Talleyrand had, by now, reached the motorcycle. Laughing, he jumped on the back, and the bike roared off. In seconds, it, its passengers, and its precious cargo were out of sight.

[1]F	I	[2]N	A	[3]L	■	[4]C	R	[5]O	S	[6]S	W	[7]O	R	[8]D
A	■		■	U	■		■		■		■	R	■	R
[9]N	O	T	I	C	E	D	■	[10]E	X	O	T	I	C	A
T	■		■	I	■		■		■		■	G	■	W
[11]A				D			■	[12]				A		S
S	■		■	L	■		■	■	■		■	M	■	■
[13]T	E	E	N	Y	■	[14]M	Y	[15]S	T	E	R	I	E	[16]S
I	■	■	■	■	■		■		■	■	■	■	■	U
[17]C	A	[18]M	E	[19]R	A	S	H	Y	■	[20]S	C	[21]R	A	P
■	■		■	O	■	■	■		■		■	I	■	E
[22]D	U	R	A	B	L	[23]Y	■	[24]B	O	N	J	O	U	R
R	■		■	O	■		■		■		■	T	■	H
[25]E				T			■	[26]				A		E
A	■		■	I	■		■		■		■	C	■	R
[27]M	U	S	I	C	I	A	N	S	■	[28]M	O	T	T	O

CHAPTER FOURTEEN

'Did you see that?' Hugo breathed. Having shown such little reaction to the seismic events that had happened since they had all met up at the café, this was easily the most animated anyone had seen him. 'That was a Norton Big 4!'

A hefty blow on the shoulder from Andrea brought him back to their predicament and a suitably contrite expression.

Everyone that had crouched down in the face of a direct hit from some flaming debris – which was anyone who wasn't Uncle Jasper – now cautiously stood up.

'Ball of fire,' the baron muttered to Kia. 'For a moment there, I thought the Moomins might have been right. What on earth was that?'

But Kia had seen too many strange sights to be distracted from the central issue.

'That,' said Kia, struggling to keep her anger in check, 'was our only hope of survival. Without Holly's copy of the puzzle, we have precisely zero chance of fixing anything, let alone that comet. And you!' She rounded on the baron. 'You just… gave it to him! What were you thinking?'

'I was thinking,' the baron said, calmly, 'that I'm going to have to buy myself another paper.'

He placed another copy in front of Holly, who inspected

it, looked up and nodded.

'It's mine.'

The baron, never happy being the centre of attention, shuffled uncomfortably.

'I didn't trust him,' he said, dismissively. 'So I swapped them round.'

Relief swept through the assembled group like a dose of salts. Kia was already on her way over to give him a big kiss, but Hugo got there first, grabbing the bewildered baron by the shoulders and planting a loud smacker on both his cheeks. Then he looked him earnestly in the eyes.

'Bravo. You did what I could not. I had no idea what was going to happen, especially to Odile. She was supposed to be gathering information on them. But I knew Marlowe and Talleyrand were not what they seemed.'

'How did you know?' Claire demanded. 'Why didn't you do anything? And how can you remain so calm when the entire city suddenly looks like its burning to the ground around us? What exactly has happened to you since yesterday?'

'Tell them, Hugo,' Andrea urged. 'It may help make some sense of it.'

Hugo sighed.

'You're right,' he said. 'Considering what else we've seen today, it doesn't seem so weird any more. But I'd like to use 5 Down as an introduction.'

Holly was surprised to have a clue number thrown at him, and he gestured at his paper.

'Yes,' Hugo confirmed. 'I spotted it earlier.'

Holly dutifully peered at it, then just stopped himself in time from saying the clue number out loud. Things were complicated enough without being despatched to some unknown location.

'We have – "Last character round, playing game", five

letters, O at the beginning, E in the middle.'

The baron was the first to make a suggestion.

'Well, "round" could be that O.'

'Agreed,' said Holly. 'And "playing" could mean an anagram of "game"...'

'Omega,' said Kia. 'The last letter of the Greek alphabet.'

'Figures,' Hugo nodded. 'And the next?'

Holly located 15 Down.

'That's a four- and five-letter answer,' he said. 'We've got quite a lot of those letters already. "Like this, any base can be turned into a source of protein". The first word is S blank Y blank. Can't be many of those.'

'Stye,' announced the captain. 'I had one of those last year. Had to put a steak on it. There's your source of protein. Four, five. Stye steak.'

'Well,' said Holly, 'if only because the five-letter word starts with a B, I think we'll pass on that dish. No, "like this" will be "so" to start, which leaves enough letters, including the Y, B and S that are already in there, for an anagram of "any base", which gives us – Soya Beans.'

The captain sniffed.

'Could also be a source of protein, I suppose.'

Kia looked confused.

'You really think Omega Soya Beans is going to explain anything?' she asked Hugo.

'Let's write it in,' Holly said, 'and see what happens.'

Hugo put his hand on Holly's arm.

'Please, don't.'

Holly looked at him in some surprise.

'This really is you?' he asked. 'How can this be you?'

'What does anyone know about omega?' Hugo threw the question open. There was no immediate response.

'Other than being a Greek letter...' Kia faltered, at last.

'Yes,' Hugo conceded. 'A letter and a symbol.'

‘Ohms,’ the baron said. ‘Omega is the symbol for ohms, which measure resistance.’

‘Resistance, exactly,’ said Hugo. ‘This is what happened. This morning, the four of us awoke, to find that we were in the Resistance. We seemed to know this, instinctively. Just like we all dressed like this, instinctively. We all have code names. We are a four-man cell, and that also has a code name. Our commander, who we’ve never seen, is called Olivier. He sent us a text, telling us to be at this café at a certain time. What the battle is, what we have to do, we have no idea. But we know who the enemy is. Or, at least, his minions.’

Everyone conjured up images of Marlowe and Talleyrand.

‘Were you given any inside information on them that might be useful?’ Kia wanted to know.

Hugo shook his head.

‘Just three names, accompanied by the word “agent”, and the leader, along with the most basic descriptions. And the only word next to the leader’s name was “visionary”.’

‘You mean,’ Kia faltered, ‘someone with original ideas for the future?’

Holly shook his head.

‘Given our recent experience,’ he suggested, ‘I would say it means he has some way of inducing visions. You remember how he waved his hand before everything turned red?’

‘That all came from him, you think?’ marvelled the captain. ‘What an underhand trick. Still, it was very real.’

‘Silent. Artificial.’

Uncle Jasper had picked up on two words, providing a synonym for one and an antonym for the other. He shrugged.

‘Noiseless. Fake.’

'You're right,' said Claire. 'That cloud should have made a hell of a racket, and the fires all around? And yet there was nothing, no extra noise at all. And that's why you were the only one who didn't fall for it. You clever old thing.'

The clever old thing just shrugged again.

'But what about your code names?' The captain asked Hugo, his captivated mind racing happily through the endless possibilities. 'Your group are the Hugo-nos, surely?'

The humour was lost on the French leader.

'Actually, as of this morning, I am Voltaire. This is Colette.' Andrea nodded, earnestly. 'Odile became Sand, and Gilbert is Hugo.'

The captain pulled a face.

'That muddies the water, rather, doesn't it? Two Hugos?'

'It doesn't make life any easier,' Voltaire admitted. 'And it doesn't explain why we should collectively be the Soya Beans, but there it is. The name of their cell, the Maniacs, is more self-explanatory, certainly. Two of them, Nasi and Murgh, you've already met.'

There was an explosion of mirth from the captain. 'So… we've joined the Resistance, and we're fighting the Nasis!'

'Captain!' Kia admonished. 'These Maniacs – what do you know about them? And why did Talleyrand suddenly stop being French and become this… Murgh?'

Another muffled chortle came from the captain.

'Durably?'

It was another unexpected contribution from Uncle Jasper.

'You think it was when we solved Durably Bonjour?' Holly asked.

'Durably,' the synonym man repeated. 'Hard-wearingly.' He shrugged his shoulders. 'Hard-ly?'

'Hardly,' Holly repeated, with audible suspicion. 'And Bonjour?'

‘I’m guessing that just signifies French,’ the baron suggested. ‘So, if Uncle Jasper’s right, Durably Bonjour becomes Hardly French, which Talleyrand obviously was. So, when that was written in…’

‘…He reverted to his native accent,’ concluded Kia. ‘Somewhere around Basildon, at a guess.’

Holly looked dazed.

‘Durably becoming Hardly, Noticed becoming Spotted – the Compiler seems to be taking it up a notch, and a very lateral notch at that.’

‘Indeed,’ said Kia. ‘And he’s sent a bunch of Maniacs to stop us. I don’t suppose there’s any doubt he’s behind them. And true to form, he’s also provided us with assistance – in the form of some Soya Beans.’

‘Great,’ beamed the captain. ‘At least we won’t starve.’

CHAPTER FIFTEEN

'This has gone on way too long. How do people spend so much time in cafés?'

Claire and her tutors looked sheepishly at each other. They conducted most of their lessons in this exact spot, finding its atmosphere helpful.

'No, no,' Kia continued. 'We've got enough information for the time being. We need to get going. Our next move – what's top of the list?'

'Start at the bottom. Cordelia's bottom.'

The captain's seemingly flippant response generated some frowns, until the baron latched on.

'No, that's right. Cordelia kept going on about the bottom line. She said we had to go to that location.'

The captain nodded as though that was self-evident.

'Musicians Motto,' Holly said. 'Worth a shot.'

'Right,' Kia agreed. 'It's got to be worth a quick look. Just you and me, mind. We might need to get out fast.'

She registered two very puzzled expressions.

'Oh, that's right,' she said. 'The explanations never got that far, did they? Well, then – Voltaire and Colette, is it now? Want to join me and...'

She glanced at Holly and giggled.

'...Colin?'

That was a name too far for the captain.

'Colin?' he demanded of Holly. 'That's your code name for today?'

'No,' said Holly. 'That's actually my name.'

'Is it?' asked the captain in genuine surprise. 'I never knew that.'

'Anyway,' Kia continued, turning back to the French couple. 'Fancy a trip? Can't tell you where. It's not a secret, I just don't know. And it's risky.'

The Resistance fighters were only too keen to get things started. Kia gestured to Holly, who got up and joined them.

'Right, then,' Kia said, putting one hand on Holly's shoulder and the other on Voltaire's. 'And you two are holding hands already, that's nice.'

She signalled their readiness to Holly, who had a quick look round to make sure nobody but their group was watching, then gave his new fellow travellers his most reassuring smile.

'Twenty-seven Across,' he said.

'*Shap*' went their environment.

This word turned out to be even more alien to French speakers than to English ones. Voltaire was instantly a head shorter, legs bent at the knee, arms out in readiness for whatever else may come hurtling at him.

But it was Colette who was the biggest cause for concern for Kia and Holly. She was already down on hands and knees, eyes tightly shut, and uttering the longest string of expletives they had ever heard. For the first time, Holly didn't regret the rudimentary state of his command of the French language. After a quick scan of their surroundings, to make sure they weren't in any immediate danger, he bent down and held the woman's arm.

'It's OK, it's OK, it's OK.' He heard himself echoing what Kia had said to him on that ship after his first transportation.

That was fitting, he thought, as Colette's reaction and current pose was exactly the same as his had been that day.

Slowly, the woman's eyes opened. Her breathing calmed down.

'Where are we?' she gasped.

'That's difficult to say,' Holly said, regretting not being able to give a more impressive answer. 'It's wherever the words Musicians Motto took us.'

When he was sure that he was no longer needed, he stood up to survey his surroundings in more detail.

For the second time today, he realised, he found himself on the side of a hill. He quickly upgraded that to a mountain, when he realised that the rolling, snow-covered landscape just below them was actually a layer of cloud. There was no way of telling how high up they really were – not too high, he guessed, as the atmosphere was still very humid.

He also credited the moisture in the air with the amount of vegetation, sporadic but lush. There were occasional tufts of tall grass of a deep green. More sparse were the trees, which were low, with a very wide canopy of scarlet leaves covering their twisted branches. The rocky terrain provided an equally colourful background, being a rich, dusty gold.

Their mountain was one of a multitude that stretched into the distance in every direction. They varied in height and shape, but formed a unified whole. The sun was low in the sky to their left. It would normally have seemed very red to them, but couldn't compete with the trees.

Colette had registered the view by now and gingerly stood up, utterly spellbound, as was Kia. The only person still looking ill at ease was Voltaire.

'We can get back from here?' he anxiously asked Holly. He got a confident nod in reply. 'Good. I can't stay here long.'

'Trouble with heights?' Holly asked.

'No, I left my cigarettes at the café.'

Holly wanted to make progress, whatever that may have been, but seeing the look of sheer wonder on Kia's face made it impossible for him. He walked up behind her, gently resting his hands on her shoulders.

'Some Peak District, eh?'

'I've never seen anything like it,' she whispered. 'I hope it's not just another one of that dreadful man's visions.'

They stood there, enjoying the moment, until Kia felt the tug of responsibility.

'Where on earth are we?' she asked, managing to push things on without having to miss a second of that view.

'Well,' said Holly. 'The faint green tinge on the side of that tree tells us that we're facing north, which means the sun over there is in the west, which means it must be evening. In which case, we've travelled very far indeed.'

Kia finally turned round, sporting a lopsided grin.

'You really did earn that orienteering badge, didn't you?'

'That's always assuming that wherever on earth we are is actually still on earth.' He smiled. 'If not, all bets are off.'

They forced their attention on to their immediate surroundings. Kia gave a small start. She had forgotten they hadn't come alone.

'There is nothing here,' Voltaire said, shrugging in puzzlement. 'Absolutely nothing.'

'Yes, there is,' Colette called out.

Unlike her companion, who had remained rooted to the spot since they had arrived, she had wandered some way off.

'Up there,' she pointed, beckoning them over with her other hand.

As they approached her, a small building came into view some fifty yards further up the mountain. It blended in nicely with its location, its timber construction having been rendered the same colour as the leaves on the trees. The exaggerated curves in the roof gave it the appearance of an oriental temple. A rudimentary, meandering path led up to it.

After exchanging a few apprehensive glances, they set off, Holly in front, Kia and Colette together in the middle, and a wary Voltaire bringing up the rear.

The temple – which they decided en route was what it was – had seen better days, but looked sturdy enough. The door was solid, but moved easily at the slightest touch.

Peering inside, they saw a single room that had clearly not had a visitor for a very long time, judging by the plant life that was growing freely though the gaps in the floorboards and the walls, and around the rudimentary benches that were arranged in three rows. It almost concealed the one thing that was worth seeing, which Kia spotted, just as they were about to give up and go back outside.

They ventured further in, towards the object in the far corner. They had to move some foliage aside to make out what it was. It turned out to be a frame of heavy timber, consisting of two A-shapes supporting a thick, square, horizontal beam. This in turn bore the weight of a bell, some three-feet high, and of solid bronze, suspended another foot off the ground by a hefty piece of rope.

'I'm guessing this is important,' suggested Holly.

'Well, it's the only musical thing around,' agreed Kia. 'But I don't see that it tells us anything.'

'Apart from what it's telling us,' Voltaire chipped in.

Kia and Holly assumed he had either misheard or mistranslated something, but were too polite to say. Their expressions conveyed as much.

'There's writing on it,' Voltaire explained. 'Around the bottom edge.'

He pointed, then squatted down to get a better look,

having to bat away leaves and lean in to follow the edge round.

'It says… Ooh lá lá, there's a big crack on the other side. No, no, that's not what it says. It says… Preserve Harmony.'

Kia frowned.

'Why does that make me think of Portsmouth?' she asked.

'It was that sailor,' Holly remembered. 'At the pub. He was going on about the guilds. And he mentioned that the Worshipful Company of Musicians, or whatever they were called, used the slogan Preserve Harmony.'

'So that's the Musicians' Motto?' Colette asked. 'That's why we're here?'

'It would appear so,' said Holly.

'It's rather elaborate for a reminder, isn't it?' said Kia. 'If that's all it is.'

No-one had any other suggestions, so they retreated outside, three of them keen to have a last look around, the fourth just keen to go back.

'It's definitely evening,' said Holly, pointing at the sinking sun. 'The landscape's turning red.'

Kia squinted at the sky.

'It's not that unusual to see the moon during the day, is it?' she asked.

'No, not at all,' Holly replied. 'There it is, over there.'

He nodded at a faint crescent to the left of the sun.

'Oh,' Kia said, faintly. 'What's that, then?'

She pointed a shaking finger in the opposite direction, where a hazy, pale circle, less than half the size of the moon, could be seen just above the horizon, with a faint, black tail, fading into the darkening sky.

CHAPTER SIXTEEN

'Lingering – dallying – waiting.'

'W-A-T-T F-O-U-R?'

'A kindly halo?'

'Unknown directions.'

The quartet nodded contentedly and sat back, Great Uncle Sid having given an affirmative response to Uncle Sid's guess that what they were waiting for was Kia and Holly.

Uncles Sid and Gordo had just come in from next door, having heard the others arrive. Great had let them all in, having been the only one in the house.

Uncle Jasper, the captain, the baron, and Claire had waited momentarily at the café after their leaders' departure in case there was a speedy retreat, before realising that such a retreat would be back to the house, the café location not having come up as a clue number, as far as they knew. They were just about to set off, after the captain had been dissuaded from ordering another coffee, when Gilbert turned up, accompanied by a tall blonde.

The captain had been very proud of his achievement of remembering the Frenchman's name and got annoyed when Gilbert refused to answer to that name, insisting that he was now Hugo. He also refused to tell them what he had been up to, or the identity of his companion, who looked vaguely familiar, until he could report to his commander, Voltaire. Didn't he mean Hugo? No, he meant Voltaire.

They had then all trudged back to the house in awkward silence, Claire and the baron doing their best to keep a cheerful conversation going, ending up just talking to each other in the absence of any other takers before giving up altogether. Now back in the lounge, the new Hugo and the captain found themselves sitting opposite each other, both making a big show of avoiding eye contact.

The sound of a female in distress in the kitchen came, ironically, as a relief.

'Colette!' her compatriot cried, jumping out of his seat.

By the time he made the door, the returning foursome were already making their way through it. The Frenchwoman was being supported at the elbow. She had found her second trip much less traumatic than her first, but she was still in no hurry to repeat the experience. The gallant Gaul offered her his seat, and she accepted it readily, murmuring 'Thank you, Hugo,' causing him to cast a triumphant glance in the captain's direction.

Holly spotted the young woman sitting next to her.

'We saw you on television,' he said, trawling through a memory. 'You're the saviour woman.'

The uncles, the captain and the baron all registered exasperation at not having worked that out themselves. The woman in question merely raised her eyebrows, never having thought of herself in that way.

'So, you found him,' Holly said, 'like you said you would.'

'No,' Hugo corrected in his usual, serious way. 'I found her.'

Now that his commander had returned, he was finally able to offload the intelligence he had gathered.

The long, dusty green coat had made Marlowe easy to follow. He showed no sign of knowing or even caring whether he had a tail, other than taking a fairly circuitous route. Hugo assumed this was standard procedure and, consequently, nothing to worry about. As it had taken them past his flatshare, it actually made it easier for him to keep track of where they were.

The Englishman finally stopped outside a newsagent's, making a show of inspecting a display of postcards. The Resistance fighter couldn't help snorting with contempt as his quarry conversed so obviously with another man, despite them both being at pains to look in opposite directions. This other man was tall and wore a dark blue suit, along with the telltale shades.

Something about the exchange told Hugo that the suited man was getting some instructions. When the pair split up, it was this man who now seemed of most interest.

After another brief but equally convoluted journey, the man stopped outside a house at the end of a terrace. He stood there for a while, occasionally checking his watch, before going up to the door and ringing the bell. The door was opened by a young, blonde woman who let him in.

Hugo made his way to the garden fence at the side of the property, and was about to climb over it when he suddenly had to scramble for cover as the couple came outside, apparently so she could light a cigarette. He strained to listen to their conversation. He couldn't make out much, but enough to spot the Italian accent he was expecting and something about her making a sketch for him. Then they went back inside.

He knew the enemy's methods and that he didn't have time to consider his next course of action. He let his instinct take over. It told him this woman might be a valuable asset. That reduced his options to one.

Clearing the fence in one leap, having made sure of a safe landing area, he slowly approached the door she had been helpful enough to leave open. He was in time to hear the woman's remark, about flames reflected in his sunglasses, and didn't like the sound of it. When the man suggested she might need saving, and was about to remove those glasses, he knew he had to act.

Grabbing the first thing that came to hand, Hugo burst in and gave the man a hefty whack on the back of the head, which hit the table and remained motionless, in contrast to the sunglasses, which shot across the table and on to the floor. Fortunately, the man's eyes were now closed.

He held his hand out, expecting the woman to scream, or at least recoil in horror, but she took it without question. He would have been less surprised by this if he'd realised that he had appeared through the patio door with the sun behind him, just another in a long line of silhouetted saviours.

Hugo had always been mystified by the English preoccupation with garden ornaments, but as he replaced the stone gnome that had come in so handy as a weapon, he decided that, should he ever make it back to his homeland, he would take one with him as a souvenir.

Still holding the woman's hand, he didn't stop until he was back outside the café, where he was frustrated to find his comrades absent, being therefore unable to divulge the information he'd managed to gather on his new companion's assailant.

'He said his name was Arfa.'

Camille was now the centre of attention, sitting on the sofa in the lounge. She wasn't sure what was going on, and wasn't much bothered, but wanted to be helpful, especially in the eyes of her latest hero.

'Short for Farfalle,' Voltaire agreed, turning his attention to the rest of the room. 'Farfalle Puttanesca, to give him his full code name. Masquerades as an Italian. The other members of his cell are Nasi Goreng, the man you know as Marlowe, and our friend Talleyrand, code name Murgh Makhani.'

His scout snorted.

'Typical of the British to name their agents after dishes they wouldn't be seen dead eating.'

'I imagine Toad-in-the-hole was already taken,' suggested the baron.

Hugo pulled a face.

'How would a name like that compare with Velouté, or Béchamel…'

'Saucy. How very French,' commented the captain. 'Although it's common knowledge you only invented all those sauces to hide the fact that your meat was rancid.'

'Pfuh! You don't even have a cuisine. You only have a kitchen.'

'Well,' the captain murmured. 'I think we can all see why Camembert here drinks at the Coffee-Nosed.'

'Boys!' Kia commanded, as Voltaire had to put a hand on Hugo's shoulder to calm him down. The captain, by contrast, only had to restrain himself from laughing. The uncles clearly had no such restriction.

'Maniacs,' Voltaire said. 'No, not these two. Our enemies. These three agents and their leader. We've already seen him. He was driving the motorcycle. But, of course, we haven't really seen him, as he always wears that mask.'

'And what's his code name?' asked the captain. 'Beef Stroganoff?'

'Not a bad guess, as it happens,' answered Colette. 'His name is Fugu. Fugu Yakitori.'

'Hmm,' the captain commented, appreciatively. 'I could murder a Japanese.'

‘Please,’ Voltaire implored. ‘May I remind you that they have already murdered one of ours? And that they have prioritised their next target?’

He took the sheet of paper that Hugo was holding out and unfolded it.

‘The intelligence they have gathered,’ he said, ‘mostly from our meeting at the café, confirmed that your team poses a threat.’ He held the object up for everyone in the room to see. ‘And from this young lady they have learnt that this man poses their biggest threat.’

The image of Uncle Jasper made them all gasp, particularly the man himself.

‘That’s actually a really good likeness,’ the captain told Camille.

‘Oh, thanks.’

‘You do know,’ the captain sounded reluctant to ask, ‘that he’s sitting over there?’

‘Oh, yeah,’ Camille said, giving the subject of her portrait the briefest of glances before turning back. Yesterday’s idol. She had moved on.

Relieved at this let-off, the ex-saviour stood up, motioned to the other two uncles to follow him, then gestured to Kia that they were going next door, before the trio left the room. Great Uncle Sid looked so forlorn at their departure that Kia went and patted his hand.

‘So, where are we?’ she asked no-one in particular. ‘We have a comet hurtling towards us. Unless we do something about it, that’s the end. But we have no idea what that something may be. And even if we did, we have a bunch of Maniacs ready to stand in our way.’

Ignoring Camille, who didn’t even seem to be listening, she got an acknowledgement from each of the French team.

‘But these saboteurs are unwittingly telling us that there is something we can do,’ she continued, ‘because otherwise they wouldn't be here. And you lot wouldn't have woken up today as Resistance fighters.'

She went over to the window, forcing herself to search the sky, despite dreading the possibility of setting eyes on that terrible new arrival. But the unbroken layer of cloud still admitted nothing but the hint of a sun.

'And we have a clue, passed from one librarian to another. But we don't know what it means.'

This produced a determined frown on Claire's face.

'Our biggest source of hope, meaning no disrespect to any of you,' Kia continued, 'is that Holly is here.'

There was no dissent on this point from anyone, other than Holly, who sceptically shook his head.

Kia watched the uncles conversing at the gate, her anxiety increasing as, while his companions headed for the neighbouring house, Uncle Jasper turned and set off in the opposite direction.

'So,' Kia concluded, having run out of positives. 'Where do we go from here?'

CHAPTER SEVENTEEN

Uncle Sid had run out of peanuts and was still nervous.

He was, by nature, an optimist. Even Holly's arrival, on what had until then seemed a perfectly pleasant day, had presented him with no more than a promise that things would get interesting, despite having heralded momentous events on two previous occasions.

But the consequent bombshell that this might be the last crossword had thrown him into turmoil. It was all very well, the captain advocating a normal, puzzle-free life for them all, but what would that mean for an anagram specialist who couldn't even communicate in any other way? His daily purpose in life would disappear. All he could see ahead of him was a huge void, with more nothing beyond.

Uncle Jasper's last words had unsettled him even further. Despite the five words having the same meaning, they had still managed to be vague.

'Shielded – secure – protected – sheltered – safe,' he had said, pointing back towards the house they had just left. The only sense Uncle Sid had made out of this was that, as Uncle Jasper seemed to have been singled out as the primary target of these Maniacs, he would take himself off somewhere to minimise the risk to Kia.

It was in this troubled frame of mind, back in the

house that he didn't think of as Gus's, that Uncle Sid was desperately seeking some distraction. This took him, as it often did, to the twig-like shape of Restless Matter. This was appropriate, as it served as a fitting description for Uncle Sid himself.

He had enlisted the help of Uncle Gordo. As usual, this had taken little effort. They were as determined as ever to reanimate the object that, contrary to its name, was lying peacefully on the table.

'Sag…' Uncle Sid started.

'…M-O-W-E-D!' Uncle Gordo concluded.

This was their way of saying gas mode, ever hopeful that this time they would be successful in transforming the rigid formation into its ethereal state. Uncle Jasper would normally have been with them, ready to precede a repetition of Uncle Gordo's word with 'Thus – cover', thereby making the so-lid mode command that would make the thing revert to its tangible form before it dissipated beyond recovery.

But, yet again, the command was redundant, and their eager smiles faded.

'Solver. What you need. What you're not.'

The old man, still in his pyjamas, was standing in the doorway. The uncles eyed him with suspicion. It was a mystery to them how he had managed to grasp the local rules and customs in such a short space of time.

They heard the front door close.

'Parcels?' called Uncle Sid, relieved at the idea that Uncle Jasper had returned. June Parcels was his pet name for his colleague.

But the man who pushed his way roughly into the lounge wasn't wearing a boiler suit, but a formal, dark blue ensemble. And dark glasses.

'No, it's not the postie,' Farfalle Puttanesca smirked, without a hint of an Italian accent.

Having brushed the old man aside, he turned back, as if he'd only just noticed the pyjamas and slippers.

'Do you know what time it is, grandad?' he asked.

The old man thought for a moment.

'Peacetime,' he said.

The new arrival nursed the back of his head and snorted.

'For you, maybe,' he growled.

He advanced on the two men by the table.

'Where is he?' he said, in a low voice.

He met a united front of ignorance.

'How?' asked Uncle Sid.

'Never mind how,' snapped the young man. 'It's who you've got to worry about. Your handyman friend. Where is he?'

A shrug and a shake of the head were all he got.

'Word is,' he explained, with exaggerated patience, 'that he's spent the last few weeks working at the same location, a very local location. Chances are, that's where he is now. And it's important we find him, as we need him to… help us with our enquiries.'

A few seconds of zero response was enough to make his fake Latin temperament rise up in him in a very real way. It was now his turn to grab whatever came readily to hand. In the absence of any garden gnomes, he settled on a strange, gnarly object lying on a tray on the table. He grasped one end of it and manoeuvred a particularly sharp point at the other end against Uncle Sid's throat.

'Address,' he insisted. 'Which road? Which… road?'

'L-O-R-N,' Uncle Gordo said, hurriedly.

'No need to spell it out,' Farfalle snarled. 'So, Lorn Road. What number?'

He applied more pressure to Uncle Sid's neck.

'Ninety-six!'

Farfalle leered at Uncle Sid.

'You see? You *can* talk. And you might need to talk again. Which is the only reason I'm going to let you live. And don't think about going to warn him. We'll see you. We've got all CCTV covered.'

He withdrew the pointed object and looked closely at it for the first time.

'Well,' he snorted. 'That's the most useful this thing is ever going to be.'

He threw it contemptuously back on the table and made his way towards the door.

'Lorn Road, number 96,' he repeated. 'You'd better be right.'

He stopped as he was walking past the slippered old man, fixing him with a glare.

'Or I'll be back. And next time, I'll take it out on this old codger.' He reached up and jiggled his sunglasses. 'How would you like to be two hundred years old, grandad?'

The codger stared back, the disdain amplified over his half-glasses. Eventually, he uttered a short sound that was the closest thing to a laugh the uncles had heard from him.

'Before the peace. Punks like you. Snapped their necks. Like twigs.' His eyes wandered, chasing a memory. 'So many.'

He turned and shuffled out of the room as though the Maniac didn't exist.

Farfalle gave the uncles one last stare, desperately trying to regain his status as the scariest thing in the house. Then he left, slamming the front door as he did so.

The two uncles were exchanging worried glances, wondering who on earth their new lodger was, when he made them jump by reappearing in the door.

'Nice work, by the way. Ninety-six. Anagram of sixty-nine. And L-O-R-N for Lawn Road. Teamwork. Impressive.'

Nodding in appreciation, he vanished again.

After a brief pause, the uncles chuckled.

'L-O-R-N!' maintained Uncle Gordo in a show of innocence.

'Rail!' Uncle Sid hissed.

Uncle Gordo feigned indignation.

'S-E-W R-O-O-D!' he protested.

CHAPTER EIGHTEEN

Next door, the French trio had retired to the garden, mainly to try and contact the elusive Olivier to discuss strategy, but also because Voltaire didn't like to smoke in the house. Hugo had packed Camille off with a promise to call round at her flat the next day. Fortunately for him, the idea that there might not be a tomorrow was beyond her comprehension, and she left happily enough.

Great Uncle Sid had retired again, bidding them all 'A copper key, universal'. This wasn't his usual use of copper, that being Cu for the element, but DI for detective inspector, followed by the key of E, and a U for the film classification universal, all joined together to make 'adieu'. Everyone was familiar with this formula and reciprocated – all except Claire, who was far too in awe of the man to question anything he said, no matter how incomprehensible.

His departure had come as a relief to Kia. She had been dying to tell Claire, the baron, and the captain of their visit to the mountainside but knew how upsetting it was for Great to hear about their jaunts to all these outlandish locations, and she wanted to spare him the details. In the event, Claire seemed instinctively to have been holding back for the same reason.

'So? Where did Musicians' Motto take you?' she

demanded, the second the old man had closed the door behind him.

She listened avidly to the description of the mountain, its colourful features and its setting within so many others. She nodded impatiently on hearing about the temple, as though she'd been expecting it. She remained silent, right up to the point when the mysterious object in the corner turned out to be a bell.

'That's it,' she said, in a trance. 'A bell. That's what the chart shows. Cordelia's bottom line. They're the frequencies of a bell.'

'Do you think it's this bell?' the baron asked.

'Well,' Claire reasoned. 'The location doesn't ring a… doesn't sound familiar, so that doesn't explain why I would recognise that particular chart, which I think I do. Did you ring it?'

Holly and Kia looked sheepishly at each other.

'Er, no,' Kia admitted. 'There was a big crack in the side. And we thought only the words were important. Does "Preserve Harmony" mean anything to you?'

But Claire had never heard the phrase before. The captain, who had totally forgotten about the guild of musicians, suggested it might refer to a particularly well-blended jam.

'Right,' said Holly, feeling it was time for some action. 'We need to get back there, ring that bell and see what happens. You coming?'

Claire declined. There was something bothering her, and she needed to figure out what it was. The baron and the captain opted to stay as well.

'What do we hit it with?' Kia asked, suddenly. 'I suppose we could find a branch out there?'

'Oh!' the baron said in surprise. 'You might try this.'

He held out a heavy, rubber-headed mallet.

‘I just found it on my paper,’ he said, with a puzzled expression. ‘I think Uncle Jasper must have left it there.’

‘That’s his, all right,’ confirmed Kia. ‘I’ve seen him use it to knock ceramic tiles into place.’

‘So have I,’ the baron agreed. ‘He also uses it as a sounding device, hitting pipes and walls to see what sound they make. It’s baffling, like watching a water diviner.’

‘Not as baffling as figuring out how on earth he knew we’d be needing it,’ Holly commented.

‘Yes, well, we may be baffled,’ said the captain. ‘But not one of us is shocked. This is Uncle Jasper we’re talking about.’

‘True enough,’ said Holly, dismissing his curiosity for the time being. ‘Let’s go, Kia. Claire, keep thinking about those frequencies. Baron, be your usual inspiring self. Captain – try not to be too distracting.’

Having already taken Kia’s arm and checked the relevant clue number, he said it and disappeared before he got any reaction.

The light dimmed immediately.

They had arrived in exactly the same spot as before. Only half the sun was now peering over the horizon, the entire scene bathed in pale red, making the trees with their scarlet foliage less conspicuous.

The cloud line had sunk noticeably since their last visit, revealing more of the surrounding mountain range. There was still no indication of how tall the mountains actually were, but seeing the steep slope below them extending so much further down made Kia and Holly feel a lot more precarious. They certainly didn’t relish the prospect of climbing any further to reach the temple. But, when they managed to break the hold of the terrifying view below them, what lay above them turned out to be several times worse.

Despite also having hit the horizon, the comet had clearly grown. Its form was still slightly darker than the surrounding sky, and the side facing the sun had acquired a fuzzy, pale pink crescent. The tail on the opposite side, which had previously tapered, now widened slightly, extending far into the distance before fading away.

Holly was the first to regain his composure. He had to give Kia's shoulder a firm shake before she could tear herself away. Even then, it took her a minute to remember where they were and why they were there. He pointed further up the slope and set off. She followed, careful to keep her eyes down on the terrain in front of her.

The path seemed longer than last time, and the gradient more arduous. The relief they felt at reaching the temple was short-lived. The door was wide open, and they both remembered closing it after them out of an instinctive respect for what they had all taken to be a religious building. The breeze was still negligible, so could not have played a part. Apprehensively, they peered inside.

In the failing light, they could just make out that much of the vegetation that had grown freely through all available gaps in the woodwork had been either trampled flat or torn aside. Unable to see more from the doorway, and seeing no reason to believe the place was anything other than deserted, they stepped inside.

As their eyes adjusted to the darkness, they were dismayed to see that the benches had been smashed and flung against the walls, making holes in some places. The serenity that had greeted them before had been replaced by a feeling of unease that reeked of blasphemy.

'Let's get this over with,' Kia suggested.

Holly agreed wholeheartedly, and descended on the far corner, mallet at the ready.

But the frame that had borne the weight of the bell had

suffered the same fate as the benches, lying in splinters to one side. Kia inhaled sharply when she spotted it.

'Can we hang the bell from something else?' she asked, still standing behind Holly.

He shook his head slowly and stood aside to reveal the reason for this answer.

The sides of the crack had been forced further apart, and the bell lay in two separate pieces in the dust.

CHAPTER NINETEEN

Uncle Jasper had indeed set off for 69 Lawn Road. Just because he was lying low, he figured, didn't mean he couldn't use his time to his advantage. He was in the middle of replacing a bathroom suite on the second floor of the property. This was one of his least favourite tasks, second only to wallpapering on his hate list. It would be the perfect day to break the back of the work, as he couldn't be of any more use to the team.

After all, he had already left them his best rubber mallet, along with a canvas bag filled with an assortment of other implements he wouldn't need today but they might. He wasn't one to rain on anyone's parade, and it was right and proper that Claire should get her moment in the sunshine, but it had seemed quite obvious to Uncle Jasper that the most likely explanation for the spikes on Cordelia's chart was the sound of a bell. This had not come from any musical understanding, which he didn't possess, but purely from scientific reasoning. He was a voracious reader of science journals, and he seemed to remember coming across something similar. Which bell it could be, he had no idea, that was their job, but it didn't occur to him for a moment that they wouldn't find the right one. Thinking ahead took him quite naturally to the problem of what to strike this bell with, and problem-solving was what he did, particularly if it involved finding the right implement for the job in hand.

So the plan was to get stuck into the work and keep the radio on, in case there was any mention of the comet having disappeared, giving him the satisfaction of knowing that his mallet had played its part. Far from downing tools to go and celebrate with his companions, he would then carry on until there was a convenient break. The world may have been saved, but that was no excuse to leave a task unfinished.

He was similarly sanguine about the prospect of this being the last puzzle. In contrast to Uncle Sid, he had plenty of other strings to his bow. He had enough work lined up for the next two years, at least, and could finally get on with it unhindered. His limited communication skills were not an issue. It didn't bother him if he didn't converse with another human being from one day to the next.

It was this mood of general contentment that came to an abrupt end as he turned the corner into Lawn Road and stopped, seeing a man wearing a greatcoat and sunglasses standing outside a house some way down.

Uncle Jasper had no idea of his companions' valiant attempts to give the Maniacs a false scent, so felt no confusion as to what may have gone wrong. As it happened, Uncle Sid's ruse had worked. The man was at least standing in front of the wrong house, the one at number 96. But Uncle Gordo's homonym had only worked in theory, not in practice.

Farfalle had relayed the message over to his colleague. Not being local to the area, this man had simply asked a woman in the street for directions, and she had of course heard 'Lorn' as 'Lawn' and, helpfully, sent him to the very road he was meant to avoid.

Efficient as ever, Uncle Jasper had archived the name Marlowe, identifying this man immediately as Nasi.

Remembering the captain's quip about the name almost caused him to smile, but his current immobility stretched to his face.

Nasi was in profile, surveying the other side of the street. Uncle Jasper started edging backwards, hoping to escape before being seen, and was about to make the cover of one of the many plane trees when Nasi turned and looked straight at him. Uncle Jasper continued until the tree blocked his vision of the man, who hadn't moved. Then he turned and accelerated to a fast walk.

It wasn't far to the next side road. He shot a quick glance over his shoulder to see if he was being followed. As there was no sign of anybody behind him, he stopped, peering over a postbox. But before he had the chance to sigh with relief, the greatcoat hove into view, and he set off again at a faster pace.

He didn't turn round again when he hit the main road. He thought it best to carry on as though the tail was still there. Up ahead there were shops and considerably more human activity, which brought him some comfort. He assumed the Maniac would be less likely to try anything in the presence of so many other people, until he remembered what had happened to Odile. But he did welcome the opportunity to blend in with a crowd. The idea that this would be virtually impossible for someone wearing a white boiler suit and a bright red hat didn't occur to him.

Passing through the parade, he stopped at a couple of the shop windows, finally daring to check the street behind him for the telltale reflection off a pair of sunglasses. Fortunately, it still wasn't a bright enough day for any of the locals to need shades, so the total absence of flashes of sunlight was obvious.

He needed a plan. Until he came up with one, he needed to keep going, putting as much distance as he could between himself and all the members of that cell. He was conscious that, although it was Nasi he had seen, and that had seen him, any one of his fellow Maniacs could pop out at any minute.

He passed the old town hall, long bereft of official, administrative duties, now mainly providing a bewildering array of day classes for the elderly. He toyed with the idea of diving inside, but decided against it. He knew too many of its patrons, having done odd jobs for nearly everyone in the neighbourhood at some time, and was sure he'd be greeted by people waving and shouting his name. He kept going, past the petrol station and the hotel, neither of which provided any inspiration.

He was now on the left side of the road. Ahead of him lay the junction where, on the right, the hill went back down towards home and the café where everything had kicked off that morning.

The notion that this right turn was the one manoeuvre he shouldn't make, however appealing, was reinforced by the figure standing on the corner – a figure wearing a greatcoat and a wide grin.

Uncle Jasper wasn't one for overreacting, but he recoiled as though he'd walked into an invisible wall. Visible or not, it managed to knock some sense into him.

The jangling of keys that made it impossible for him to creep up on anyone unannounced meant that he was carrying with him the means of access to half the properties in the area, and he cursed himself for not realising this earlier.

He shot into the side street and out of the Maniac's line of vision. As luck would have it, the first house on the right was a detached Victorian pile surrounded by trees. He had done a number of jobs there, mostly small repairs. The owners were currently on holiday and had lined him up a few things to do, after he'd finished in Lawn Road and before they got back.

His filing system didn't let him down. He went straight to the right pocket and, out of the several sets of keys he found, chose the one with the blue string. The front door was open in seconds.

He closed it behind him, as quietly as he could, making his way through the secondary door that was decorated with stained glass. Once in the hallway, he was glad to find all four of the room doors shut, meaning he couldn't be seen from the road. These doors would be locked, so he was safe, even if someone broke into one of those rooms.

He tried to work out what to do. He knew he shouldn't leave the house. He had no idea who was out there, and he certainly couldn't think of a better hiding place. Entering an adjacent room was out of the question, far too many windows. Going down into the cellar or up the stairs seemed a bad idea, as both options cut off his means of escape.

But he wasn't any good at doing nothing, that was a waste of time. He even tried to remember what needed to be done around the house, in case there was some small, quiet task that could occupy him while he waited until he considered the coast to be clear.

All these thoughts were swept aside, as he heard a creak behind him. He turned, to see Nasi Goreng, in his heavy green coat, standing at the top of the stairs, his glasses low enough on his nose to allow a flickering glow to be seen above them.

And this time, he wasn't smiling.

CHAPTER TWENTY

'This is driving me nuts. I need a library.'

Claire had been staring at the frequency chart for what seemed an eternity, given the lack of results. She, the baron, and the captain were the only remaining occupants of Kia's lounge. Claire had remained standing, transfixed, muttering occasionally. The men had long since taken a seat in respectful silence.

'You need some peace and quiet?' the captain suggested, relieved not to have to hold his tongue any longer, but disappointed his superhuman effort in that regard may have been in vain.

'No, I need to look something up,' Claire answered. 'But at least now I know where to look.'

'Any particular library?' the baron asked.

'Yes. Mine.'

The captain's perplexed look revealed that his mind was wandering around a pile of charred remains on a cloud.

'No, not that one,' the baron whispered. 'The one she works in now. The little one in Derry Road.'

'And I need to go there now,' Claire decided. 'I can't wait for the others to get back. I have a feeling they won't have been successful.'

'Well, in that case,' the baron said, 'given what's out

there, you're going to need a chaperone. And I happen to know of two guys who aren't doing anything at the moment.'

The captain gestured towards the garden, still playing host to a French conference.

'Shall I go and get them?' he asked. 'Oh, I see,' he added, on getting an exasperated look from his colleague. 'Ready when you are.'

The baron, popping his head round the back door to tell the Resistance workers that they were just off to the library, Kia and Holly should be back from God-knows-where any minute, and would they mind keeping an eye on the place, elicited no more than a weary nod and an acknowledging wave of a cigarette. It seemed unlikely the Soya Beans would ever be surprised by anything again.

The baron took charge of the route, taking the smallest streets available, keeping an eye out for enemy presence. On top of his guide and lookout duties, he also had to prevent his companions walking into oncoming traffic on several occasions, Claire because she couldn't take her eyes off the chart, and the captain because his mind was always elsewhere. Despite the journey not being the most direct, it still took them only fifteen minutes to reach their destination.

The purpose-built library was from the 1930s, situated on the inside corner of an L-shaped street. The end they reached first was semicircular, with five double-height windows arranged symmetrically. The baron had been here a few times, but saw it now in a new light, and noticed for the first time a square plaque above the middle window, bearing the motto NON SIDI SED TOTI. He couldn't help smiling, as his distant memory of Latin told him this meant 'Not for self but for all' – appropriate, he thought, given the mission they were on.

Claire led the way inside, nodding at the young man in

the corduroy jacket behind the desk between the entrance door and the exit door. He looked up in surprise.

'Not in today, are you, Claire?' he asked.

'No, Bill,' she assured him. 'Just doing some research. Lunchtime rush building up, I see.'

The library consisted mainly of one large room, mostly lit by the five high windows at one end. Next to them, a stand bore a selection of the day's newspapers. There was a children's section at the opposite end with some suitably miniature furniture. Between them was a sparse, random layout of tables and chairs.

The room was empty, save for two figures in hoodies, sitting at a table in the middle, their backs to the door. Bill raised his eyes to the ceiling, and then he returned to his work.

Claire led her friends towards a screen in the opposite wall, but before they got there, the captain spotted a collection of various instruments to one side.

'Free access to musical instruments,' he enthused. 'That's got to be a good thing. I expect you can play them all by now.'

Claire laughed.

'I did pick up that clarinet once,' she said, 'but I couldn't get a note out of it. It was really embarrassing. It put me off trying any of the others, which is a shame because there is one I'm dying to have a go at.'

'I know!' agreed the captain. 'The drum kit.'

Claire shook her head.

'The piccolo?' he tried again.

'The cello,' said the baron, staring at it without needing to look round for the confirmation nod.

'But could you imagine the noise?' she lamented. 'I know what kids sound like, learning to play stringed instruments. I couldn't put anyone through that.'

The two men looked expectantly at her until she became uncomfortable.

'What?' she asked.

The baron indicated the instrument that was propped up against a chair.

'Oh, I couldn't,' Claire protested.

'Yes,' the baron said. 'You could.'

Claire looked imploringly at the captain.

'Perfect time,' he said. 'End of the world, remember? And you're never going to have a smaller audience, unless you come out busking with us.'

She turned the look on the baron.

'Try it,' he shrugged. 'If you like the feel of it, and we live through this, we'll get you a teacher.'

Claire gave in. Picking up the bow in her right hand, and grabbing the neck of the cello with her left, she settled herself in the chair.

'Oh,' she winced. 'This is going to be so screechy.'

But it wasn't. Two dramatic arpeggiated chords burst out, filling the entire library. These were followed by a few notes, then another chord, before the melody resumed and died away, and Claire had to stop. Her mouth was open, and she was trembling from head to foot.

There was a pause as the echoes were allowed to die with dignity. Then the captain turned to the baron.

'I'd cancel that teacher,' he said.

The baron smiled.

'Elgar,' he said, refusing to wipe away the tear that had already reached the corner of his mouth. 'It had to be bloody Elgar.'

Bill was staring open-mouthed from behind the counter, before becoming self-conscious and burying his head back in his book. The couple in the hoodies hadn't moved. The baron assumed they were wearing headphones.

Claire looked incapable of any voluntary movement of her own, so the baron gently took the instrument and the bow from her and laid them on the floor. Then he took her hand and raised her to a standing position. Her expression had at least moved from horrified to elated.

'Focus,' he told her. 'Weird as it seems, we've been there, and we know exactly how it feels. And we had the luxury of running with it. But you don't, because we're all depending on you to figure this next bit out. So force yourself to file it away. Or use it as more incentive to make sure there is a tomorrow.'

'Absolutely,' she breathed.

Swallowing hard, she nodded a few times, as she tried to divert all her thoughts to the matter in hand. With one last suspicious look at the cello that was now lying innocently on the floor, she turned back to the machine that had been her original destination and took a deep breath.

'This is a new feature,' she explained. 'It's only a small library, but it houses one of the best music reference sections. That's why I wanted to work here. But they're cutting back on staff to save money, so they've just come up with this automated system. I haven't even tried it out myself, yet. You say what you want into this microphone, and it finds it and delivers it to that window over there.'

She pointed to a dark recess in the far corner.

The baron didn't seem convinced.

'Looks expensive,' he commented. 'I wonder how many wages they'd have to save before it pays for itself.'

'Yes, well,' Claire said. 'Ours not to question why, ours but to do and…well, hopefully not.'

She took a small notepad from her pocket and opened it.

'This is the definitive paper on bell frequencies,' she told them. 'I'm pretty sure they'll have it.'

Holding the pad in front of her, she leant over towards the microphone and pushed the button to activate the machine.

'*Heaven's Bells*,' she announced. '*A Compendium of Harmonics*, Cavaciuti & Andre, Slender Reed Press, 1977.'

They waited while this information was silently processed.

'I expected it to whirr,' the captain whispered. 'But I suppose nowadays everything's digit…'

The machine interrupted him.

'*Seven Smells*,' announced a woman's voice, calm but authoritative, her words appearing on the screen. '*A Company of Heretics*. Have a Snooty and Honorary Sender Repress, Nineties Event is Heaven. I'm sorry. That doesn't appear to be currently available.'

The captain took the notebook from Claire before she had a chance to try again.

'You're probably still a little shaky,' he said. 'These machines aren't very forgiving.'

He cleared his throat.

'*Heaven's Bells*,' he began, in his best Shakespearean intonation.

'*Devon Spells*,' replied the machine.

'*A Compendium of Harmonics…*' the captain continued, raising his voice.

'*Acorn Pendulum Off Arsenics*.'

'Cavaciuti & Andre…' he shouted.

'Andalusian on Tray.'

The baron caught the captain's arm just as it was about to deliver a fatal blow to his tormentor.

'You don't look so forgiving yourself,' he said, patting his friend on the shoulder. 'Let me try something.'

To the surprise of the others, he droned the same information, using just a single note and exaggerating every consonant. The device was silent for a moment, before repeating every word correctly, with its on-screen confirmation, much to the captain's annoyance.

'It was a hindrance,' explained the baron. 'A deliberate obstacle. So there had to be something in the grid to overcome it.'

The captain wasn't convinced.

'I don't remember it saying anything about daleks,' he said.

'Close enough,' chuckled the baron. 'It was Lucidly Robotic. We had no idea what it meant at the time, but every solution seems to have its moment, if you wait long enough.'

Their wait seemed to be over.

'Please make your way to the dispatch portal,' the machine purred. 'Your item will be with you in five minutes.'

It was the last thing this voice would ever say. With a loud crack, the screen split into several pieces. As the horrified trio stared at it, smoke started seeping out, slowly at first, but soon in billows that made them back away.

'I'm afraid your delivery has been delayed... indefinitely.'

They didn't need to look at the man standing in front of an open door in the far corner to recognise the nasal Essex drawl of Murgh Makhani. When they did, they could see more smoke swirling behind him, along with a bright, flickering glow.

'Oh, no!' wailed Claire. 'Why do my libraries keep burning down?'

CHAPTER TWENTY-ONE

The two hooded figures had jumped out of their seats and were advancing on the gleeful Maniac, who stood his ground.

'Now, boys,' he gloated. 'You don't want to be old before your time, do you?'

He reached up and removed his sunglasses. His eyes mimicked the fire that was now raging behind him.

The man in the darker hoodie turned his head.

'Look away!' he shouted.

Claire, the baron and the captain did as they were told, simultaneously shielding their eyes. They had seen first-hand the consequences of that fearful gaze.

The second man had not moved, and he was still facing the demonic stare. Murgh laughed and peered closer at him. Getting no reaction, his sneer soon turned into a scowl. Eventually, with a roar of disappointment, he put his glasses back on and started for the exit.

'Clear!' the first man bellowed.

The trio opened their eyes, anxious to check they were all unharmed. On wider inspection, it turned out they weren't.

'Bill!' Claire screamed.

Her fellow librarian had not been able to tear himself

away from that awesome sight. Youth and vitality had been sucked out of him, like air from a vacuum-sealed pack of bacon. His withered, wrinkled form lay lifeless across the counter. Strangely, his hair was still brown, giving it the impression of a wig. It changed colour as they watched, silvery-grey spreading from one side to the other, like a pond freezing over.

This restored the Maniac's good mood. With a triumphant cry, he grabbed his victim by the back of the collar and hoisted him into the air like he was a straw-filled dummy. Then he rushed out of the door, carrying his trophy with him. A rattly engine could be heard starting and revving, before roaring into the distance.

Claire was staring at the door that was still swinging slightly back and forth. Trying not to scream again, she jumped when something touched her hand. It was the first man, hoodie still firmly in place. He had a young face, despite looking rather weather-beaten, and he showed a couple of days' worth of stubble.

'*Heaven's Bells*, was it?' he asked, in a gruff voice.

She stared at him as though he'd spoken in an alien language.

'Some sort of compendium?' he persisted.

'Harmonics,' she whispered.

With that, the man turned and went over to the door the Maniac had been shielding. Without hesitating, he walked straight into the flames and disappeared.

This time, Claire couldn't help screaming again, but the other man, who still had his back to them, held up a hand.

The fact that this character seemed to have suffered no ill effects after experiencing a face-off with a Maniac on full beam was too intriguing for the captain. He went over to the man and put a hand on his shoulder.

'Mate,' he said, having to speak up over the crackling of

the flames. 'Are you OK? We've seen what those creeps can do. You must have had your eyes really tightly...'

He stopped and drew back as the man turned round. He hadn't been affected because, underneath the short, neat fringe, there were no eyes to cover.

In fact, there was no face at all.

Before the startled trio could figure out how to react to this, the first man reappeared, walking calmly out of the inferno, his hands in his pockets. There was smoke coming off him, but no flames, as far as they could see.

As he approached them, he pulled one hand out of its pocket, reached inside his jacket, and retrieved a black, hardback book with gold lettering on the front and spine. He handed it to Claire.

'There you go,' he said. 'It looks like the stars are with you today.'

He slapped his friend on the shoulder, and they made for the exit.

'Excuse me,' the baron began.

The two men stopped, but didn't turn round.

'How did you know?' the baron continued. 'I mean, when you gave us the all clear. How did you know he'd put his glasses back on?'

The man pointed at the entrance door, which, like its counterpart, contained several panes of glass.

'I watched him in the reflection.'

The baron felt rather sheepish at this simple explanation, and it was a moment before he realised how thick the smoke had become. He herded his friends outside, by which time their helpers were nowhere to be seen. Murgh and his ghoulish prize were long gone.

A crowd of onlookers was growing. They could be heard lamenting the loss of the library's many functions. People spoke of political talks they'd attended, knitting classes and language workshops. One man had held a memorial get-together for his stepfather just the previous weekend. No-one mentioned taking out books.

Claire was inconsolable, unable to accept she'd seen lightning strike twice.

'All that knowledge,' she cried. 'All those riches, those amenities. All gone. I couldn't save a single thing. What would you choose to rescue out of all that? To come out empty-handed!'

Her agitation increased when she noticed her companions staring at her with faint grins.

'What?'

'You really don't know, do you?' the baron marvelled.

'Know what?'

'Claire,' the captain whispered, making a show of looking around to make sure he wasn't being overheard. 'You're carrying a cello.'

She looked down in astonishment to see that she was indeed carrying the instrument under one arm and that the bow was in her other hand, awkwardly sharing it with the treatise on bell harmonics.

'The power of instinct,' commented the captain.

'Quite so,' agreed the baron, as a fire engine turned into the far end of the street, sirens blaring. 'And my instinct tells me this is no time to bask in the afterglow. We need to get back to the house.'

This time, the baron took them by the most direct route. He was now carrying a large, stringed instrument, which Claire had reluctantly relinquished in order to prioritise her little black book, and so felt they were too conspicuous to spend a moment more out in the open than was absolutely necessary.

Kia and Holly had returned, in the meantime, and immediately wanted to be brought up to speed. Voltaire,

Colette and Hugo had heard their voices and come in from the garden, where they had had no luck getting in touch with their leader, Olivier. Claire took herself and her dissertation off into a corner to search for answers, while the baron told the story of another ill-fated library. His mostly seated audience was enchanted by the discovery of a cello virtuoso, enlightened by the baron's use of Lucidly Robotic, and horrified by the appearance of the arsonist Maniac. But the biggest gasp came from Kia at the description of their two benefactors.

'The stars were with you indeed,' she said, awestruck. She turned to Holly. 'That was Fireproof Aries and Faceless Taurus. I think I told you about them last time you were here.'

'You did,' he said. 'And you didn't sound too keen to run into them, if memory serves. So that just leaves – Backpack Pisces, was it?'

This was getting too surreal for the French scout.

'So, if we find a man with a rucksack full of fish…' said Hugo, his face a mixture of cynicism and incredulity.

'You'd make bouillabaisse?' suggested the captain.

Hugo snorted, but seemed quite taken by the idea.

Voltaire showed his impatience with this frivolity, but it was Colette who spoke out first.

'Come on!' she commanded. 'We need a plan. What are we going to do?'

'We're going to eradicate these – these Maniacs.'

Claire had pre-empted the home team, and she was coming out of her corner, fighting.

'Is it true,' she asked Kia, 'that if you solve something, everything affected by that clue goes back to how it was?'

'Yes, that's true.'

'So, if we wipe these abominations off the face of the earth, we get Bill and my library back?'

'Well, yes,' confirmed Kia, 'but, looking at the bigger picture, that's all meaningless if we can't deal with the comet. That bell we were meant to use – it was lying in pieces. They must have known it was what we needed, so they went and smashed it. That's it. Game over.'

Claire shook her head.

'No, that was a red herring, as I knew it would be. It was only there to remind you of the motto Preserve Harmony. I've found the real bell.'

She held out the black book, open on a page that showed the same chart as the one Cordelia had brought.

'It's Big Ben.'

CHAPTER TWENTY-TWO

'Well, as far as the Case of the Librarian and the Bell goes, I don't think Operation Bill and Ben is going to be easy.'

The captain was very pleased with this play on words, but gave Hugo a sympathetic look.

'What, you don't think we'll get the cultural references?' the Frenchman protested. 'We get all your best TV programmes.'

The best thing the television could show at this moment, having been switched on again, was the news channel Great Uncle Sid had left it on, several hours previously. The sound was very low, but the reporter's voice was quite audible when everyone else's had fallen silent, which they now had.

The helicopter was still hovering above Parliament Square, revealing the military build-up to have increased exponentially since they had last seen it. The reason for this was still unclear, the PM having once again denied any involvement.

'How can he not know of this?' Colette demanded. 'Is it a military coup?'

'Unlikely,' said the baron. 'We haven't had one of those for a while.'

'Well, then your prime minister is lying?'

Kia shrugged.

'He's a politician,' she said.

Holly smiled at the response which could have been his own.

'It's an unusual situation,' he offered as an explanation, 'but we think there may be a higher authority behind the army's movements.'

Colette's jaw dropped.

'You mean,' she said, pointing upwards, 'from on high?'

'Sort of,' was the best Holly could come up with, waving his newspaper.

Colette's expression was a mixture of surprise and exasperation.

'Always, the puzzle,' she complained.

'Are you seriously saying,' Voltaire asked, 'that whoever devised that thing is deploying thousands of soldiers…' he paused to see if he could make this question sound any less absurd, but he couldn't, '…to stop you from ringing a bell?'

'I know,' Holly conceded. 'It sounds ridiculous. But what's even more ridiculous to me is that, surely it's all pointless? That bell goes off every hour on the hour anyway.'

The confused looks told him that something was wrong.

'*News at Ten*?' he persisted. '*Bong*! And the quarter bells? *Bing bong bing bong, bing bong bing bong*,' he sang, causing more consternation. 'No? Really?'

'Doesn't ring a – familiar note,' said the captain.

'The bells don't make a sound,' Kia confirmed. 'We've never heard Big Ben. Don't know why not. Never really thought about it.'

Holly had to sit down.

'I can't believe it,' he muttered. 'It's used on the news every night. And it's always used to count down to big events, like New Year's Eve. And you say you've never heard it.'

He stared into the distance, talking more to himself.

'The bells have only ever stopped ringing during wartime and, even then, not in both world wars. So the fact that they've been silenced now implies the Compiler is somehow stuck in a war. In his head. And putting the Blitz in a cloud. That's one hell of a preoccupation.'

'He must be in preoccupied territory,' the captain couldn't help contributing.

Everyone groaned, except Hugo. Despite his best efforts, he laughed out loud. But when that died away, all they could hear was sobbing.

Claire hadn't said a word since her revelation about the chart. Unnoticed by anyone, her former bravado had waned, and she had slowly withdrawn into a nightmare world of shrivelled faces and smouldering ruins. She wasn't even aware she was crying and jumped when Kia put a hand on her shoulder. She looked up, but could find no words.

Kia sat next to her. Despite desperately wanting to provide some reassurance, she was finding the means elusive.

'It can be really difficult…' she tried, but felt as though she'd already reached a dead end. 'When you lose someone…' she began again, but with the same result. 'Particularly when you think there might be the slightest chance…'

Three strikes and she was out. She gave up the fight.

'It was a nice library,' she conceded.

Claire stopped sobbing and grabbed Kia's hand.

'Give them back to me,' she whispered.

Kia stared at her for a moment, her face a study in conflict. Then she put her arms around her. Claire's worried expression didn't change. She wasn't sure whether this was solidarity or just consolation. She wouldn't be in doubt for long.

Kia let her go and stood up.

'Claire's right,' she declared. 'We have no idea what's going to happen tomorrow even if we do deal with this comet. If we can right some obvious wrongs now, it will at least create some happiness. And who knows, it might even make things easier later on. We get rid of these bastards – pardon my French, Colette – and we get rid of them now. Holly, baron, anyone – see if there's anything suitable in the grid.'

Her minions were only too glad to be given something to do, and they set about their task with vigour, mostly with their heads down to conceal their grins, to Kia's annoyance.

Despite home advantage being expected to play a part, it was the away team who scored first.

'I had to look that word up,' said Hugo. 'It made no sense.'

'Which word?' asked Holly.

'Oh, it's in 2 Down.'

They all turned to the clue, which read 'Patient, pursuing pecan for one fruitcake (7)'.

'Does everything you do revolve around food?' the captain wanted to know.

'Well, yes, of course,' admitted Hugo. 'But this was the first time we went to that café, and I asked the owner if he had any cream for the coffee. He called me a fruitcake.'

Chuckles could be heard around the room.

'That's just a word for an eccentric person,' Kia explained.

'Yes, I know that now. But how is a fruit cake eccentric? And how is that an insult? It would be like me calling you a tarte au citron.'

'I've been called worse,' the captain shrugged.

'I think Hugo's on to something,' said the baron. 'I mean, "fruitcake" might be a mild word, but basically it just means a mad person, doesn't it? Like "maniac"?'

A serious mood descended.

'Do it,' commanded Kia. 'How does the clue work? And why does the pecan have to be for just one fruit cake?'

'Little, individual cakes?' suggested the captain. 'With one pecan on top of each? You'd have to be pretty patient to do that.'

'Not if you have any feeling for presentation,' protested Hugo.

'It's not "for one fruitcake",' said Holly, frowning. 'It's "pecan for one", as in "pecan for example". And as we have the first and third letters as N and T…'

'Nut,' concluded Kia.

'And working backwards,' said the baron, 'if the meaning is "fruitcake", then this word has to be "nutcase".'

Holly nodded.

'OK,' said Colette, her face showing that she wasn't OK at all. 'I'm beginning to see how this works, and I can see that "patient" "pursuing" "pecan for one" means that a word meaning "patient" goes after "nut" – but how do you get "case" from "patient"?'

'Oh, "case" can mean a medical case,' Holly said. 'As in "The hospital sees 2,000 hepatitis cases a year". That's just one of many meanings.'

Voltaire raised an eyebrow.

'Oh, yes,' Claire was happy to volunteer. 'Apart from the medical meaning, it could be an instance or example, a police investigation, a lawsuit – or, of course, a form of a noun or adjective,' she directed at Colette, who smiled and bowed her head.

'The pupil becomes the teacher,' she said.

'Or it could just be a suitcase,' suggested the baron.

'Or a basket case,' added the captain.

'Or a bad case of wasting time,' Kia concluded. 'What's the second clue?'

'Er – it's "Deadly, small perishables",' announced Holly. 'Also seven letters.'

'English pastries?' suggested Hugo.

The captain tutted.

'Only a tarte au citron like you wouldn't like a Chelsea bun,' he said.

'I've got this,' said Kia, with confidence. 'We have an S at the end, and "small" is usually just an S. So that leaves a six-letter word for "deadly" to go in front. We already have an M for the first letter and an R for the third. I make that "mortal", giving us "mortals" as the solution. And "mortals" make "perishables".'

There was no triumphant smile, just a look of grim resolution.

'And if Nutcase Mortals are indeed our Maniacs,' she went quickly on, stifling the round of applause that had already broken out, 'that would imply they're vulnerable. We can eradicate them.'

She gave Holly the Nod of Annihilation, and he dutifully readied his pen.

Then the phone rang.

'Is that my phone?' Holly asked. It had been so long since he heard it ring, he barely recognised the sound.

'No,' said Kia, haughtily. 'It's the same phone, but it's my phone.'

She lifted the portable device from its cradle and pressed the button – twice, in the event, putting it on speakerphone for all to hear. Before she could say anything, a voice appeared, a low, demonic voice.

'Kee-yah.'

Kia dropped the phone in fright. It landed on the sofa next to Claire, who recoiled from it as though it was going to bite her.

'Fu-gu,' the phone rasped.

No-one dared to say anything. Everyone conjured up the image of the masked man on the motorcycle.

'I can hear you all – breathing.'

Realising that everyone was suddenly holding their breath, Kia decided she needed to take the initiative.

'What do you want?' she asked. 'You'd better make it quick, Mr Yakitori,' she added, her bravado returning. 'You haven't got long.'

'Well, there's the thing.' The head Maniac's inhuman tone was slow and measured. 'Being just a solution away from oblivion focuses the mind. Makes one take… precautions. So, yes… a few strokes of the pen, and you may think your troubles are over. But there's a caveat.'

Holly's pen was wavering. He was itching to stop this monster in mid flow, but Kia held up a restraining hand.

The monster broke into a quiet laugh.

'Every master has another master,' it growled. 'Don't we, Mr Holly?'

Holly's pen-wielding arm fell loosely to his side.

'Mine may have made us expendable,' Fugu continued, 'but not defenceless. So now, you have a decision to make. You can eradicate us, but then you'll never get your hero back. Heroes are so thin on the ground, and thin heroes can be turned.'

Kia tensed, and her face darkened.

'How many more can you afford to lose, my girl?' the Maniac gloated. 'The hour is getting late. The Sand has already trickled away, n'est-ce pas? And we've certainly settled the Bill. It's not our time that's running out. It's yours.'

CHAPTER TWENTY-THREE

Uncles Sid and Gordo came running at Kia's summons – a frantic banging on the wall between the two houses. They conveyed what they could about their encounter with Farfalle Puttanesca, but could provide no information on Uncle Jasper's whereabouts, and were visibly disappointed that their misdirection seemed to have failed.

'They've got him,' Kia fumed. 'I know they have.'

Every one of the Maniac's jibes had hit their mark. Colette and Hugo were having to placate an increasingly agitated Voltaire, distraught at the mention of his fallen agent. Claire was staring disconsolately at her charts, thinking of her fellow librarian. She hadn't known him that well, but that made his demise even more painful.

But Kia was the most affected, and she was all rage.

'How?' she demanded. 'How did they get him? How could he be so stupid?'

'Maybe they put a well-stocked skip out as bait?' suggested the captain, but under his breath. He couldn't help himself, but he also wanted to keep his head.

Fortunately for him, their attention was drawn to the television, showing more aerial shots of the Pitch-Black Army, which was still making its relentless journey southwards. There were lengthy tailbacks in either direction on the M1 after the dark mass had completely destroyed junction 25, the intersection with the A52. Loughborough had been spared, the army passing to the east. Then it was Leicester's turn to be relieved as it failed to prove worth a detour. But the inhabitants of the market town of Kettering were getting decidedly jittery.

This item was interrupted to go over to an astronomer who was falling over herself in her enthusiasm to convey the exciting news that, before the comet put an end to all life on earth, it would pass in front of the sun, thereby providing the first comet eclipse mankind had ever experienced. This involved not only shrouding the planet briefly in its shadow, but also its ion tail, which always faced away from the sun, and which the breathless scientist assured everyone would be harmless.

'That's lucky,' commented Colette. 'We're not going to get fried before we get squished.'

Kia dismissed these distractions with an ease that surprised even herself. She knew what her priorities were and had her instructions ready. But before discharging them, she went over and sat next to Claire.

'We are going to wipe these Maniacs out,' she promised her, quietly. 'But we're going to have to do it the long way round. We have to find Uncle Jasper first, if we can.'

Claire smiled and nodded.

'If it was a question of Bill versus Uncle Jasper,' she said, 'even I'd go for Uncle Jasper.'

Kia gave Claire's arm a squeeze, then stood up.

'Right, listen up,' she commanded. 'Top priority – find Uncle Jasper. He could just be wandering about, so we need a search party. But in a group, no solo efforts. If he has been taken, it's because he was on his own. Any other thoughts?'

'I looked through the grid,' the baron offered, 'to see if there was anything that might tie in with Uncle Jasper.

I thought, if they have got him, they'd have to take him somewhere pretty secluded.'

'Go on,' said Kia.

'Well, we've just heard they've got control of all the local CCTV – not that it seems to be doing them any good, or they wouldn't have had to pay these two a visit.'

The uncles nodded at the logic.

'So, I wondered if Camera-Shy Scrap might be an interesting location, somewhere CCTV might not operate.'

'Or somewhere we can take the fight to them without being seen,' mused Holly. 'Sounds plausible.'

'Risky,' was Kia's assessment. 'It could be anywhere. Probably very remote. And if there's a scrap involved, whoever went there would have to be up for that fight.'

'E-Y-E M-I-T-E.'

Uncle Gordo was standing to his full height. It was the first time Holly had seen him not wearing a smile, and he was surprised how formidable the good-natured man looked without it.

Not to be outdone, Uncle Sid leapt to his feet.

'Named!' he declared.

'Yes,' murmured Kia. 'I didn't think there'd be any shortage of volunteers.'

Holly took her to one side.

'Are you sure?' he whispered. 'Uncle Gordo?'

Kia's eyes widened in reply.

'Don't be fooled,' she said. 'You don't want to be around when he goes off on one.'

Shrugging, he turned back round.

'OK,' he said. 'In the absence of anything else, I think it's worthy of a look. I'll take you two there. But we have no idea what's waiting for us, so we must be ready for anything. The slightest hint that the danger outweighs the advantage, I pull us straight out. But at least we'll know what's there, and we can then decide what to do afterwards. Agreed?'

He got resolute nods from the two men, but the French contingent felt they would be better suited to the task. Hugo in particular argued that the counter-intelligence knowledge they seemed to have woken up with that morning would surely prove invaluable on such a mission. Kia apologised, but thought their scouting skills would be put to better use out on the street, looking for clues as to Uncle Jasper's whereabouts while keeping an eye out for the enemy. They accepted this assessment, but with some reluctance, although Colette couldn't help looking relieved at not having to take that particular form of transport again.

Holly checked the clue number, and the trio formed their familiar battle-ready stance of an outward-facing triangle. After some loud inhaling and exhaling – mostly from Uncle Sid – and the customary fussing from Kia, the three men tensed in preparation for whatever unspeakable horrors they may face, and the destination was uttered.

The destination turned out to be a vast room entirely surrounded by bookshelves.

'Oh, hello,' said Cordelia. 'Fancy seeing you again so soon.'

CHAPTER TWENTY-FOUR

The Record Holder was back in full regalia, they noticed. In case this hadn't been impressive enough, she had even added a tiara.

The would-be fighters relaxed and disentangled themselves.

'Genial halo,' she said to Uncle Sid.

'W-O-N F-O-U-R Y-E-W,' Uncle Gordo whispered to him, before wandering off to have a look round, being the only one not to have visited Cordelia's library before.

'Ooh!' she squealed, before anyone could return her 'hello again'. 'I must be a clue destination! That's the only way you could have come straight here!'

Holly and Uncle Sid both winced and cast an eye up to the doors at the top of the long, central flight of steps, remembering what they had to go through to reach her last time, particularly the murderous Hall of Obsolescence.

'What was it?' she gushed. 'What was the solution that wafted you all to me?'

Holly shifted uncomfortably.

'Er, Camera-Shy Scrap,' he muttered.

Cordelia pulled a face.

'Well, that's not very flattering,' she protested. 'But I suppose it explains how pumped up you all were when you arrived. Surely, you're not stupid enough to try and fight me?'

'Oh – no,' said Holly, finally empathising with all the children at his school that he'd sent to the headmaster's office. 'We weren't sure what it meant. We assumed it was more about figuratively taking the fight to the enemy in a place where we wouldn't be seen.' He looked around. 'I presume you don't have CCTV in here?'

'Heavens, no. I'd have the Minions' Union on my back in seconds for maltreatment.'

Holly noticed for the first time that the librarian was alone.

'Where… is Nigel?' he asked, still not sure whether that referred to one of her assistants or all of them collectively.

'I've given him the day off. It seemed appropriate, as this might be the last day, so I can't be that draconian an employer. But I did make it clear that, if there is a tomorrow, I want him in bright and early. Hang on… What do you mean by fighting the enemy? How are you going to combat a comet from in here?'

'Oh, that's on hold. Those Maniacs you mentioned this morning? Well, they're real enough, and they're now our primary concern. They've got Uncle Jasper.'

Cordelia's look of outrage was fleeting.

'I suppose that makes sense,' she said. 'It makes them unsolvable, at least until you find him. And they knew you'd make him the priority, putting the recovery of a team member ahead of dealing with a threat to the entire world, just like you did last time.'

She gave him a disapproving look, but not without affection.

'Know where to look for him?'

'Not really. That's why we're starting here.'

'Well, I haven't got him,' she declared. 'Unless Nigel

filed him away somewhere. Maybe in the DIY section.'

'So why are we here?' Holly wondered. 'There must be something in here that will allow us to further the fight.'

'Dear me, you are obsessed with fighting. And who are you fighting, exactly?'

'A group of English fifth columnists, one masquerading as an Italian, another a particularly weaselly fake Frenchman by the name of Talleyrand…'

'Talleyrand!' the librarian snorted. 'Well, how much of a heads-up do you need?'

Holly's eyebrows demanded enlightenment.

'Charles Maurice de Talleyrand-Périgord,' she sighed, 'to give him his full moniker, was Napoleon's chief negotiator. Despite working tirelessly for peace to further France's cause, his name has become a byword for crafty and cynical diplomacy. I thought you were a teacher.'

'Maybe if he'd been a mathematician,' Holly mumbled. 'At least I am acquainted with his other nom de guerre, Murgh Makhani.'

'Oh, yes, that's much more appetising,' agreed Cordelia. 'Let's hope he's next on your menu.'

'Well, we must have been sent here for a reason, so if you don't mind, I'm going to leave these two reprobates to figure out what it is.'

'Oh, I'll keep an eye on them,' she twinkled.

Uncle Sid's look of panic was not assuaged by Holly's reassuring wink.

As he was about to say 'grid', Holly noticed the new chair in the middle of the floor. It was a chunky, wooden affair that looked as though it had been assembled out of railway sleepers. It was quite large, but nothing on the scale of the one Holly had made disappear on his previous visit. It was adorned with primitive equine sketches that reminded Holly of prehistoric, French cave paintings.

Cordelia followed his gaze.

'What?' she demanded. 'I like horses.'

Ignoring Uncle Sid's imploring eyes, Holly went back to the house alone and relayed what he had found, such as it was. Kia was initially unhappy that their search party for Uncle Jasper was already two men down, but had to concede that, if the clue number had a location, there must be something useful there.

'And if there is,' she confirmed, 'they'll find it. I wish I could be that confident of success in our own quest.'

Nevertheless, she organised the remaining squad into two groups. She would take the baron and the captain in one direction, and Holly would accompany the French trio in the other. If either group was lucky enough to come across the missing man, he would be firmly escorted back home. If he managed to evade them all and make his own way back, Claire would be there to fill him in on developments.

'After all,' Kia argued, 'if they haven't got him, he will have no idea that both sides are looking for him.'

Both groups turned right out of the house, there being no likely hiding places in the opposite direction. Once at the square, they split up, Kia's threesome going back towards the café, Holly taking his troupe in the direction of Lawn Road, in case the handyman was indeed immersed in his bathroom renovation, oblivious to the furore revolving around him.

Hugo's tracking skills had been no idle boast. He stopped on the corner of Lawn Road, just as Uncle Jasper had done.

'What if,' he surmised, 'they had found out where he had been working for the last few days, and there had been an agent waiting for him somewhere in this street?'

Voltaire and Colette nodded pensively. Holly wasn't convinced.

‘It’s possible,’ he said. ‘But we could just go to the house and see if he’s there…’

Hugo was adamant.

‘No, I’m sure he never made it to the house,’ he insisted. ‘He would have stopped here, and then moved as quickly as he could behind this tree.’

He made some exaggeratedly furtive steps until he reached cover, reminding Holly that mime artists were always French.

‘And then…’ Hugo continued.

And then a hatchet buried itself in the tree mere inches from the scout’s head.

He instinctively crouched and whirled round simultaneously, to see a long-haired, old woman, dressed in black and wearing a beret, bearing down on him.

‘Sand?’ he gasped, as he avoided her grasp just in time. This allowed his former colleague to retrieve her weapon, which she then prepared to swing at him again. Her movements were undeniably agile for a woman of her age, but he still easily managed to dodge the blows that were raining down on him, with their accompanying grunts and moans.

Eventually her relentless attack moved to within the orbit of the other French couple, Colette having to pull Voltaire out of the line of fire as he stared, transfixed in horror, at the change in his friend.

‘Can’t you do something?’ Holly shouted from where he was standing a short way off.

‘She’s still Sand,’ Colette wailed. ‘We can’t hurt her. What can we do? She’ll give herself a heart attack like this.’

‘Confuse her,’ Holly decided. ‘Split up, lose her and she’ll calm down. She’s no danger to anyone else. If we find Uncle Jasper in the meantime, we can deal with these Maniacs and maybe we’ll get your friend back.’

Seeing the sense in that, they set off down the street. Holly watched them scattering in three directions, as their superannuated assassin swung out vainly at them.

'That's the worst zombie film I've ever seen,' he muttered grimly to himself. Turning back to the street they'd been heading for, he tried to get that image out of his head. But the image that greeted him was infinitely worse.

Fifty yards down the road, a man was watching him, a man wearing a blue suit, sunglasses and a contented smile.

In his panic, a range of Italian dishes paraded themselves past Holly before he managed to identify Farfalle Puttanesca. This panic increased when, as if hearing his name, the man started walking slowly towards him.

Checking that everyone else was now out of sight and likely to be out of danger from this new and far more deadly threat, Holly figured the quickest escape route would be saying a clue number, leaving his stalker isolated and temporarily harmless. The first number he could think of was, once again, 1 Down. At least this time he knew where that would take him, and he quite fancied another trip to the Peak District.

He said the number and was instantly back on that path, bathed in sunshine and wrapped in the same gentle breeze as before. The view along the valley was as impressive and comforting as on his last visit – except in one respect. This time he could see that he wasn't alone.

Further along the path, his smile having acquired a distinctly sadistic edge, the Maniac was still advancing.

CHAPTER TWENTY-FIVE

Holly's mind was reeling, and he felt nauseous. How could the man have followed him? It broke a rule Holly thought was unbreakable. Something was as wrong as it was possible to be.

The Maniac was closing in, but was in no hurry, confident his prey couldn't escape him. Holly had to get away but, in his desperation, couldn't think of anything but trying another clue number. Maybe some locations would be out of bounds.

The next number that occurred to him was the last one he had used. Surely, Cordelia's library wouldn't allow such an intrusion.

Apparently, it would. The backdrop changed, but the man didn't break his slow stride, not even bothering to take stock of his new surroundings. Holly did, long enough to see an astonished librarian stammering 'What? What?' standing next to a table with a huge, open book, alongside the two uncles, who spotted and recognised the man in pursuit. They instantly advanced on him, fists clenched, ready for the scrap they had been expecting when they arrived.

A voice stopped them in their tracks.

'Mist opportunity!'

It was a breathless voice; one Holly recognised but couldn't place. But as he had no wish for any confrontation between his team and a Maniac, he decided he couldn't wait for the owner of the voice to reveal itself and uttered another clue number. This time, he was glad to see his pursuer was still with him, although it took a moment to make him out in the sudden darkness.

They were now on the side of a mountain. The sun had long gone down, but the sky was clear and the moon was bright enough to bring out the red in the short, wide trees. Even the gold-coloured ground seemed to glow.

Holly had arrived at the same spot as before. His predator had already reached the point from where Colette had spotted the temple further up the mountainside. His grin was still firmly in place, and he was reaching for his sunglasses.

Having run out of known clue number locations, and ruling out the possibility of saying 'grid', that being the last place he would want to introduce a Maniac, Holly considered running, but figured the terrain was so rocky he'd be flat on his face before he'd taken three strides. That only left the option of the first fist fight he had ever had. He knew he'd be fighting blind, arms flailing haphazardly as he kept his eyes closed to protect himself from those deadly flames. He'd be a sitting duck. He was dead in the water, and he knew it.

He was just squinting in preparation for screwing his eyes as tightly shut as he could, fists at the ready, when that voice called out again.

'Mist opportunity! Endless topiary!'

Someone behind him grabbed his arm and the scenery dissolved into another. This one was brighter, although cloudy, and noticeably more horizontal. But the only detail Holly considered worth registering for the moment was the absence of a well-dressed assassin.

Letting his head fall forwards and covering his eyes with his hand, Holly forced himself to relax. The fact that his legs nearly buckled told him how tense he'd been. Deep breaths were the order of the day and would be for some time. It was only when it struck him how odd it was that he felt he could relax, despite not having identified either the voice or the location, that he looked up. As soon as he did, the view told him everything he wanted to know.

He was standing in a garden, a walled garden with walls that were transparent and partly covered in brick-coloured ivy. He had been here before, and it held happy memories. By way of verification, he held up a hand. Sure enough, it appeared disembodied, his sleeve having taken on the appearance of the lawn behind it. Fortunately, this defining characteristic of the Chameleon Realm no longer brought on the nausea and dizziness it had caused him the first time. Raising his elbow further made his sleeve reveal the brickwork of the walls, green ivy and all.

And then he finally put a name to his rescuer's voice.

'Lady!'

He turned to be greeted by a red mop of hair. The Wise Lady had her head down, one isolated hand resting on what Holly assumed was the back of a garden chair, and was having more trouble than him getting her breath back. She held up the other hand to signal that she needed another moment.

This gave him time to try and figure out what she had called out. He started with what he'd heard as 'missed opportunity'. Knowing that the Wise Lady dealt with inserts, or hidden words, he toyed with 'sedo', 'edop', and 'doppo' before giving up and moving on to the other phrase, 'endless topiary'. This suggested the obvious 'stop', an understandable instruction if he kept changing location just as she was about to catch up with him. Assuming both phrases to contain the same word, an assumption supported by the beginning of the word 'opportunity', he ended up wondering if she'd actually said 'mist opportunity', but what that might mean, he had no idea.

His curiosity was such that, when the woman finally lifted her head, still panting slightly, it was the first thing he could think of saying.

'Mist?' he asked. 'As in, fog?'

Lady raised her eyebrows and gave him a slow, appreciative nod.

'Semi-starved,' she confirmed.

Far from elaborating any further, she gave him a big smile and ran her hand up and down the side of his arm.

'Alcohol, lying,' she purred, quickly changing it to, 'Menthol, lying!' She put a hand to her mouth in mock embarrassment.

Holly laughed.

'Good to see you too, Lady. And thanks for getting me here. I thought my number was up.'

She waved that away, then gave him a reproachful look.

'Stuff a stocking,' she complained.

'Well, I had to be fast,' Holly protested. 'You saw what was coming for me?'

She nodded.

'Beatlemania champion.'

She looked so sad, and yet Holly was relieved by how clued up she was about the current situation. He would have hated having to break some of the recent developments to her, particularly the threat the Maniacs posed to her beloved team.

'So, you know,' he stammered, 'that this crossword could be…'

'Grief, in a lament,' she nodded.

But she managed another smile and squeezed his arm again.

'Happy outing,' she said. 'Another excursion.'

He was moved that she felt it appropriate that he should be here to share what might turn out to be the last adventure in this remarkable place.

Mention of the puzzle had brought something else to her mind.

'Stop a performance,' she commanded, snapping her fingers and pointing to Holly's jacket.

He removed the paper from the jacket's inside pocket and held it so they could both see the clues. Lady peered and pointed at one of them.

'Barn owl,' she insisted.

Holly was intrigued to see which clue needed to be solved now. It was 25 Across, which read 'Wrapped in flannel, a sticker is pliant (7)'.

'Does "wrapped in" mean this one of your clues?' he asked, getting immediate confirmation. 'So, inside "flannel a sticker", we find – "elastic", which means "pliant"?'

'Dislodge last icicle,' Lady confirmed.

'This is important?'

Lady's response was to tap the next clue impatiently. The second of the horizontal pair was 26 Across. Holly read 'Mean to declare time (7)'.

'Claret' was the only word he could see embedded between others, but received an exasperated tut when he suggested it.

'Beaver agenda!' she snapped. 'Fave rag, exceptional!'

Holly was annoyed at himself for assuming it was a hidden word clue just because it was the Wise Lady who'd drawn his attention to it. The common centre to both her utterances was the word 'average', giving him the answer before he had to study the clue. A quick glance told him that 'aver' came from 'declare', and 'age' was a duration of 'time', 'mean' being one of several forms of 'average'.

'Elastic Average?' he queried.

She patted his hand with an all-in-good-time expression on her face. Then she tapped on another line in the grid.

'Musicians' Motto,' Holly read out. 'No, that turned out to be a red herring. The bell was broken, but it was the wrong one. That location's no longer useful.'

Lady shook her head.

'Archangel,' she informed him.

She was about to say something else, when they heard a banging noise behind them. Turning round, Holly noticed the two rectangles, apparently hanging freely in the air, that Kia had explained were windows in Lady's otherwise camouflaged house, the interior rooms only visible because the windows' shutters were closed, acting differently from the rest of the house due to being later additions.

One of the rooms revealed was a cluttered cottage kitchen, and it was from here that the sound was coming. Great Uncle Sid was banging on the window and shouting something inaudible. He didn't seem to be able to make eye contact with them, looking around desperately. Holly realised that, for Great to be visible to him, the shutters would have to be closed, meaning the old man couldn't see out. Presumably the window itself was open, and it was the shutter that was taking a hammering.

Holly glanced at Lady, expecting some sympathetic concern at the poor man's plight. But she merely raised her eyes to the sky and sighed.

'Brash utterance!' she shouted.

The banging stopped. Great could be seen fiddling with a catch, and then the shutter swung round on its hinges to reveal, when fully open, the brickwork it now covered. The window, in the meantime, reverted to being part of the house and disappeared, along with the occupant of the room.

Lady again expressed her annoyance.

'New hats?' she bellowed.

'Sauce!' came the reply.

The woman looked astonished, and then she started nodding vigorously.

'Sauce!' the old man shouted again.

Lady peered earnestly at Holly and pointed to where the voice was coming from, reinforcing its importance.

'Sauce?' he asked.

She nodded again. Leaning closer, she then said something that really knocked him for six.

'Fugu Yakitori.'

He could only stare at her. She pointed back at the house, for a moment, and then repeated it, ensuring Holly could see there was a connection.

'Fugu Yakitori.' And then, as an afterthought, 'Mist opportunity.'

Then she broke into a radiant, gentle smile and stroked his cheek.

'Grubby exterior,' she whispered.

With that, she gave him such a hefty shove in the chest, he actually lost his balance and landed on his back. By the time he hit the ground, it was no longer the soft grass of Lady's garden, but the hard tarmac in the middle of a deserted road.

He sat up with difficulty, nursing his bruised elbows. Why had Lady sent him here? As with everything else, there had to be a reason.

The road was a dual carriageway, probably an A road, Holly guessed. The section he found himself in was cutting through a low hill with an embankment on either side, after which it meandered slightly into the distance for about a mile, surrounded by undulating fields. Fortunately, there wasn't a single vehicle to be seen.

Holly was just thinking it would nevertheless be a good idea to get up and off the road, when a noise disturbed the peaceful, idyllic setting. It started behind him as a low growl, but as it grew, which it did at an alarming rate, it acquired a higher accompaniment, an angry sound, swirling and seething.

He turned, barely having time to register the thick, dark blanket that was rushing towards him, covering the road and everything around it. It was all he could do to take a deep breath before the wave of the Pitch-Black Army swept over him.

CHAPTER TWENTY-SIX

'Hunter poet!' Uncle Sid hissed, grabbing Uncle Gordo's arm.

Cordelia watched his eyes darting fearfully up the stairs. Uncle Gordo had put his foot on the first step.

'No, indeed,' she agreed. 'Not up there.'

Uncle Gordo suddenly remembered the story.

'H-A-U-L?' he asked.

'The Hall of Obsolescence, yes,' she confirmed. 'I've never so much as peeked through those doors. Even Nigel hasn't been tempted, but then he's not a curious chap, at least not in the sense of inquisitive. I'd have had them bricked up years ago. But it's just as well I didn't, or you wouldn't have been able to get out.'

Uncle Sid shivered at the thought of having so narrowly escaped those swirling blades, only to reach a dead end. Lost in that scenario, he flinched when Cordelia put a hand on his arm.

'My, you are jumpy,' she said.

She surveyed the man, whose clothes were particularly crumpled today. There was clearly something bothering him.

'Same nickel,' she suddenly threw at him.

He frowned.

'Simnel cake?'

'My favourite,' she laughed. 'It's been my salvation on countless occasions, and it could be again.'

She watched in glee, as confusion played around his face and that of his companion.

'A cake shop,' she offered in explanation, revelling in the fact that it wasn't a very satisfactory one.

Finally taking pity on them, she adopted a more serious tone.

'We're all worried about this Final Crossword thing, aren't we? The idea that, when tomorrow dawns, if it dawns at all, there'll be no reason to get up? That's actually a more frightening idea than being wiped out by a comet, isn't it? The lack of purpose, the absence of a role to play? And then having to interact with the everyday world, finding some worthwhile occupation, having to...'

'...U-R-N D-O-E?'

'...Make a living, I suppose, yes. I hadn't meant occupation as paid employment, merely as a way of passing the time, but we creations of the grid do live a subsidised life, for some reason, so there's no reason to suppose that would continue.'

A gloomy mood set in as each of them tried to imagine what a post-grid life would look like.

'Same nickel,' said Uncle Sid, in a distant voice.

Cordelia decided that was enough maudlin speculation.

'Come over here,' she said. 'If this is to be the last day, there's something you should see before that too becomes redundant.'

She led them over to a large, rectangular table with a candelabra at both ends. In the middle lay a huge, leather-bound book. It was closed. As they approached, the words *Principia Cruciverborum* in gold lettering came into view.

'This,' Cordelia said, resting an affectionate hand on it,

'is our Good Book. It contains all the rules and regulations that govern this place.'

She turned the heavy cover to reveal the frontispiece. The subtitle read *First Laws for Second Chances*. The librarian shook her head.

'Never did figure out what that meant,' she said, ruefully.

Turning the page revealed the List of Contents. The first section concerned The Cryptic Clue, And The Varieties Thereof. Uncle Sid pointed at Chapter One, The Anagram. Cordelia was only too happy to turn to the relevant entry. The three of them leant over to see the first sentence, which read 'The anagram, the rearranging of letters, the transformation of one reality into another, is a world in itself, and the crown in the crossword compiler's arsenal'.

This was enough for Uncle Sid. Disregarding the issue of what possible use a crown would be in an arsenal, he straightened, chest out, and gave Uncle Gordo his most imperious gaze.

'K-N-O-W W-H-E-Y,' came the good-natured response.

'Now, boys. Play nice. Here, look at this instead.' Cordelia flicked through to the end of the book. 'Where is it? Ah, there you go.'

The page she'd chosen consisted of just a heading – Fail-safe. Tucked into the binding was a loose sheet of paper. When Cordelia removed it and showed it to them, they saw the same graph she had brought them earlier.

'This is the original,' she explained.

Uncle Gordo pointed away from it, to indicate the version she'd given Kia.

'K-N-O-T R-E-E-L?'

'Oh, no, Nigel had to make a tracing of this one. He tried several time to photocopy it, but the copy kept coming up blank. It was almost as if this silly little piece of paper didn't want...'

Her eyes widened, and she gasped.

'That's it, isn't it?' she asked. 'That's what brought you here!' She waved the diagram in the air. 'This is the Camera-Shy Scrap!'

Her triumphant look made them feel rather sheepish.

'Sorry, boys,' she commiserated. 'There'll be no fighting today.'

It was at this point that the fight came to them.

A noise made them turn round, and there was Holly, tensed, motionless, in the far corner of the room. Following his line of sight to the opposite corner, they saw the reason for his stooped poise. An all too familiar figure in a blue suit and sunglasses was slowly advancing, solely focused on his prey, oblivious to his new audience.

This was one intrusion too many for Cordelia.

'What? What?' was all she could manage, moving automatically to shield the *Principia*.

The uncles set off on their own trajectory, an intercept point between the Maniac and the Solver.

But before they had a chance to reach full speed, a voice brought them to a complete standstill.

'Mist opportunity!' it shouted.

They saw Holly look over at them with a perplexed expression. Then he seemed to come to a decision, and they heard him utter a clue number. He instantly vanished, along with his adversary.

The uncles looked at each other in frustration and amazement.

'Idle ways?' asked Uncle Sid, getting a tentative nod in response.

'That was the Wise Lady?' Cordelia demanded. 'So, at least I got to hear her voice. And if she's on the case, then Holly's not alone.'

The uncles did their best to get some comfort from that.

'And there's an image that I will cherish for the rest of my days,' she went on, to their surprise.

In explanation, she nodded at the candelabra Uncle Sid had instinctively grabbed as a weapon, and she giggled.

'How romantic,' she said. 'Uncle Sid, in the library, with the candlestick.'

CHAPTER TWENTY-SEVEN

Holly needn't have bothered taking that deep breath, as it was instantly knocked out of him.

He was being thrown around like a rag doll. He could feel strong, rough hands grabbing him and moving him brusquely on. The movement was constant, depriving him of the ability to gather his thoughts. Also missing were his bearings, as he felt he was being propelled in every conceivable direction.

The noise was still swirling round him. Added to the mix were occasional grunts, the shouting of distant, muffled orders and the underlying dull beat of marching.

From the inside, the army wasn't quite as pitch-black as its exterior. Sporadic, vague smudges of light, all of the darkest red, revealed some grim, resolute faces, none of which paid Holly the slightest attention.

Just as he felt he would pass out for lack of oxygen, the army seemed to have had enough of him and spat him out. He flew a full ten yards clear of the advancing darkness. Fortunately, his landing place was now a field rather than a road. He fell to earth on his front, blinking in the sunlight and gasping for air.

By the time his sight and breathing had returned to anywhere near normal, the military machine was no longer even audible. He didn't have to lift his head very high to see the evidence of its scorched earth policy, a sharp line dividing the lush green of his immediate surroundings with the barren soil beyond.

For the moment, his mind could only accommodate two issues. The first was the question of why the Wise Lady had left him where she did. Given that everything here seemed to happen for a reason, what benefit was he supposed to have gained from that experience? He took it for granted that she knew what the outcome of the encounter would be and wasn't just trying to kill him off.

The second was trying to get his head around the information he'd managed to glean about the soldiers as they'd indifferently used him as the ball in a giant pinball machine.

They were all women.

In the absence of any better explanation, he decided that maybe the two issues were, in fact, one and the same.

He struggled to his feet, trying – and failing – to identify one part of his body that wasn't aching. In light of the fact that he had some thinking to do, and that staying upright wasn't worth the considerable effort, he sat back down on the grass.

His next decision was not to go back to the house until he had worked out what he should do next. The Wise Lady's words were bothering him, and he needed time to figure out what they meant. And he had some 'sauce' to go with that – Great Uncle Sid's solitary word of advice. That also remained a mystery.

He tried to remember Lady's exact words. The last ones, 'grubby exterior', were the clearest in his mind, and the easiest to solve. She had simply said 'bye' as she pushed him under an army. The rest was far more mysterious.

Why, for example, had she attached so much importance

to the line Elastic Average? He didn't even know where to start with that, but it did remind him that he hadn't yet written it into the grid. After a moment's consideration, he could see no reason not to. In fact, making it official might reveal something useful.

Letters duly entered, he waited expectantly. He looked around, but registered no change. He felt within himself, looking for a revelation to make itself known. All he noticed was that he wasn't aching any less.

Lady's repetition of Mist Opportunity towards the end of their encounter was another puzzle. She clearly meant 'stop' by it as she was breathlessly chasing after him to whisk him out of Mr Puttanesca's warpath. But why say it again later? He couldn't think of anything he was doing himself that needed to stop, so presumably she wanted him to stop someone else from doing something. But without any more information, that was another dead end.

What unsettled him most was her mention of the name of the Maniacs' leader. Hearing her say something that didn't sound like it needed solving was bad enough. He vividly remembered the chill they'd all felt when she suddenly renounced hiding words and spoke normally following a blast from the Culprit's sonic device. But as she had reverted to type this time, there must be an insert involved here, and the only thing Holly could find within the name Fugu Yakitori was another name, Guy. And that wasn't ringing any bells.

It occurred to him that Lady had taken pains to link this word to that of Great Uncle Sid. Try as he might, Holly failed to see any connection between the words Guy and Sauce. The only person he could think of who might have the imagination to do that was the captain. He even toyed with the idea of going back to the house to find out, but dismissed it, albeit reluctantly.

These deliberations having ground to a halt, it was time to move on, but where? He still felt too impatient to return home. Surely there must be a more productive location?

Then he remembered Lady's reference to Musicians' Motto, and her pronouncement of 'archangel' when he suggested that road was now closed. That could only have meant the word 'change', but what had changed? Was the bell back in one piece? But that would be irrelevant, if that wasn't the bell in question.

His curiosity demanded that he go back to that location to see what had changed. His common sense resisted, reminding him that it was where he had left the Maniac on his tail, who could still be marauding there like an angry wasp. But curiosity was a bully and had its way.

He gritted his teeth, but was pleased to see that standing up was less painful than last time. He dusted himself off, removing most of the earth that had attached itself to his jacket and trousers. Then he steadied himself, preparing as best he could to take whatever evasive action might be needed.

When he said the number, the change was immediately apparent.

He was still on a slope, as expected, but it was halfway up some steps, rather than a mountainside. He was hemmed in by high stone walls on two adjacent sides, a lower stone wall further away on the third. On the fourth side, the steps went down to a pavement which ran for quite a distance, with a long, grey building on the right and a wide river on the left.

The identity of this river soon became apparent as the familiar figure of the London Eye loomed up ahead. This also told Holly that the building was County Hall.

Turning fully around, Holly was once again confronted by a stone lion, but rather than roaring in his face as the one in St Paul's had done, this one had turned his back on him and was up on a plinth that was big enough to have a wooden door in the side. Going to the top of the steps brought Holly, as he had expected, on to the eastern end of a heavily militarised Westminster Bridge.

So that was Lady's change. The grid had replaced the red herring of a broken bell with the real target and changed the location of a clue number. And it was only when Holly was staring in awe across the Thames at the majesty of the Palace of Westminster, and St Stephen's Tower that housed the fateful bell in particular, that he realised what the elderly couple had been trying to tell him and why it was imperative he was now here.

When 'sauce' appears in a cryptic clue, Holly remembered, it often referred to the letters HP, the famous HP Sauce, the invention of a Nottingham grocer, who registered that name for it after he'd heard that it was being served in a restaurant in the Houses of Parliament, adding a picture of the building to the label in case anyone hadn't made the connection from the initials. That was Great Uncle Sid's coded message. And as far as Lady's contribution to this warning went, there was only one Guy associated with the Houses of Parliament.

The words 'sauce', 'Guy' and 'stop' combined to tell Holly that he was there to foil the Maniacs in their plot to make sure Big Ben never sounded.

Devastating as this conclusion was, something else managed to distract him from trying to imagine what that plot was and what he ought to do about it.

The daylight had faded slightly, but not because of any clouds, which had largely dispersed. A haze had appeared over Lambeth Bridge on his left, approaching fast, a mist that had a slight twinkle to it. Faint sparks seemed to be raining down in slow motion. In an effort to find its source, Holly followed the trail way up into the sky, where it narrowed until it reached a small, black disc that had just encroached on that of the sun.

It was the ion trail of a comet, and the eclipse had started.

CHAPTER TWENTY-EIGHT

Lambeth Bridge, and everything south, had disappeared behind a shimmering curtain. Curiously, that curtain didn't extend very far to the east. Holly knew that it would only just cover where he was standing, along with everything on the other side of the bridge as far as he could see. He also knew he only had seconds before it reached him. He worked hard to disregard any speculation about what affect this mist might have on him, preferring to concentrate on the likelihood that he'd be lucky to see his hand in front of his face.

The soldiers who were busily barricading the bridge had seen it too. Roughly half of them were staring, rooted to the spot. The other half made up for their comrades' inactivity by rushing around twice as fast. Their shouted communications, already loud, now became a constant frenzy of orders and acknowledgements.

Holly's priority was to make it to the bell tower. What he did then would depend on what he found there. Having despaired of his chances of making it through the heavy military presence on the bridge unchallenged, he now realised that the eclipse was providing the perfect cover, a fleeting opportunity that mustn't be missed.

His target was on the left as he looked across the river.

Given the likelihood of almost zero visibility, he figured his passage there would be a lot easier if he started on that same side and felt his way along the wall. Making a hurried count of the number of ornate lamp posts he would be passing before reaching his goal, he ran to the railing, reaching it just as the edge of the comet's trail rushed past him.

Other than the expected dimming of the light and the shortening of his view, he registered no ill effects. There may have been a slight tingling, but as that mirrored the subtle visual phenomenon surrounding him, he may have imagined that.

He knew this camouflage wouldn't last long, so he set off immediately, putting one hand after the other along the top of the wall. He closed his eyes. He couldn't see where he was going anyway, and he was finding the sparkly snowfall distracting. But that instantly took him back to a similar journey on Waterloo Bridge, just two bridges away, when he was about to enter a very different London, and he quickly opened them again. The main difference between then and now was the absence of gunfire, and he hoped it would stay that way.

He had only covered a short distance when he came up against a pile of sandbags. Moving his hand gingerly around it, he found he couldn't reach the top. Deciding he would be unlikely to scale the thing without ending up in the Thames, he saw no option but to go round it and hope it didn't go all the way across the bridge.

It ended after just a few yards, enabling him to pass it and make his way back to the wall where, for some reason, he felt safer. He knew it was irrational to think he was less likely to run into anyone there, but he did at least know it was leading him in the right direction.

Had this been one of the spy thrillers he used to enjoy, he realised, the hero would have donned the uniform of the army he had infiltrated and sauntered through without attracting any unwanted attention. Holly was therefore delighted when a seemingly abandoned jacket and cap ensemble faded into view to his right, until it became apparent that they were still very much operational and he had to move on swiftly before the soldier wearing them turned round.

His theory of the wall providing privacy was instantly disproved, as another uniform suddenly appeared right in front of him, also very much occupied, the young soldier staring straight at him. Holly froze, until he realised that neither of them was now moving and thought it would be better if one of them was. The new recruit seemed helpless to pursue him, merely uttering a non-committal 'Hey!' which struck Holly as more of a cry for help than a military challenge.

Emboldened by this encounter, he upped his pace, crouching slightly, and fended off several human obstacles like a rugby player making a dash for the touchline. By the time he reached the final lamp post, he was out of breath, but still unrestrained.

By his reckoning, he should now be standing as close to the bell tower as the bridge would allow. Shielding it from him was an eight-foot, wrought-iron railing with spikes along the top, on the other side of which he remembered a path between some manicured grass leading up to the campanile door, even though, at this moment, he couldn't see any of that.

Holly knew that whatever plot was being executed to prevent the bell from ringing out would not be found on his side of the railing. What he didn't know was how to get to the other side. Climbing seemed inadvisable, and going round to the front gate was out of the question. It would take time he didn't have and was likely to be heavily guarded.

The answer, when it struck him, did so forcibly on his shoulder, almost knocking him to the ground. When he turned to see the cause, he saw that it was someone with the same predicament as himself, but without the fear of the injuries the iron spikes might inflict.

Despite only being two yards away, Holly couldn't make out the whole figure. It was already perched on the railing, four feet off the ground, trying to find a purchase on the spikes that would cause the least damage. But Holly's breathing slowed when he recognised the black-and-white motorcycle suit. It stopped altogether when he moved closer to confirm his worst fear. As the head came into view, he could see that it was completely covered by a black mask.

Holly considered the possibility that the whole eclipse environment was another of this character's induced visions, but dismissed the idea. It had all been predicted on the news, after all.

The adrenalin really kicked in when Holly realised the opportunity he now had. Fugu Yakitori was clearly in a hurry to clear the railing so he could carry out, or at very least mastermind, his own particular Gunpowder Plot. All Holly had to do was detain him, and hope that the chief Maniac was a lone wolf, or that breaking the chain of command would be sufficient.

He grabbed a handful of leather jacket and pulled as hard as he could. His adversary must have been feeling around rather gingerly for a benign spot amongst the twisted ironwork and came away easily enough, knocking Holly over properly this time before landing on top of him.

Using a hand on Holly's face for leverage, he was instantly back on the railing, scrambling more desperately. Holly got up in time to grasp the same bit of leather. Having learnt from his previous mistake, he swung the masked figure round and on to his back on the ground, where he pinned him down, holding both his arms.

Despite the constant struggling, Holly was surprised, bordering on smug, at how easily he could restrain the owner of the scary voice he had heard on the telephone earlier. But then he discovered why.

'Imbécile! Crétin! Salaud!'

A torrent of abuse was not unexpected, under the circumstances, but the French was a surprise. And the high-pitched register didn't make any sense at all. He could only stare when the irate character managed to grab the top of the mask and drag it off, remembering only at the last second to avert his gaze from the deadly flames that were sure to appear.

But the only sign of flames was the colour of the hair that was revealed. Holly was astonished to find himself uncomfortably face to face with the redhead he had last seen in an office in Somerset House, a woman who had gone by the name of Miss Oliver.

'Of course!' he gasped. 'Olivier!'

He couldn't help being taken back to their first encounter, and her endearing giant of a son, the original bearer of the name Oliver, who would have had so little trouble picking his mother up and depositing her on the other side of the railing.

He relinquished his hold, and shuffled backwards, allowing her to sit up.

'Of course, Olivier, you moron!'

'But you're dressed…'

'In a Fugu suit, yes. How else am I going to get near them to stop them? You do know what they're doing, don't you, Monsieur Holly?'

'Well, not specifically…' he admitted. 'Er… how do you know my name?'

She picked herself up.

‘There’s no time for this,’ she said, still finding time to dust herself off, as Holly also got to his feet. ‘Help me get over this fence, and there’s just a chance…’

But before she could put her mask on again, a blinding point of light appeared from the direction of the bridge, illuminating everything in its narrow path. It formed a tunnel of visibility from across the river, narrow enough not to reach the sides of the bridge, but wide enough to reveal the disconcerting number of firearms that were now trained on the obviously non-military couple, accompanied by the call, ‘Halt! Identify yourselves!’

Olivier proceeded to identify her companion with another string of well-chosen expletives.

‘How are we supposed to stop these Maniacs,’ she concluded, ‘if we get apprehended by the army, you…’

Holly never got the chance to protest that this mysterious source of light was not of his making. The ground suddenly shook, caused by an explosion they could feel more than hear. This was followed by a rumble that slowly got louder.

It was impossible to tell where this sound was coming from. The guns were now pointing in every direction, Holly noticed with some relief. Not so reassuring was the look on the Resistance leader’s face.

‘We’re too late!’ she wailed, looking wildly around.

Visibility briefly deteriorated again, as the mysterious beam of light disappeared. But then the edge of the ion trail swept past them, continuing its journey north. The eclipse was over, at least where they were, and the air reverted to its normal transparent state. But what had seemed a blessing to Holly instantly turned to horror.

St Stephen’s Tower was already leaning slightly. The source of the rumbling sound became apparent, as increasing clouds of dust could be seen billowing out from the base of the stricken building, once again making it hard to see, particularly at street level.

The tower gave a sudden lurch downwards, and then it slowly started falling across the path Holly had taken just minutes before.

Olivier screamed, not in French or in English but in the universal language of sheer frustration. Pausing only to throw her mask angrily at a bewildered Holly, she ran into the swirling dust.

'No!' Holly shouted, but she was already out of sight. The only things to be seen were soldiers appearing out of the gloom, running in the opposite direction.

He watched, mesmerised, as the building continued its awful slow-motion descent, before it started breaking up. It was only when he saw the strangely familiar sight of large chunks of masonry hurtling directly towards him that he forced himself to abandon the dreadful scene.

CHAPTER TWENTY-NINE

Pyracantha. Firethorn.

Holly found the names of this evergreen, thorny shrub as fascinating as the object itself. The thorns were self-evident, and the fire described the colour of the berries that developed in late summer and continued well into the autumn. The much-needed nourishment for the birds that this provided was the reason Anna had been so keen to install this bush at the back of the garden. That and its very efficient role as a burglar deterrent.

It was also a very good listener. Holly had slumped next to it, into his garden chair which he had found in its usual place, finding some comfort in the familiarity of the scene.

'I considered following her into the swirling dust,' he told it. 'Either I could have dragged her out - unlikely I'd have been able to find her - or we could have gone together. The inexplicably recurring siren luring the Solver to an appropriate death, crushed underneath Big Ben, the landmark he'd failed to save.'

Standing around, feeling they were eavesdropping on a private conversation, were Kia, Uncle Sid, Uncle Gordo, the baron, the captain, and Claire.

'But that wouldn't have solved anything,' he continued, still addressing his spiky friend. 'Then, I hoped the bells would somehow ring out as the building collapsed, just by knocking against each other. But that didn't happen either. So I ran away.'

No-one, not even the captain, could think of anything to say that would lighten the mood. The clouds had come across and thoughtfully shielded them from the sight of the comet, but had only succeeded in making the setting even more dismal. Indeed, the atmosphere was so gloomy that the two uncles wished Holly had left them in the library.

He had gone straight from the devastation on Westminster Bridge to Cordelia's lair. The librarian's cheery greeting had stuck in her throat as soon as she saw the look on his face. Acknowledging the sentiment with the faintest of smiles, he had gone straight up to the uncles and grabbed each of them by the arm, before thinking better of making such an abrupt exit.

'Forgive me, Cordelia,' he said, staring at his feet, 'but the world is crumbling, and we're running out of time to set it right. If, indeed, that's even a possibility.' He sighed and looked up, wondering whether this would be the last time he'd be on her eye level. 'It's been an honour – and I sincerely hope we meet again some day.'

His next word was 'grid', leaving Cordelia contemplating an empty space where the three men had been standing, the uncles' increasing unease at Holly's demeanour, and the wink Uncle Sid had still managed to give her at the last second.

Once back, they had found Kia, the baron and the captain pacing worriedly in the garden, having abandoned their search for Uncle Jasper. Claire provided the only point of stability, sitting on the ground with her knees under her chin. The French trio had still not returned, status unknown.

The uncles had imparted their only bit of news first, that Camera-Shy Scrap had turned out to refer to the piece of paper they already had and not the secluded punch-up with the Maniacs that they had hoped for.

Holly then filled them in about all that had happened since he had seen them last. His audience was horrified at his description of the hatchet-wielding old woman, who had seemingly been brought back from the dead, and even more horrified on learning that the Maniacs could match his clue location hopping. A cheer had gone up when he got to the part where the Wise Lady had whisked him to safety, followed by gasps at his encounter with the Pitch-Black Army and his revelations about its personnel.

An awed silence developed at his depiction of being inside the eclipse of a comet, a phenomenon his listeners hadn't experienced as it had passed some way to the west of them. This silence only deepened as they heard the fate of their French comrades' leader and the devastation of a sizeable part of the Palace of Westminster.

At this point, Holly gave in to the clamouring of his eyes and let them close. He would gladly have fallen asleep, let everything take its course, and deal with the consequences in the morning, but he knew that wasn't an option. When he finally found the strength to lift his eyelids, there was his pyracantha confidante, patiently waiting to hear those final thoughts.

'I think "ran away" is a little harsh,' said Claire, the only one not to have got lost in one of the episodes of Holly's epic tale. 'More like a tactical retreat?'

The others nodded eagerly, glad to have been brought back to the present and relieved that someone had found the words of encouragement they hadn't.

The baron remembered something he'd meant to say during the narrative, but had kept back for fear of interrupting the flow.

'That beam of light from across the bridge, the one that

gave you away to the soldiers,' he said. 'I think I may be able to shed some…'

A ripple of laughter spread throughout the group.

'You may be too late,' warned the captain. 'You may have bolted the stable door before the horse has…'

More laughter, which increased when Holly finally smiled.

'All right, nice one,' conceded the baron. 'The point is – I solved another couple of lines of the grid just before you got back.'

The lighter mood produced some sarcastic 'oohs'.

'Whatever. The first is the line starting at 6 Down. "Curse son with firm desire", seven letters, first is an S, third is an O, and it ends on an E.'

He gave the others a moment to consider their options, which they all did, except Kia, who just raised her eyebrows impatiently.

'OK,' the baron continued, taking his cue from the eyebrows. 'I figured the S took care of "son", "firm" could then be the CO for "company", which takes care of the O, which leaves a four-letter word for "desire". Which means the "curse" at the beginning is actually a noun, rather than the verb implied in the clue.'

The absence of suggested synonyms highlighted the absence of Uncle Jasper.

'That's "urge",' Holly volunteered, as much to break the silence as to provide the solution, 'which gives us "scourge", a curse or plague.'

The baron nodded. Spurred on by the indifference this produced, he moved swiftly on.

'And the next one is – let me see – yes, it's "Kid star gets support", also seven letters.'

Again, there was no reaction. This time, everyone wanted him to get on with it.

'Did you know Shirley Temple has a cocktail named after her?' was the captain's contribution. 'Imagine having something non-alcoholic named after you.' He looked appalled. 'Thank goodness for Captain Morgan.'

'I wouldn't have got this one,' the baron cracked on, 'if we hadn't had every other letter already. I think it's a word for "kid", used as a form of address. I think it's "sunbeam", as in "Didn't see that coming, did you, sunbeam?" So "star" and "support" become "sun" and "beam".'

Holly and the uncles nodded. Claire and the captain cheerfully shook their heads at one another. Kia just smiled.

'That sounds about right,' Holly agreed. 'I think Scourge Sunbeam is a very apt description. It certainly scuppered any chance of success we may have had.'

'Pity I didn't get it sooner,' the baron grumbled. 'If you'd been able to write it in, it might not have appeared.'

'Maybe,' said Holly, finally bothering to take his paper out. 'Maybe not. At least, if I write it in now, it might not come back later.'

He entered the words and surveyed the result with some satisfaction, surprised at how much they had completed.

'What's the other line?' he asked.

'Oh, that's not so useful,' the baron answered. 'At least, I couldn't make anything of it.'

'Well, that's true of most of them,' commented Kia. 'It will probably come into its own eventually. What was it?'

'Eleven Across. "Leave a group performing", seven let…'

'Abandon.'

Holly had almost whispered the word to his ever-attentive shrub, and it took a few moments for him to realise that everyone had overheard him and was looking at him in silent surprise.

'I remember that one,' he explained. 'It conjured up an

image that stayed with me. He's used it before. Maybe he's getting sloppy. Let's hope so.'

'A group performing,' Kia mused, 'a-band-on. "Abandon", synonym for "leave". That works.'

'Thank you,' said the baron. 'The second one took a little longer. It's "A backside's sound – that's what's owed". And it's another seven…'

He was interrupted again, this time by gales of laughter coming from the captain and the uncles.

'Boys, boys,' Kia admonished. 'Have we really sunk that low?'

'The word "sound",' Holly said, trying for Kia's sake to keep a straight face. 'Does that mean it's one of Uncle Gordo's clues?'

'Oh, he got it immediately,' the captain just managed to find enough oxygen to say. 'But he doesn't like to blow his own trumpet.'

The ensuing avalanche of merriment swept Holly and Claire along with it. Kia smiled benignly, but made a point of staring fixedly at the homonym expert, Uncle Gordo, who duly caved in to the pressure, as soon as he had the breath to do so.

'A,' he wheezed, 'R-E-A-,' he inhaled deeply, '-R-S.'

Once an explanation had been given, the clue instantly became less amusing and everyone calmed down.

'OK,' said Holly, the first to regain his composure fully. 'It sounds like "a backside's", which is "a rear's", which in turn becomes "arrears", "that's what's owed".'

'Which gives us Abandon Arrears,' Kia said, in a hollow voice. 'And guess what? We have no idea what it means.'

Her tone was so bleak that Holly couldn't even muster the enthusiasm to write the words into the grid.

Kia went and found the companion chair to Holly's, hidden in the far corner. She sat down heavily and put her head in her hands, covering her eyes.

After a brief, awkward silence, Uncle Gordo went over to Holly.

'K-N-E-A-D-S E-W-E,' he whispered in his ear. Then he patted him on the shoulder before herding everyone else quietly back into the house.

1 F	I	2 N	A	3 L	■	4 C	R	5 O	S	6 S	W	7 O	R	8 D
A	■		■	U	■		■		■	C	■	R	■	R
9 N	O	T	I	C	E	D	■	10 E	X	O	T	I	C	A
T	■		■	I	■		■		■	U	■	G	■	W
11 A				D			■	12		R		A		S
S	■		■	L	■		■	■	■	G	■	M	■	■
13 T	E	E	N	Y	■	14 M	Y	15 S	T	E	R	I	E	16 S
I	■	■	■	■	■		■		■	■	■	■	■	U
17 C	A	18 M	E	19 R	A	S	H	Y	■	20 S	C	21 R	A	P
■	■		■	O	■	■	■		■	U	■	I	■	E
22 D	U	R	A	B	L	23 Y	■	24 B	O	N	J	O	U	R
R	■		■	O	■		■		■	B	■	T	■	H
25 E	L	A	S	T	I	C	■	26 A	V	E	R	A	G	E
A	■		■	I	■		■		■	A	■	C	■	R
27 M	U	S	I	C	I	A	N	S	■	28 M	O	T	T	O

CHAPTER THIRTY

Holly moved his chair over to Kia's. Had it been brand new, it would only have made a loud scraping noise on the broken concrete path. Being decades old, it had the added rattle of a tambourine from all the bits that had worked themselves loose over the years.

Her hands still covering her face, Kia was oblivious to this noise, as she was to the fact that they were now the only two occupants of the garden.

Unsure of what to say, Holly took a moment to survey his setting, marvelling at how alien such a familiar location looked.

'Are you sure this is my garden?' he settled on as an opener. 'It was a jungle, last time I saw it.'

Kia initially showed no sign of having heard him, but eventually lifted her head.

'I know,' she sighed. 'I've seen it.'

'Ah,' said Holly, pleased his patience had paid off. 'Well, that begs a very obvious question.'

Kia settled into a more comfortable position in anticipation of a question and answer session she had been expecting, but was still very much in two minds about.

'Well,' she said, 'as long as you're sure it's me you're talking to and not that bush, fire away.'

Questions about Kia had monopolised Holly's mind for weeks now, barely allowing any other thoughts to intrude, but now that he had the opportunity to ask them, he started getting cold feet. The idea of how he'd feel if he let this chance go by forced him to take the plunge.

'You say you've seen it,' he faltered. 'How is that possible?'

Kia shrugged.

'I just can,' she said, simply.

'In flashes, between your world and mine?'

'No, all the time.'

Holly was startled.

'So, when you say you've seen it…'

'…I mean I can see it right now, yes. It's like a shadow, a faint grey picture – not so much superimposed on all this colour, more like coexisting.'

Holly sat back in his chair, having trouble taking this in.

'Good Lord, you mean you can see two different realities all the time?'

'Well, yes, but yours is very faint. And, of course, it's only two versions when things are different. The back of my – our – house, for instance, is the same, so there's only one version. I can only see two gardens now because you've let yours go.'

Holly looked around, desperately trying to memorise this tidier layout so he could duplicate it when he got back to make her life easier.

'But you can't touch it?'

'What do you mean?'

'Well, if I left, say, a garden rake lying around, could you fall over it?'

She laughed.

'You? A rake?'

Holly was glad he'd got her to laugh, however unwittingly.

'No,' she went on. 'It's just an image. I'd walk straight through it.' She frowned. 'The only thing in your world I have ever had any control over is that little picture frame on the mantelpiece in the living room.'

Holly shot forward in his seat.

'The little round one? I've noticed that move! I probably wouldn't have, if I'd dusted more regularly. I keep moving it back. I assumed it was caused by buses rattling by, shaking the ground.'

'Or maybe,' she suggested, 'a train along the front of the house?'

He smiled, glancing automatically at the building to make sure it was still in one piece.

'Well, yes, that would do it,' he murmured, then turned his attention back to Kia. 'I take it, no-one else here shares your… double vision?'

'No, just me.'

He nodded. Staggering as this answer was, he had expected it. Everything seemed to revolve around this remarkable girl.

'And the uncles all live over there,' he said, gesturing in the direction of Gus's house. 'Does that mean you live here all alone?'

'Mostly,' she replied. 'Great stays over sometimes, when he's in the neighbourhood. It used to be just me and mum. That was fun. Then I went through my rebellious phase, nothing serious, just staying out late, mostly for the sake of it. Mum would lock the front door so I had to ring the bell. But I found a way round that. You see that kitchen window? There's a way of leaving it unlatched so that it looks locked. So I'd go next door – the uncles were always up, I swear they never sleep – and Uncle Jasper would help me over the fence, and I'd climb in and be fast asleep in bed when mum came to wake me up for school. She never could figure out how I did it. I think she was quite impressed, really.'

She had acquired a faraway look as she reminisced, which now faded.

'But eventually she wanted to get away from the house, started to find it depressing, and I preferred to stay. I couldn't leave this house. It's a very good HQ. So she moved round the corner.'

'I see,' Holly said, dubiously. 'And your father?'

'Oh, I see him from time to time,' she smiled. 'Not as often as I'd like. Oh, I've just remembered.'

She reached into a pocket and pulled out a small, dark blue exercise book, which she handed to him.

'I dug that out after you were here last, and I've been carrying it round ever since. It's my maths book, from school.'

He flicked through a few pages, apprehensive at first as to how he'd react to seeing his old subject after so many years, then enchanted by the familiarity of the questions that were set, and finally delighted by the apparent ease with which she solved them.

'So you can see my reasoning,' she said, proudly.

He lost himself in the symbols for a moment, before the current predicament's clamour for his attention grew too loud. But that in turn threw up another question.

'Assuming it all works out today,' he ventured, without looking up.

'Never in doubt,' she asserted, giving him a stern look which he could feel, even if he couldn't see it.

'Well, let's assume it anyway, that this is the last crossword, and tomorrow the sun rises on an unscathed world – what will you do? What would you like to do?'

'No idea,' she admitted. 'I haven't given it a thought. It's never been an option. I suppose – something that involves travelling? Apart from the odd, frantic few minutes in some rather outlandish locations, I've never been away from here. I'd like to spend a bit of time in some genuine wonders of the world.'

He stared at her, trying to assimilate all this information, until he became aware that it was starting to get dark. He reluctantly abandoned his line of inquiry and, with an appreciative nod, put the book away.

'Getting back to Uncle Jasper,' he said, 'things to do.'

But he still allowed himself to be drawn back to his previous meeting with the handyman.

'I can't believe it was only this morning he was doing magic tricks with that solid/gas/liquid thing. He was like a kid.'

'Restless matter,' Kia confirmed. 'He has a real nose for that stuff.'

Holly stood up, stiffly.

'I'm going in to… er… clear my head for a moment. Sort out what to do next.'

'Good idea,' said Kia, relieved the questions had finished. 'I'll… er… do the same, but out here.'

With a last smile, Holly shuffled through the door and into the kitchen. Hearing voices in the living room, he decided to stay where he was for the moment and sat on one of the two chairs at the kitchen table. He needed to focus, and to be able to hear his own thoughts. He leant his head back and closed his eyes, forcing himself to take slow, deep breaths.

He stopped suddenly, feeling that he was no longer alone in the room. Opening his eyes confirmed that he was right. Sitting on the other chair was Anna.

She was smiling at him, and he was happy just to smile back. That precious moment that seemed to happen on each one of his visits had finally arrived, and he was going to make the most of it. He knew he must have dropped off for a moment and was only dreaming. He knew that she couldn't touch him, and that he would never hear her voice.

'Hello, Holly Oak,' she said, giving his knee a squeeze. 'Happy Valentine's Day.'

CHAPTER THIRTY-ONE

'You can let me go now, Holly. I'm not going anywhere.'

Holly couldn't speak, and he didn't allow himself to blink, in case Anna turned out to be just an apparition after all.

He had tried to stand up, but his legs had given way. He was now on his knees, with his arms around Anna's shoulders, looking into those eyes. Letting go was not an option.

'I'm so sorry,' she said, cradling his face in her hands, which made him instinctively close his eyes, immediately opening them again with a start. 'It would have been so much easier, letting you think I was just a figment of your imagination, a memory that came and went.'

She gently rubbed her nose against his. He started again when he felt her breath on his face.

'But I couldn't do it,' she went on, stroking his cheek. 'I'm so sorry.'

She looked at him with concern. He hadn't managed to say a single word, having enough trouble just filling his lungs.

'Kia said you were like this on that ship,' she commiserated. 'Oh dear, it was selfish of me...'

'No!'

He kissed her, briefly at first, as though to stem the flow of words, then lingeringly, still resisting his natural inclination to close his eyes.

'No,' he repeated, finally pulling away, taking one of her hands in his. 'No – this is – the most unbelievable – I never thought...'

He gave her a quizzical look.

'How can you be real? Are you sure you're real?'

She used her free hand to give him a playful but firm slap on the cheek.

'Ha!' He made the sound Anna used to make when they were watching a weepie and the mood suddenly lightened after a particularly emotional scene – what she called a snotty laugh. 'I didn't see that coming. So it really is you!'

He pulled her closer and held her tightly, confident enough now to abandon his vigil and close his eyes. He lost himself in the moment. Anna had to tell him twice that she couldn't breathe before he heard her. He let her go immediately, and they just stared happily at each other.

He was burning to know if she'd been here the whole time, how she got here, what she'd been doing. But he wasn't going to ask any questions yet, in case that jinxed everything.

As he had noticed last time, she had certainly aged – a few wrinkles, a touch of grey in the hair – and he was glad it wasn't his imagination that had added these realistic touches, but the passage of time.

That reminded him that she hadn't looked so happy on his previous visit.

'So – that day of the cloud,' he hesitated to ask. 'Was that really you then, as well?'

She lowered her eyes in embarrassment.

'Fancy me being jealous. After all this time.'

'Jealous?' He tried to hide his delight. 'Of Lorraine?'

She gave him a sly look.

'It was me that slammed the door behind you when you left. But it was just as well I did,' she hurried on, before he could take her to task, 'because otherwise you wouldn't have been in contact with her when you went back, and I'd have been stuck with her. I mean, she'd have been stuck here.'

He shook his head. If this was a dream, it was the best one ever.

'You really haven't changed,' he murmured. 'Thank God.'

Then he looked worried.

'Have I? I don't think I have, but… Do I look much older? Have I got more… boring?'

She laughed and lightly punched his chest.

'That old chestnut?' she scolded. 'Still consider yourself boring?'

She sat back and made a show of looking him up and down.

'You've put on a little weight,' she conceded. 'And I recognise every item of clothing you're wearing as something I bought you.'

Holly smiled, but was acutely aware that he would have loved to have shown her that he was finally wearing the watch again that she had given him, the one that would constantly remind him of her face, the one that the baron had lost somewhere in St Paul's.

'But boring?' she asked, more seriously. 'I watched you both times you were here before. The way you dealt with overwhelming odds, the way you involved everybody, the way you never gave up, your ingenuity, your sense of duty, of right and wrong, your – spirit – just made me realise how lucky I was to meet you, and why I have loved you all these years.'

Holly had regained his speechlessness. He was more

confident than ever that he wasn't dreaming, because he knew he could never have dreamt up those words. His customary self-restraint was holding, but only by blinking furiously. He was determined not to give way to tears, mostly because they would prevent him from focusing on this precious image. And anyway, how would they make any sense, when he was the happiest he'd been in sixteen years?

This use of logic was totally alien to Kia. Holly's current tunnel vision meant he was oblivious to the fact that Kia had been standing at the kitchen window for some time, and she was now wearing the biggest smile and was crying buckets.

She only dodged out of sight now when the baron appeared at the doorway. He had heard voices and thought it was time for some action.

'Holly, I really think we…' he began. 'Oh. Oh! Oh, my God.'

Still kneeling on the floor, Holly turned his head and sensed more embarrassment than shock.

'You knew about this?' he asked.

The baron shuffled his feet.

'Well, yes, I might have…'

'So, I take it everyone knows?'

Holly got a sharp nudge from Anna.

'What were they supposed to do?' she asked, softly. 'It was my decision. You always seemed to appear at the most catastrophic moments. How was revealing my presence going to help? No. I got to see you, and you briefly got to see me, and that would have to be enough. Only, today – it wasn't.'

It was her turn to look embarrassed.

'I couldn't stand it any more. I gave in. I'm sorry.'

Holly gave her a stern look, intending to give her a mock lecture on self-denial, but burst out laughing instead.

It fell to the baron to provide the serious tone.

'Look, I'm sorry, too – and I can't conceive of how you're feeling right now. But I do know how everyone else is feeling right now, and we really need to be doing something.'

With that, he went back into the living room, no doubt to bring the captain, Claire, and the two uncles up to date on the kitchen sink drama that was unfolding.

'Well, this will test whether I was right before,' Anna said, adjusting the collar of Holly's jacket and brushing off his shoulders. 'You're now going to have to file this away, and concentrate on the matter at hand, because they're all counting on you. You can't let my being here interfere with that. If it did, I'd never forgive myself. I can only hope that having my support gives you more confidence. You must try and turn my moment of weakness into your source of strength.'

'How can I?' he pleaded. 'How can I think about dealing with all this, knowing that I have to save you as well?'

'But that's just it,' she said, stroking his hair. 'You've saved me twice already.'

CHAPTER THIRTY-TWO

Holly decided that acting as though nothing had happened was the best way to proceed, despite entering the room holding hands with the wife he'd thought dead for sixteen years. This nearly succeeded, apart from the two uncles grinning, whispering and nudging each other like schoolchildren. But when the captain led them all in a round of applause, the game was up. Holly happily acknowledged the clapping, even playing to the crowd by giving Anna another long kiss.

'Now, Holly,' she admonished. 'It's not a royal wedding.'

'Yes,' Holly said, thoughtfully, to renewed cheers. 'I rather think it really is.'

Kia had used the commotion to slip in behind them, red-eyed but still beaming, and was heartily joining in.

The baron came up and shook Holly's hand.

'The best man, is it?' Holly mused.

'Certainly the best man to go searching for our French beans,' the baron said, ignoring the captain's rebuke about thinking of his stomach at a time like this. 'I'm worried about them. They've been gone too long.'

'You shouldn't really be going out on your own,' Holly said. 'Those other things are still out there, somewhere.'

'I'll come along,' suggested Claire. 'We'll check out the

square, and if they're not there I can at least drop this cello at home.'

The baron eyed the large case dubiously.

'Probably not the best way to be inconspicuous,' he said.

'Nonsense,' Claire replied. 'That church at the top of the hill past the hospital? That's now a recording studio, orchestral stuff – film scores, mainly. People are in and out of the station carrying instruments all the time.'

They both turned to Kia for the final word.

'Fine, off you go,' she said. 'But don't be long. We're going to need you.'

The pair set off, Claire pulling a face when the baron wouldn't let her do any heavy lifting. Holly saw them to the door.

They hadn't been gone two minutes before the French trio reappeared from the opposite direction. The scout Hugo brushed aside the concern for their well-being, indignant at the idea they'd allow themselves to be caught, or even that the baron would have spotted them, had they been coming back from the square, so adept were they at blending in with their surroundings.

'How do you make a tarte au citron invisible?' the captain wanted to know. 'Oh, of course. You eat it.'

Hugo had been the one to lure their aged, axe-wielding colleague away from the others, leading her a suitable distance before losing her without any trouble. They had given themselves twenty minutes to rendezvous at a particular street corner. Poor Sand seemed focused enough on her targets for them not to worry that she might be a danger to the public.

'But they obviously know about this place being your centre of intelligence,' Voltaire warned them, 'so it's only a matter of time before they turn up.'

Kia agreed.

'I suspect the only reason they're not here by now is that, having blown up Big Ben, they think they've already won.'

'Excuse me?' spluttered Colette. 'They've what?'

Kia provided the abridged version of the recent events at Westminster, thinking it prudent to omit the sad fate of their leader for now. And telling them her identity, and the fact that they'd met her before in two different guises, would certainly have been a complication too far.

'Oh, I see,' said a shocked Voltaire. 'Well, anyway, if we're going to deal with them, we'd better do it fast.'

His call for speed, however, didn't stop him pausing to be intrigued why two people he wasn't aware of having a connection were suddenly sitting on the sofa holding hands.

'We were married a long time ago,' Holly explained. 'But for the last sixteen years, she's been dead to me.'

'Ah, Monsieur Holly,' Voltaire scolded, putting a paternal hand on the lucky man's shoulder. 'You see how much time you've wasted with your obstinacy. In affairs of the heart, forgiveness is everything.'

Colette changed the subject, keen to spare Voltaire the embarrassment of realising just how wrong the end of the stick he'd grabbed was. The uncles had already started sniggering.

'I think I've solved two of your clues,' she announced, succeeding in her aim of attracting everyone's attention.

'Cryptic clues in English,' Holly marvelled. 'That's impressive.'

'If she's got them right,' Hugo commented.

'Well, there were many letters in there already,' Colette said, bringing out her newspaper. 'So I couldn't go far wrong. You think it will help?'

'I'm sure it will,' Holly said, getting his copy out of his

jacket. 'What have you got?'

'It's 4 Down,' she replied. 'It reads "Arrived, having done away with singular, cryptic handles", and it's four and five letters. The word "cryptic" drew me to it.'

'OK. And how do you think it works?'

'Well, I thought "arrived" might be "came", especially as we know the first letter is a C. Then, remembering how you described these clues as blueprints, I wondered if "having done away" meant that it contained an anagram of "done". And I know from spending so much time looking in dictionaries that an S can sometimes stand for "singular", as opposed to "plural".'

There was a stunned silence, apart from a low, appreciative whistle from the captain.

'Which makes "code names",' she continued, not sure whether to take this reaction as admiration or disappointment, 'which works with the four letters we already have. The only bit I can't figure out is "cryptic handles", which sounds like a secret way of opening something, and makes me think I've got it all wrong.'

'No, no,' Holly assured her. 'Spot on. Nail on the head. A handle can also be a name or nickname, so a cryptic one would certainly describe a code name. Well done. Full marks.'

'All right, then,' said Colette. 'You said these solutions work in pairs, and I did get the next one, but it makes no sense.'

'You definitely got it right, then,' confirmed the captain. 'None of them make any sense.'

'Let's see,' said Holly. 'After 4, comes – 23, which is "Second person loses heart, twice, around a plant", five letters.'

'Now, I know,' said Colette, 'that "plant" can also mean "factory", and that's what seems to be implied here, but I think it is just a garden plant after all. Look at the letters. There's a Y, a C, and an A.'

'YMCA?' suggested the captain. 'Only tried it once. Certainly made me lose heart.'

'It can only be "yucca",' Colette ploughed on, 'which is the same in French, fortunately. But why it's "yucca"...?'

Holly and the uncles peered at their papers, the latter shaking their heads, disappointed at the lack of anagrams or homonyms. Voltaire knew this was all beyond him, but was willing his compatriot on. Hugo was trying to look as disinterested as possible. The captain was a picture of concentration, ever optimistic that the secret of solving these clues would suddenly reveal itself to him. Kia and Anna had caught the glint in each other's eye. Kia sat back contentedly. Anna rested her head on Holly's shoulder.

'I mean, I know the second person is "you",' Colette went on, happening to be looking at the captain.

'Me?' he queried.

'No, "you". First person is "I", second person is "you", third person is "he", "she" or "it". Obviously.'

'Of course,' the captain nodded earnestly.

'So "second person loses heart" is "you" without the middle, which accounts for the Y and the U. But "twice"? Why isn't that YUYU?'

'Because,' Holly murmured, 'the "twice" actually refers to the "around", which is C for "circa", meaning "approximately" or "around". Then the "a", and you get "yucca".'

'That's a shame.' Colette looked crestfallen. 'I was hoping I was wrong. Because Code Names Yucca is nonsense.'

'Oh, you'd be surprised,' said Kia. 'Write it in, Holly, and let's see what happens.'

Surprised at how gung-ho Kia was being, Holly nevertheless complied. Nervous glances were exchanged, everyone looking for a result.

'Well, that fell as flat as one of my mother's soufflés,' muttered Hugo.

'Quiet, Hugo,' chided Colette.

'Hugo?' the man replied. 'I'm not Hugo. I'm Yucca.'

'Don't be ridiculous,' snapped Voltaire. 'I'm Yucca.'

'Grow up, you two,' commanded Colette. 'There's only one Yucca here, and it's me.'

Holly stared at them each in turn, then down at his grid and its pair of new entries.

What had he just done?

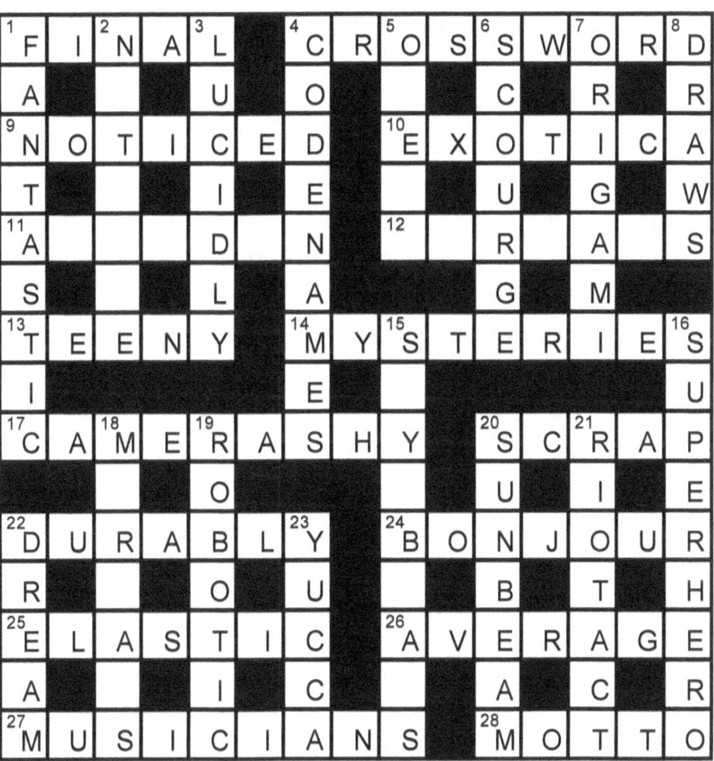

CHAPTER THIRTY-THREE

'What was that? Some sort of code name reset button?'

The nine of them shared a bewildered expression, wondering how the day could get any more weird. The captain, as usual, was the first to give that bewilderment verbal form.

'We'll just have to deal with it,' said Kia. 'The Soya Beans here are going to be the most affected, obviously. It's going to make communications amongst themselves rather awkward, as well as between us and them. It's not ideal.'

'Well, quite,' agreed the captain. 'I mean, what do I call you now?' he asked the scout. 'The agent Yucca, also known as Hugo, also known as Gilbert? Yakahakag, for short? Or was he a Finnish racing driver?'

Everyone was too preoccupied even to groan.

'Who needs three yuccas?' he summed up.

'But it's not three yuccas, is it?' the Resistance leader said, his face betraying a revelation.

'What do you mean?' Kia asked.

'Well, we're not the only group of agents, are we? If our code names have changed, maybe those of the Maniacs have changed as well. And they won't know why. They may not even have noticed. Each of them may take for granted that his code name is Yucca. And we might be able to use that to our advantage.'

'But we have no way of knowing if their names have changed,' said Holly.

'Yes,' said the Frenchwoman. 'We do.'

She produced the mobile phone she had found in her colleague's hand after her demise at the café.

'This belonged to Marlowe, or Nasi Goreng,' she explained. 'Or – hopefully – Yucca.'

She held the phone out to Holly.

'No point giving it to me,' he said. 'Better pass it to someone who knows how to get into the thing.'

Kia took it and turned it on. Pressing a few buttons, she quickly found the list of contacts.

'Have you been into this list before?' she asked. 'And did it contain the names of the Maniac agents?'

Getting an affirmative response to both those questions, she triumphantly held the phone out for all to see the screen.

'Just "X" and "Yucca" in that list now,' she announced. 'I'm guessing "X" is our friend Fugu and that the other name is now connected to the numbers of all the other agents.'

Holly found himself staring at one of his favourite thinking points on the wall, conscious of the obligation he felt to come up with a plan, fortunately unaware that everyone was indeed looking at him for the same reason. Anna had sat back to minimise any distraction she may be causing.

'Right,' he said, at last. 'Here's what we're going to do. Above all else, we need to eradicate this team. That not only eliminates the very real threat they pose, leaving us free to deal with other matters, but may also reverse the things they've been responsible for. We can't just write the Nutcase Mortals line in the grid, much though we'd like to. It would solve them out of existence. Unfortunately, it would mean we may never find Uncle Jasper. But we can use that clue number's location. I bet that's where they've got him, wherever that is. So, getting there is easy, but there are going to be guards, I imagine, so we need to get them out of the picture. And we seem to have been handed the ideal means to do so.'

Kia held up the phone.

'That's right,' Holly confirmed.

The Resistance leader picked up the thread.

'We can send all the Yuccas a message,' he suggested, eagerly, 'supposedly from their leader, telling them to congregate somewhere out of the way while we go in on a rescue mission. Hopefully, they won't have realised yet that they all have the same code name, and they will assume the message is meant for them personally.'

Holly nodded.

'Assuming Fugu isn't there himself,' the scout said, 'telling them he didn't send that.'

'Well, yes, assuming that,' Holly said, 'and I think that's a fair assumption to make – that should give us enough time, depending on what we come up against, to grab Uncle Jasper and get back here.'

The two remaining uncles were the first to jump into action.

'To legs!' shouted Uncle Sid.

'Whoa,' said Holly. 'Hang on a moment.'

'W-Y-E W-E-I-G-H-T?' protested Uncle Gordo.

'Well, first off,' Holly said, 'we have to send that message. Kia, if you wouldn't mind? How about "X maintaining radio silence. Go immediately to Whitestone Pond and await further instructions"?'

There was general agreement on the wording.

'Send,' Kia said, pressing the appropriate button.

'That should keep them occupied long enough,' the younger Frenchman said, 'as long as they don't notice that the message is coming from another Yucca.'

'Let's go, then,' Kia said, echoing Uncle Sid's sentiment.

'Hang on,' said Holly, to their obvious annoyance. 'Firstly, if this ruse is to work, then there's no point blundering in there before they've had a chance to act on the message.'

This was met by frowns, then looks of resignation, followed by several of them reluctantly returning to their seats.

'Thank you,' he resumed. 'Secondly, this enforced wait is actually a blessing, as it gives me time to go and find the baron. I think he has to be a part of this.'

Such was the mood of dejected impatience that this received barely an indifferent nod. The only person to react to the idea at all was Anna.

'Must you go out there?' she wanted to know. 'On your own? Couldn't I come with you?'

He took her hands and shook his head.

'If it was just a walk to the newsagent's and back, a nice stroll to the village,' he told her, 'then, yes, of course. It's so tempting to dismiss tomorrow and just spend the last few hours of today with you. I'd love to whisk you off to the Peak District, where Kia and I went this morning. Or show you the magical view from that temple on the mountain. I can think of nothing nicer. I genuinely can't. But we both know that if we give in to that, then all this will end fifteen minutes after midnight tonight. So we put that aside and carry on, which means having to go out there. And if it is dangerous out there then it's the last place I want you to be.'

He kissed her hand.

'Believe me,' he assured her, 'I can only bear to leave you now because it's the only way I know I might be able to see you again.'

With that, he turned and slipped out of the front door,

almost unnoticed.

But Anna wasn't remotely reassured. She knew him better than anyone, and she knew he had no intention of involving anyone else in this escapade.

He was going to attempt to rescue Uncle Jasper on his own.

CHAPTER THIRTY-FOUR

Anna was only partly right. Holly had no intention of tackling the Maniacs on his own, but a two-man party was as far as he was prepared to go.

The baron was waiting outside the Luminous Steed, as arranged in a hurried whisper as he and Claire were leaving the house.

'We dropped the cello off at her place,' he said. 'I told her I was just popping to the corner shop. She's going to be mad when she realises I'm not coming back.'

'Not as mad as the troupe at the house,' Holly said, grimacing. 'We should particularly prepare ourselves for a bout of Gallic wrath.'

'Gallic and avuncular,' the baron agreed. 'Not a healthy combination.'

'We'd better be successful, then. That ought to count for a certain amount of forgiveness.'

The baron took a deep breath.

'So, what's the plan?' he asked.

'There isn't one, really,' Holly admitted. 'That's why I wanted this to be a compact team, in case it all goes wrong. Minimise the casualties.'

'That sounds reassuring.'

'That's not to say I don't have full confidence in its

members, or at least one of them.'

He motioned to the baron to follow him round the pub and down the street.

'Also,' he went on, 'the smaller the number of people, the less chance of being seen, and that's the priority. If they can follow us wherever we go, then there's nowhere to hide, and we don't want to take any of them straight back to the house. We can't rely on the Wise Lady stepping in again to rescue a dozen people.'

'Right. So, why are we going down here?'

'We don't want to be seen to disappear – if that makes sense – and we can't go back to the house. There's an alley further down this road which should be secluded enough. And then straight to the Nutcase Mortals location, whatever that is.'

He went on to give the baron a brief outline of what had happened to all the code names, how they had taken advantage of that, and how this had increased their chances of success, given that Holly had already decided the two of them would be going on their own. The younger man took it all in without any questions.

They had reached the alley, actually a covered passage leading to a mews. Going into that mews would bring them back into the light and into direct view of the houses. The traffic in the road, a one-way street, had backed up due to some roadworks, and the two men were currently in the sight line of a double-decker busload of people. The only course was to wait for more privacy for their disappearing act. They stood there awkwardly in the shadows, wondering how they would be able to justify their presence if challenged.

'How's the guitar concerto coming along?' asked Holly. 'You were going to use the tune from St Paul's?'

'Yes, I'm going to have to be careful how I use that,' said the baron. 'I wouldn't want the auditorium melting at every performance.'

'Guaranteed to bring the house down,' Holly agreed.

'Quite. No, the planning's coming along. I know which instruments I'm using, how many sections there will be, what the main harmonic structure is. Now it's really just finding the time to put in all the detail, and time is a problem. The captain keeps organising writing sessions, rehearsals, busking. Keeping up with him is hard enough, let alone finding time for anything else.'

'Couldn't you just ask him to calm down a bit? Let him know you also have things to do?'

'I could, I suppose. But he's so keen. And it's like – it's like having a younger brother, and you feel obliged to help him, which is nice, because it makes you feel needed, but more than that…'

The baron lowered his voice as far as the idling engines would allow.

'There's something very familiar about the younger brother bit,' he whispered. 'Which makes me think, maybe I had one, in that previous existence.'

Holly was always intrigued to hear the baron talk about his theory that he had lived another life before he arrived here, one that he couldn't remember. But he also found it rather unsettling, and he never knew how to respond. Nod wisely, he decided.

'Anything else distracting you from composing?' he asked. 'Claire seems nice.'

The baron slowly shook his head.

'Claire's very nice,' he said. 'Very nice, very musical, really gifted. She's still settling down to what counts as normal around here. More normal than living on a cloud, anyway. That must be some adjustment to make, and she's coping well. So I wouldn't want to make that any more complicated than it already is. But yes, I had noticed. She's lovely. I mean, nice.'

He sighed.

'But – well – Kia's very nice, too, and I'm afraid I've put her on a bit of a pedestal.'

'I hadn't noticed,' Holly lied.

'No. Nor has she,' the baron laughed. 'It's always been from a distance – more of a distance since Robin's been on the scene.'

He turned his serious face on Holly.

'Did you notice he's done nothing for Valentine's Day? Not a mention. That can't be right. And if she genuinely hasn't noticed, then she deserves him.'

He shrugged.

'But she's still the one who makes me trip over my words. She's a tough act to follow.'

He shrugged again.

'I don't know.'

A medley of car horns started up.

'Somebody's dithering,' Holly commented.

The baron raised his eyebrows at him.

'No,' protested Holly. 'I didn't mean – that wasn't meant...'

The baron slapped him on the shoulder, and they both chuckled.

'I'm sure such dilemmas would never have darkened your orderly, mathematical existence,' the baron joked. 'Maybe I should ask Anna...'

'Oh, look!' announced Holly, pointing at the bus that was finally setting off. 'The traffic's moving. How convenient. Time to go.'

The rest of the tailback was hidden by parked cars. They needed to make their move now before the next bus came along.

'Ready?' Holly asked.

The baron nodded.

'We'll crouch down, less likely to be seen and also ready to run for cover, should we need to. But the most important thing – no noise.'

The baron nodded again, and they both squatted down like sprinters at the starting line. Holly grabbed the baron's arm and said the clue number before his imagination had time to get the better of him.

Looking around their new surroundings, Holly decided even his imagination would have come up with something more interesting.

They were on the pavement of a narrow street, thankfully deserted, next to a red-brick wall, just at the point where a curved section of it suddenly came out into the pavement and snaked out of view. On the opposite side of the road was a brightly painted hoarding with razor wire spiralling along the top, above which they could see the tops of a random assortment of small, industrial buildings. But there was no audible sign of industry, or of anything else. It was eerily quiet.

Feeling exposed out in the street, Holly gestured to the baron to follow him, and he made his way, still crouching, along the round brick wall. This turned out to be a semicircle, after which it resumed its straight path, until it reached a section of plywood boards. They could now see that their road was a side street of a much larger one, just fifty yards ahead.

At that moment, someone walking along the larger road could be seen crossing theirs. Holly spotted a gap between the brick wall and the plywood, and darted in, pulling the baron after him.

They found themselves in a cramped, overgrown space littered with old gas canisters and other similarly rusty objects that defied identification. From here, they could see that the curved brick wall in the street formed part of a circular building, just ten-feet high, with a large square perched on top, also in brick, covered in graffiti. The round building had a dark green, metal door which was half open.

Stepping carefully around the debris, they made their way to this door, and Holly peered inside. It was dark, and there was a heavy, dank smell, but it seemed to be deserted. It was certainly as quiet inside as it was outside.

The door was ajar, the opening wide enough to let the men through without having to open it any further, which was a relief, as it looked as though its creaking could alert the entire neighbourhood to their presence. After a few seconds, their eyes started to get used to the feeble light.

They were standing on a concrete platform. To their right was an open door, beyond which was an office, long abandoned. In the middle was a lift with a double concertina gate. To the left of that, a spiral staircase descended steeply around the lift shaft and out of sight.

The only way forward was the way down. Holly started towards the stairs when the baron put an arm out to stop him, pointing down at an old oilcan that was directly in his path. Smiling in gratitude at having been prevented from kicking the thing down the stairs, Holly stooped to pick it up and move it out of harm's way.

But he underestimated how greasy it was. To his horror, it slipped out of his hands, hit the edge of the top step, and careered away from them, bouncing off every fourth step on its downward journey.

CHAPTER THIRTY-FIVE

Holly and the baron stared open-mouthed, as the oilcan made its haphazard way down the stairs. But what shocked them was not the indescribable racket it made, but the fact that it made no sound at all.

After waiting a second for that fact to sink in, and then looking at each other in disbelief, the baron noticed a sign, high on the wall above the stairs, that read 'Camden Town deep shelter'. He pointed at it, and then waited for the look of comprehension to arrive on Holly's face.

Holly had only encountered this phenomenon once before, during an ill-fated taxi journey on his previous visit. He remembered being told that Eternal Silence was a solution that Uncle Sid had wilfully withheld as it only affected Camden Town, an area he considered greatly improved by this new arrangement. The unique atmosphere this created then became a tourist attraction in its own right, only adding to the region's existing popularity.

This also accounted for the eerie lack of noise they'd noticed outside. Holly tentatively snapped his fingers for confirmation.

'Well, that's one sense we can't rely on any more,' he said to the baron, who merely shook his head, never having been any good at lip-reading.

One mystery may have been solved, but they were still none the wiser about the building they were in, although the style of architecture, the colour of the bricks and now the direction of the stairs indicated that it was somehow connected with the Underground system. This idea was suddenly reinforced by a trembling that could be felt in the floor, consistent with a train entering a station not far away, pausing to disgorge its occupants and then setting off again. The pair waited motionless until their feet told them everything was back to normal, then slowly made their way down the stairs.

The faint lights along the wall had been distributed sparingly, causing the stairs to fade slowly in and out. The two men kept a wary eye ahead of them as every step revealed more of the spiral. Two turns down, they came across the oilcan. After that, it became impossible to keep track of how far they were going, but it seemed a long way, and they were glad to reach the bottom without further incident.

The light improved at the bottom of the stairs to reveal the start of a bright tunnel. A door to their left was open. Through it they could see a long room. Halfway along, a huge, black cylinder came out of the wall, ending in a circular, metal grille.

Gesturing to the baron to keep watch, Holly ventured inside. Closer inspection of the cylinder showed that it housed a large fan – part of the ventilation, Holly presumed. Beyond it, hidden from the door, there was a square hole in the floor with an open, hinged cover. The top of a ladder could be seen coming out of it.

Curious as to whether it led anywhere interesting, Holly peered down the hole, but was instantly driven back by the smell. He certainly couldn't imagine Uncle Jasper surviving down there for very long.

He rejoined the baron in the passage and moved on

to the next door. This one was closed and bore a large sign, saying 'PLANT ROOM. DANGER – KEEP OUT'. Bravado made Holly do the exact opposite, but prudence ensured he only opened it slightly, just enough to catch a glimpse inside.

A glimpse was indeed enough. Holly shut the door again hastily and put his back against it, eyes wide. The baron gave him a quizzical look. Holly frowned, struggling to find a way to communicate. He had never been any good at charades. He settled for raising his hands, wiggling his fingers and miming an 'ooh' sound, as though he were trying to frighten a child. The baron raised an eyebrow, and he reached for the door handle. Holly did nothing to stop him.

The room was dark, lit only by a purple glow. This was coming from something at the back that, the baron had to concede, did look like a ghost. It was the shape of a tall hot-air balloon, filled with an ultraviolet gas, with a small blue flame dancing around inside.

Holly was now looking over the baron's shoulder, and together they watched this gentle display for a moment, before closing the door again, shrugging, and moving on.

The next doors revealed where the toilets had once been. The fittings had long since been stripped out, but there were still obvious marks to show where the cisterns and urinals had been fixed to the walls.

After that, they came to a crossroads, their tunnel carrying straight on and a wider one extending right and left. There was no illumination on either side, but they could see another crossroads some way ahead with light coming from the left, so they ignored the first junction and made their way to the second.

Peering cautiously around the corner, they saw another tunnel – technically half a tunnel, the ceiling being a semicircle. It was also wider than theirs and curved off to the right. The left-hand wall was lined with two layers of bunks, four of which showed signs of recent occupation. This caused a nervous exchange of glances.

They were hesitating, reluctant to enter such a large space where they would be visible and vulnerable, when the baron spotted something on one of the bunks. He went over and picked it up. Then he showed it to Holly.

It was Uncle Jasper's red, woollen hat.

There was no longer any question. The baron pocketed the hat, and they immediately set off down the tunnel, skirting the wall on the right, eyes darting in all directions.

They reached a point where the lights became much dimmer ahead of them, but there were steps leading down to another level where the bright illumination seemed to continue. Emboldened by their recent find, they walked straight down.

They now found themselves in the other half of the same tunnel, the floor curving round on both sides to meet a flat ceiling. It was like walking along the keel of a boat. The bunks were replaced by shelves, full of dusty folders and files.

After covering the same distance again, they came to another junction. The only available option seemed to be a tunnel to the right, that so closely resembled the first they feared they may have gone round in a circle. Holly was reminded of his circuitous route around Somerset House.

But there was a difference in the lighting. Both ends of this tunnel were in complete darkness.

Sensing they must be nearing their goal, they tiptoed along the passage, despite being aware that they could have been stamping, for all the difference it would have made to the sound.

Once past the bright patch in the middle, the area served

by a solitary, naked light bulb hanging from the ceiling, their eyes started adjusting, and they could just make out the concertina gate of another lift, this one chained shut.

Holly pieced the layout of the four tunnels in his head. Factoring in the positions of the two lifts, he realised that the complex was symmetrical – the same crossword grid rotational symmetry he'd seen in the uncles' coffee table.

Despite this revelation, the overwhelming feeling was one of disappointment. They had come this far and seemed to have reached a dead end.

This feeling was not shared by the unfortunate occupant of the lift, who was frantically, and futilely, shaking the inner gate to attract their attention. His intended audience had stopped just short of being able to make out his white boiler suit.

Unaware of the anguish just yards ahead, Holly and the baron looked at each other in resignation. Eternal Silence played no part here, as neither of them could think of anything to say. They both knew that there was no further they could go, and that, if there was anything to be gained by this trip, they must have missed something along the way. The only option was to go back.

They had just started turning when something flew into Holly's ear. He screamed, instantly putting a hand over his mouth, before realising how redundant that was. The baron hadn't even noticed and was still moving away. Holly shouted after him, still to no avail.

He looked down and saw that the object was a paper aeroplane. He picked it up. By now, the baron had noticed he was on his own and had come back to investigate.

Looking in the direction from which the missile had come, Holly still couldn't make out anything but the lift gate. He unfolded the piece of paper and frowned at it. It was a shopping list of hardware that meant nothing to him

– flanges, washers and isolating valves. He showed it to the baron, who shook his head. It was only when they turned it over that the message became clear.

'ANSWER NUTTERS' read the first line, 'BREAK LUNATICS' the second, followed by, in much larger letters, 'SOLVE MANIACS!'

They ran over to the lift, Holly dutifully getting out his newspaper and pen. There, sure enough, was Uncle Jasper with an exasperated look on his face. He waved away their attempts to open the gate. The chain and the padlock looked conspicuously new in their current, dilapidated surroundings and weren't going to give. He was still pointing insistently at Holly's paper.

But before Holly could act on this directive, Uncle Jasper's eyes widened at something over Holly's shoulder. Turning to see the cause of this consternation, Holly could just make out two red lights in the distance.

His first thought was that a train was approaching. But this wasn't that sort of tunnel. It was only when he detected a movement in them that he realised they were flames.

A face slowly appeared around those flames, followed by the rest of the man they had first met as Marlowe, soon to be Nasi Goreng. The man whose phone they had found and used. The only Yucca not to have got the message.

He walked slowly, with the confidence of a spider who knows the fly isn't going anywhere. There was ample time for Holly to write in the words that would eradicate this spider for good, along with all his kind.

But Holly couldn't move. And he couldn't think of anything but Anna and how he was letting her down. He could only stare, feeling the life being drained out of him, as the all-consuming fire drew nearer.

CHAPTER THIRTY-SIX

'I'll kill him.'

'Then I'll kill the other one.'

Worry had turned to anger. As Holly was taking longer and longer not to return, Kia had become more and more convinced that something terrible had happened to him. She had to be restrained from going out after him. Anna tried to calm her down, but without much success. The French trio volunteered to form another search party, but that didn't seem sensible either, particularly after their lack of success last time. Uncles Sid and Gordo couldn't stop pacing, frustrated that time was running out for their missing comrade. The more the captain struggled to think of things to say that might improve morale, the less came to mind. All they could do was sit and wait, and none of them were very good at that.

It was only when an agitated Claire turned up alone that they figured out what was happening. The two men had both lied about their imminent return and, to the minds of those assembled, two wrongs very much didn't make a right. It was this conclusion that made Kia, and then Claire, announce their murderous intentions.

When there was a loud knock on the front door, they thought they'd been given an opportunity to carry out their threats. It was Kia and Claire who shot out of their seats and made their way into the passage with grim determination. If looks could kill, they had as good as fulfilled their mission already.

Kia was reaching for the door latch when they spotted that the door had acquired a new feature – the intrusion of a sharp piece of metal that had frayed the wood of the door on either side of it. It hadn't been a knock at the door so much as a blow from an axe. This new addition was now rocking slightly back and forth as its owner tried to retrieve it.

'Don't open it!' Claire whispered.

Kia had no intention of opening it, or of staying where they were for a second longer than necessary. Claire was rooted to the spot, in paralysed fascination, and had to be manoeuvred back into the living room. Kia swung into leader mode.

'Move the sofa in front of that door,' she commanded the uncles, who immediately complied, before Anna even had a chance to get up from it.

'You – Voltaire – Yucca – whatever,' she barked, gesturing that the Resistance leader join her at the window. What he saw there made him gasp.

His heavily aged former colleague, beret firmly still in place, had managed to free her hatchet and was successfully hacking pieces out of the front door. Judging by her progress, it wouldn't be long before the door to the living room received the same treatment.

Everyone had moved to the window. The biggest reaction came from Claire, who put her hands to her mouth.

Standing motionless behind the axe-woman was the equally wizened form of her fellow librarian, oblivious to their presence. In his bony, wrinkled hand he held a large shovel.

'Bill!' Claire couldn't help shouting.

Muffled as her voice was from behind her hands, he seemed to hear her. He turned to the window and slowly advanced on his apprehensive spectators. He stopped when he reached them, allowing Claire to see in full detail how the artificial passage of time had ravaged his appearance. She could feel nothing but pity for him.

She was about to try and communicate this pity to him, when, with a sudden movement of his arm, he forced the handle of the shovel through a pane in the window.

Shards of glass flew in all directions. Claire screamed. Everyone recoiled to various points within the room. The two uncles moved least, instinctively forming a barrier between their companions and the assailant. Uncle Gordo picked up an old briefcase of Holly's, that hadn't been used since his teacher days, and was trying to prevent the airborne debris from travelling too far. The ancient library assistant was eagerly building on his success with the first pane by smashing as many of the others as he could reach. The uncles were quite happy just to contain the destruction, confident that none of the panes were big enough to allow a human being to pass through them.

But the front door's valiant resistance had merely delayed their other attacker, and the less substantial inner door to the room in which they were taking refuge – a room with no other means of escape – proved even less effective. It wasn't long before a cadaverous figure waving an axe was in their midst.

Kia threw everything she could lay her hands on at this intruder, but as they were mostly cushions, they had little effect, other than to elicit some shrill, exasperated screams. The captain had some success at containment, brandishing a wooden chair until, one by one, the chair's legs fell victim to the blade of the hatchet and he was forced to retreat.

There followed such a loud noise that even the axe briefly fell still. The uncles' confidence had been ill-founded. Bill had remembered that the shovel had two ends and had turned the blade on the exposed struts between the, now absent, panes. These had offered little resistance, and a whole chunk of the window frame came crashing in, pinning Uncles Sid and Gordo to the floor. Their attacker made sure it continued to restrain them by standing on it while he surveyed the rest of the room.

His eyes fell on the French trio. They were standing by the wall opposite the door, the two men shielding their companion. He held the handle of his shovel and swung it fully behind him, ready to inflict as heavy a blow as he was able, and advanced on them.

The hatchet was also back in motion. Its owner had scanned the remaining occupants of the room and had selected Anna as her primary target. She raised her weapon and bent her knees in preparation of the short leap through the air needed to come within range. One blow was all it would take. A terrified Anna was already backed against the far wall and had nowhere to go.

Suddenly, they all felt a tremor in the ground. It was slight, but enough to cause both assailants to fall forwards. There followed a desperate scramble to disarm them while they were incapacitated, the Frenchmen grabbing the shovel, Kia and the captain racing each other to reach the axe, Kia winning.

The age of the couple still caused a reluctance to physically hold them down, despite their apparent frailty being so forcibly contradicted by their actions. No-one could decide how to approach the situation, but in the event, no decision needed to be taken.

'Bill?'

Claire was the first to notice that her former colleague's

hair had darkened to resume its normal colour. And when the figure in the beret slowly lifted her head, the hair was still white, but the face was that of a twenty-year-old.

Yuccas went out of the window.

'Sand!' Colette cried, rushing over to help her friend up. Her look of delight was not reciprocated, sadly, as Sand was now in hysterics, utterly traumatised by her vivid memories of the recent past.

'Well, that was most curious,' was Bill's considered reaction, although it wasn't clear whether he was referring to his experiences as a centenarian assassin or the huge hug he had just received from Claire.

The uncles had been the first to register the seismic change, finding themselves unexpectedly free to stand up. Their burden of the splintered window frame was back in its customary place in a piece of seamless restoration. And Kia's search for confirmation of what had happened didn't have to go any further than the door into the corridor, which no longer showed any sign of having fallen foul of an axe.

The only person besides Sand not to be visibly jubilant was Anna, who had slithered down the wall, shaking violently. Kia crouched down next to her, relieved to see that, through the tears, she was actually smiling. She acknowledged Kia's presence with an involuntary splutter, which made Kia giggle.

'That was one of your snotty laughs, wasn't it?'

Anna nodded happily and repeated it.

'Can I pick them or what?' she said, wiping the tears from her face. 'He's done it again, hasn't he?'

1 F	I	2 N	A	3 L	■	4 C	R	5 O	S	6 S	W	7 O	R	8 D
A	■	U	■	U	■	O	■		■	C	■	R	■	R
9 N	O	T	I	C	E	D	■	10 E	X	O	T	I	C	A
T	■	C	■	I	■	E	■		■	U	■	G	■	W
11 A		A		D		N	■	12		R		A		S
S	■	S	■	L	■	A	■	■	■	G	■	M	■	■
13 T	E	E	N	Y	■	14 M	Y	15 S	T	E	R	I	E	16 S
I	■	■	■	■	■	E	■		■	■	■	■	■	U
17 C	A	18 M	E	19 R	A	S	H	Y	■	20 S	C	21 R	A	P
■	■	O	■	O	■	■	■		■	U	■	I	■	E
22 D	U	R	A	B	L	23 Y	■	24 B	O	N	J	O	U	R
R	■	T	■	O	■	U	■		■	B	■	T	■	H
25 E	L	A	S	T	I	C	■	26 A	V	E	R	A	G	E
A	■	L	■	I	■	C	■		■	A	■	C	■	R
27 M	U	S	I	C	I	A	N	S	■	28 M	O	T	T	O

CHAPTER THIRTY-SEVEN

Actually, he had to admit, he hadn't.

Holly had often frozen in moments of fear, although not so much lately. He remembered occasions on his first visit here when something had appeared behind him and he had conspicuously avoided turning round to investigate, let alone confront it. But it had always been temporary. This was the first time he had been completely paralysed and, had someone not come to his aid, he would never have moved again.

The baron, then? Surely his trusted companion had stepped in at his hour of need and done what he himself had failed to do? Sadly not. The baron had been as incapacitated by the burning eyes as Holly had been.

It was Uncle Jasper, the man they were there to rescue, who had saved them all. Infuriated by how easily the others had been immobilised, he had snatched the paper and pen out of Holly's hands and written the words Nutcase Mortals in himself, thereby answering a question that had intrigued them for a long time – was it just the Solver's copy of the paper that had to be used for the solutions to be effective, or did the Solver himself have to be the one to enter the words? Fortunately for them all, it seemed that in this instance, the Solver was redundant.

None of that mattered to Anna, of course, who had thrown her arms around her husband on his return and was showing no signs of ever letting go, despite Kia's best efforts to get Holly's account of their escapade. After a half-hearted rebuke, her anger at the two men's deception had totally dissipated.

The captain thought their success merited at least a case of Bentley's. The uncles were almost dancing, so jubilant were they on being reunited. The Soya Beans had almost calmed Sand down enough to stop her crying. Claire was unsuccessfully feigning interest in Bill's plan to write a thesis on *The Biological Limitations of Geriatric Killers.*

Much was made of how Uncle Jasper had remembered the line Origami Riot Act in the grid, and how it had spurred him on to write a very unambiguous note on a piece of paper that he then folded into an aeroplane, allowing it to travel considerably further than if he'd just screwed it up into a ball.

Apart from the reception Holly received, his happiest moment came when the news on television, still wittering to itself in the corner, went to an update on the army's deployment in Westminster Square, and it showed a cursory shot of a gloriously intact Big Ben, as though nothing had happened. Which of course, he thought ruefully, as far as they were concerned, it had. And he got a further warm glow from the feeling that there was still an enigmatic redhead out there somewhere.

A further pleasant surprise came when the returning group of Holly, the baron and Uncle Jasper turned out to be a quartet. Uncle Jasper had shared his lift with a short gentleman wearing a brown warehouse coat and a flat cap, and he had made sure his new friend was included in the return party which, in the absence of a key to the padlock, had been achieved by holding hands through the gate and forming a human chain.

The man wasn't remotely fazed by the way he had been transported to Holly's house. He had introduced himself as Wally and was currently enlightening anyone who would listen about the history of their recent prison.

'The Deep Shelters were built at the end of the Blitz,' he was saying, pausing only to accept one of Uncle Jasper's rich tea biscuits. 'They hadn't wanted to use the Underground platforms for shelter during the air raids, but people used them anyway. So they built eight of these shelters, doubling the capacity of some of the Northern Line stations. Space for eight thousand in each, run by the ARP – the air-raid precautions.'

He helped himself to another biscuit.

'Trouble is, by the time they were finished, the Blitz was over, so they were mainly used for storage until the V1 and V2 rockets started coming over towards the end of the war. Then they finally got used properly.'

He turned wistful and even stopped eating.

'Wonderful bit of engineering. A long tunnel on either side of the main train tunnels, access tunnels crossing both. They had canteens, toilets, endless sleeping arrangements. And two entrances at diagonally opposite ends, each with their own lift, stairs, and ventilation system.'

He jabbed Uncle Jasper in the ribs with his elbow.

'Creepy though, wasn't it?'

They both laughed.

'Creepy is right,' the baron agreed. 'It even had its own purple ghost, didn't it, Holly?'

'Well, it looked like a ghost,' Holly muttered.

'The mercury arc rectifier?' Wally enthused. 'That's a thing of beauty. Converts alternating current to the direct current that runs everything down there. To think it still works!'

'But why were you down there, Wally?' Kia wanted to know. 'What did the Maniacs want with you?'

'Damned if I know,' the man said, cheerfully. 'I was going about my business, when someone suddenly sticks a bag over my head. Next thing I know, I'm dumped in a lift. But between the look of the place and the Eternal Silence, which is a jolly handy clue, I've got a pretty good idea where I am. And then this fellow here is pushed in with me, and he's good company, so I can't say that time dragged unduly.'

'And what is your line of business?' asked the captain. 'Assuming you're not a lift engineer.'

'Bless you, no,' Wally replied. 'I work in Big Ben. I'm the Keeper of the Great Clock.'

The room went so quiet, apart from one of the captain's low whistles, that the poor man had to be reassured he hadn't insulted them in some way.

Between them, Kia, Holly, and the baron filled the maintenance man in on the reasons the Maniacs had worked so hard to prevent the bell from sounding and the role it had to play in the re-establishment of a comet-free world. All three of them instinctively left out any mention of the bell tower having been destroyed and rebuilt, not wanting to upset him.

This was probably just as well, for the man was now looking very emotional anyway.

'I've been doing this job for as long as I can remember,' he confided in them. 'And I've loved every minute.' He took a deep breath. 'But not once have I questioned why I have to keep a bell in fully functional order if it never rings. Five bells, actually – the Great Bell and the four quarter bells.'

He sat back on the sofa, shaking his head in wonder.

'To think, I'll actually get to hear them. Something nobody's ever heard before.'

Holly patted him on the shoulder, deciding not to tell

him that he had heard them and that they were well worth the wait.

'So, how do we get them to sound?' Kia asked. 'Do we have to run round with Uncle Jasper's rubber mallet?'

'Bless you, you wouldn't even tickle it with that,' Wally chuckled. 'The Great Bell is fourteen tons, give or take a few pounds. No, for starters, you can't get near the place. Have you seen the army presence? It's like an ants' nest.'

'Never mind that,' Kia said, without much conviction.

'All right, if you say so,' said Wally, with even less.

'And then what?' she persisted. 'Pull some ropes?'

The man laughed so loud his flat cap slid off.

'Spot of campanology?' he cried. 'This is no Sunday afternoon bit of bell-ringing we're talking about. Fourteen tons, remember? The hammer alone weighs two hundred kilos. But it's all ready to go. It just needs a few connections making. The trains are all going like clockwork.'

'Sorry,' said the captain. 'What has the transport system got to do with it? And I always miss my connections…'

Uncle Jasper shook his head.

'Coaches,' he insisted.

'That's right,' agreed Wally. 'Trains. The clock mechanism uses three trains – the Going Train, which controls the timing, the Strike Train, which covers the striking of the Great Bell, and the Chime Train, which sounds the quarter bells. Going, Strike, and Chime.'

'Leaving, Hit, and Ring,' Uncle Jasper echoed, as if trying to memorise the words.

'That's it. All that machinery, and yet a tick every two seconds is the only sound to tell you that it's working. Now, the Strike and Chime Trains in the Clock Room are connected directly to the hammers of the bells in the Belfry via the Link Room. That's where you need to be to make the necessary connections.'

'Just a bunch of cranks, then,' summarised the baron. 'That sounds appropriate.'

'Quite so,' said Wally. 'Anyway, it's a simple job.'

Everyone looked to Uncle Jasper, who nodded reassuringly.

'The Going Train is a work of art,' its keeper couldn't help enthusing. 'Very innovative. It uses a double, three-legged gravity escapement, which was especially invented for it, to keep it regular.'

'I don't know about the double, three-legged bit,' the captain chimed in, 'but my gravity escapement works every morning, also regular as clockwork.'

This put an end to the science lesson. In any case, Holly decided they had enough information to formulate a plan, whatever that was going to be.

As the assembled crowd split up into smaller groups, Kia sat next to Wally.

'You and Uncle Jasper managed to communicate all right?' she asked, intrigued.

'Oh, yes,' the man confirmed. 'You have to remember – when we were in that lift, we were in Eternal Silence, so it was all sign language. That's a very level playing field.'

He nodded in appreciation at his former fellow captive.

'He's got quite a head on him, that one,' he said.

That head was about to be tested, as Holly took Uncle Jasper to one side.

'Do you remember,' he asked, 'that Elastic Average line in the grid?'

The man nodded.

'Well, when I was with the Wise Lady, she singled it out as being particularly important. Any idea why?'

Uncle Jasper frowned and shook his head. The thought process continued, the frown remained.

The French contingent had gathered in a corner in

subdued conference. After a few reassuring nods to Sand, who was valiantly but vainly fighting off another panic attack, its leader approached Holly.

'Monsieur Holly,' Voltaire whispered. 'I am very sorry, but we have decided that, with the Maniacs gone, we have no further role to play here. We are spies, nothing more. Our function, our raison d'être, has disappeared. And it has been rather traumatic. Not just for Sand, but for all of us. So, if it's all the same to you, if you can spare a moment, we were wondering if you could take us home.'

CHAPTER THIRTY-EIGHT

'Say what you like, Hugo, old chap,' the captain was saying, 'but you are going to miss the food. Good old English fare.'

'Like what?' the Frenchman challenged him.

'Like croissants, and camembert,' the captain replied, earnestly.

Hugo snorted.

'I'm just looking forward to sorting out what my name is,' he muttered.

'If it's any consolation,' the captain said, patting him on the arm, 'I'll always think of you as a tarte – au citron.'

'Are you sure that saying the Omega Soya Beans clue number will take you back to France?' Holly asked Voltaire.

'Well, that's our name,' replied Voltaire. 'As to where we end up – we're from different places, but all within the Limousin region, so if you could drop us off anywhere there…'

'I don't know if it works as a taxi service,' Holly smiled. 'I'm a stranger here myself. But we'll give it a go.'

The French quartet did the rounds, saying their goodbyes, Sand managing little more than timid nods. Hugo left Camille's address with the captain and the baron, asking them to visit her and explain why he couldn't go himself. They left Claire for the big finale, but she put up her hand to stop them.

'I'd like to come along, if that's all right with Holly,' she said, staring down at the carpet. 'Get a quick look at France, say goodbye properly there. Then Holly can bring me back.'

They seemed quite relieved at the suggestion, and Holly had no objection. Not wanting to prolong the parting any more than necessary, the six of them linked up, and Holly said the number.

They found themselves in the shadow of a small, twelfth-century church, if Holly understood the well-lit placard on its wall correctly. Opposite them was a tourist office. Fifty yards ahead, bathed in street lighting, was a mini-roundabout, in the middle of which was a raised flower bed, bursting with colour, despite the time of year.

Voltaire looked around and broke into a huge smile.

'Ambazac!' he cried.

'Your village?' Holly asked.

'No, not originally,' Voltaire replied. 'But my sister Louise lives just around the corner, and she's looking after all my stuff. She'll look after us, too.'

The four émigrés stood for a moment, breathing the air. Claire couldn't stand still, she was so happy to be there.

'Holly,' Voltaire said, holding out his hand. 'Merci, mon ami. We are very grateful, for being brought back home and for being allowed to play our small part in your story.'

Holly shook his hand.

'No, thank you,' he said. 'We wouldn't have got this far without you.'

Voltaire hesitated.

'There is… one more favour I would ask of you.'

'Name it.'

'We don't want to be Soya Beans any more.'

'Don't tell the captain,' said Hugo, 'but I don't even like soya beans.'

Holly still wasn't sure what they were asking of him.

'You never wrote those words in,' explained Colette. 'Because then we wouldn't have been trained Resistance fighters any more.'

Holly looked apprehensive.

'You want to be solved? Are you sure?'

'We were here before today's grid, weren't we, Claire?' Colette asked, getting a vigorous nod in response. 'So we'll still be here afterwards, only – less burdened, hopefully.'

Holly looked to Claire for reassurance and got it.

'Not so much solved,' she said, 'as absolved.'

With a sigh, Holly took out his paper and pen. After another quick check to make sure they were all in agreement, he completed the two words.

Looking up, he was relieved to see that nothing had changed.

'Feel all right, Voltaire?' he asked.

'Fine,' the man replied. 'And I have a real urge to get out of these ridiculous clothes.'

They all laughed.

'But it's not Voltaire,' he went on. 'It's Hugo.'

He held his arms out to his companions.

'Andrea! Gilbert!'

He turned to the fourth member, his voice cracking.

'Odile!'

The four of them formed a tight huddle. Holly winked at Claire.

'All for one, eh?' he whispered. 'Shall we go?'

She stared ahead for a moment, her eyes wide.

'No,' she said at last.

The others let go of each other to look at her in surprise.

'I'm sorry, Holly,' she blurted out, tripping over her words. 'I always knew this would be a one-way trip. Ever since I came down from that cloud, I've wanted to go to

France, and here I am. And I'd like to stay, if they'll have me.'

There were enthusiastic agreements all round. Andrea held her arms out and gave her a hug. Then Claire turned to Holly, making eye contact with him for the first time since she'd asked to come along.

'Say goodbye to the baron for me,' she said with some embarrassment. 'Tell him it's his fault I'm here. He persuaded me to leave that cloud. He told me about the live music, and the rain. And the French. Tell him it's his fault I'm so happy. And I'm sure it will be easier for him to follow his heart, with me out of the way.'

She took Holly's hand.

'I'm sorry,' she said again.

Holly shrugged and smiled at her.

'Don't be,' he said. 'It's a very simple equation. If there's more for you here…'

They held each other for a moment. Then he let her go and stepped back.

'I'm going to miss you. They're all going to miss you. You're quite an asset. A musical asset.'

'Oh, that reminds me. Could you ask Bill to take that cello back to the library for me?'

He nodded, as Andrea came up to him.

'We are very aware, Monsieur Holly, that while our day has ended, yours hasn't,' she said. 'And that if you're not successful, this may be our last day. But if it is to be our last day, we want you to know that it's been a good one to end on.'

She pointed at the sky, which only showed an uneven layer of cloud.

'Good luck with the comet,' she whispered, and kissed him on both cheeks.

1 F	I	2 N	A	3 L	■	4 C	R	5 O	S	6 S	W	7 O	R	8 D
A	■	U	■	U	■	O	■	M	■	C	■	R	■	R
9 N	O	T	I	C	E	D	■	10 E	X	O	T	I	C	A
T	■	C	■	I	■	E	■	G	■	U	■	G	■	W
11 A		A		D		N	■	12 A		R		A		S
S	■	S	■	L	■	A	■	■	■	G	■	M	■	■
13 T	E	E	N	Y	■	14 M	Y	15 S	T	E	R	I	E	16 S
I	■	■	■	■	■	E	■	O	■	■	■	■	■	U
17 C	A	18 M	E	19 R	A	S	H	Y	■	20 S	C	21 R	A	P
■	■	O	■	O	■	■	■	A	■	U	■	I	■	E
22 D	U	R	A	B	L	23 Y	■	24 B	O	N	J	O	U	R
R	■	T	■	O	■	U	■	E	■	B	■	T	■	H
25 E	L	A	S	T	I	C	■	26 A	V	E	R	A	G	E
A	■	L	■	I	■	C	■	N	■	A	■	C	■	R
27 M	U	S	I	C	I	A	N	S	■	28 M	O	T	T	O

CHAPTER THIRTY-NINE

'At least we know the name of our enemy,' the baron had told Holly on his return.

Comet Ladd/Smythe, as the media had dubbed it after the two astronomers who had won the battle for first sighting, was no more visible in England than it was in France. Fortunately, the news channel had a camera somewhere more accommodating, and it showed a constant, live picture of it in a corner of the screen. On its own and out of context, it could have been any size, depending on the paranoia of the viewer.

In truth, Holly was amazed at how little paranoia and hysteria was on view. The newsreaders were cheerfully talking about this imminent extinction event as though they were watching it on another planet.

As far as the population was concerned, the answer to the age-old question of what you would do if you knew you only had hours left to live seemed to be to carry on as normal. Most of the population were either going about their daily business, or just staying at home, judging by how empty the streets were. Holly wondered whether the people in this place simply had a different mindset, having endured so many potentially catastrophic threats before. There must have been others besides that cloud and this comet, he presumed.

Maybe it was a question of faith, everyone putting theirs in an unseen power that could always be relied upon to come to their rescue. Perhaps Camille hadn't been so deluded after all. Holly had no trouble elevating Kia and her team to godlike status, but immediately rejected the idea when he realised he would now have to include himself, and that didn't feel healthy.

News of Claire's non-return had largely received a positive, if surprised, reaction, especially after Holly had given them the equation he had formulated at the time. Once a maths teacher, always a maths teacher, Anna had teased. Wishing them every success, Bill had set off to pick up the cello and make a start on his thesis while his experiences were still fresh in his mind. Wally was happily nursing the tea he'd needed to wash down the last of Uncle Jasper's biscuits, adding a running commentary to the TV's constant swirling around Big Ben.

'That's the Ayrton Light,' he was saying, pointing at the clock tower's highest level of open columns, between the two layers of grey slates. 'That's only lit when parliament is in session. There are separate stairs going up to that.'

Holly was getting impatient. He felt they'd wasted enough time and was anxious to get going. There was no knowing what they'd find when they got there, so there was no point planning anything. They would just have to wing it. All they knew was that their first task was going to be getting across the bridge, and the fortification that had appeared since they last looked was, they all agreed, getting ridiculous. But it was while they were all staring morosely at this insurmountable obstacle that things got even weirder.

The news coverage switched from the regular army around Parliament Square to its more sinister counterpart, the Pitch-Black Army, which, the anchorman could now confirm, was converging on the same location to provide reinforcements. Its destination was obvious from the fact it was approaching it from three directions. Two prongs were making a direct approach, using Birdcage Walk from the west and Whitehall from the north. A third contingent had crossed the river over Waterloo Bridge, turning right on to York Road, aiming for the other side of Westminster Bridge.

The speed of the progress being made meant that contact between the two armed forces would be made within seconds. Close-ups of the soldiers on the ground showed a considerable amount of apprehension. Several could be seen crossing themselves.

The mesmerising aerial shots of streets turning black struck Holly as looking artificial, as though he was watching a video game.

The relentless darkness reached the military outposts and kept on going until the three battalions met and merged into one. By the time all movement stopped, the black area coincided exactly with the area the regular army had previously marked out.

The first sound to break the team's stunned silence came from Kia, and it was a heartfelt wail.

'That's it,' she elaborated. 'Any chance we had of reaching that tower is gone. I couldn't actually see how we were going to get past one army, to be honest, but two?'

She put her arms up round her head.

'It's impossible,' she intoned. 'Utterly impossible. He's done us. He's finally done us. There's no… What's happening?'

There was a change in the picture they were seeing from the helicopter, but at first it wasn't clear what that change was. Slowly, they realised that the amoeba-like, black shape of Westminster Square, and the streets radiating away from it, was becoming less and less black.

Anyone seated was up on their feet now, as they all crowded around the television set for a better view.

The black was now a mid grey and kept on fading. Landmarks that it had covered were becoming visible, features in the streets distinguishable. As they watched open-mouthed, it faded altogether, leaving no trace. The Pitch-Black Army had done what it set out to do and dissipated.

But if they thought their credulity had already been stretched to breaking point, the ensuing close-up coverage of the area took it beyond its elastic limit.

All the soldiers that had been seen nervously awaiting the arrival of their so-called reinforcements were lying where they'd been standing. They were bound, gagged, and unconscious, their equipment strewn around them on the ground.

The occupants of the room stared at one another in disbelief.

'So,' the baron ventured, 'the military wasn't just there for us.'

Kia slowly shook her head.

'The Compiler didn't send in the Pitch-Black Army,' she breathed. 'It was working against him.'

There was a pause, as they digested this new development.

'We don't know that,' the captain concluded. 'He's pretty conflicted. I wouldn't be surprised if he organised both armies, just to keep things interesting, or to avoid having to commit one way or the other.'

Nobody seemed taken with this suggestion.

'It's what I would have done,' he protested.

The matter was brushed aside by a call to arms.

'Tie mist,' announced Uncle Sid.

Uncle Gordo nodded in agreement.

‘R-I-T-E T-H-Y-M-E,’ he said.

‘They’re right,’ said Holly. ‘We have to act now and act fast. There’s never going to be a better chance than this.’

The general agreement was silenced by a gesture from Uncle Jasper. He went right up to the television screen and peered at it. It was a shot at ground level of the bridge and the river.

After a moment, he slowly straightened, an enlightened look on his face.

‘Clever dame,’ he whispered.

CHAPTER FORTY

'Oh, no,' the baron insisted. 'There's no bespoke squad for this mission. It's too important. And we have no idea what we're going to find. So we all go.'

Holly hadn't had time to respond to Kia's question as to who would be going on this excursion, which they all knew would be the last, however successful it turned out. Anna had already suggested to Kia that she get in touch with Robin, in case she didn't get another chance, but Kia was annoyed that she hadn't heard from him all day, so she had dismissed the idea.

'I mean, I don't know whether I would have been on that team, or not,' the baron continued, already embarrassed by his assertive outburst. 'But I'd like to be. I think I should be. I think we all should be.'

Holly smiled.

'Well, I was about to say the same thing,' he said. 'Sink or swim, we all need to be there.'

He looked hopefully at Anna. She shook her head.

'I wouldn't be of any use,' she said. 'You'll have to give all your attention to this. I'd be a distraction too many. You really don't need me to be with you.'

He went and stood in front of her.

'It wouldn't make much difference,' he said, gently.

'You're always with me anyway.'

She stroked his face, and there was a lingering kiss. Holly was indifferent to the awkward silence in the room.

'Hold that thought,' he said, letting her go. 'Are we all ready?' he asked the others.

Everyone nodded, except Uncle Jasper, who rushed over to his canvas bag, still sitting patiently in the corner. He rummaged around, pulling out a few utensils, scrutinising them briefly before returning them. The one that received the most attention was a nondescript piece of wood, until he found what he was looking for. Triumphantly, he held up an empty, two-litre, plastic lemonade bottle.

'Good idea,' said the captain. 'In case we all get caught short.'

Ignoring him, Uncle Jasper threw a coil of rope over his shoulder and joined the other seven people in the huddle that was forming in the middle of the room. Wally hadn't needed to be asked. He had grasped the procedure immediately.

They were all linked and just awaiting Holly's say-so, but he couldn't take his eyes off the only person still on her own.

'Good luck, Holly Oak,' she said, her voice breaking slightly.

'Don't go anywhere,' he instructed her. 'I will see you again soon.'

Without breaking eye contact, he whispered the clue number, and Anna's face turned into the back end of a lion.

They had arrived at the same spot he had visited earlier – the steps leading up to the wrong end of Westminster Bridge. The scene was almost deserted, and they hadn't been observed.

As though on cue, the clouds were slowly parting to reveal the reason they were there. To their left was the moon, full and majestic. Directly above them was a seething, grotesque parody of the moon, smaller but infinitely more menacing. It was grey with a tinge of pink on the side, still lit by the sun, a straight, dark tail tapering on the other side, pointing accusingly at the moon. It had blurred edges and looked, for all the world, like it was breathing.

Telling them to look away, Holly led them up to the bridge itself. They were at first exhilarated to see their destination looming just ahead of them. The clock face read ten o'clock, Holly still finding it unsettling that it did so silently. But when they saw what lay in between, their hearts sank.

The soldiers were still lying around, incapacitated. A couple of them were even snoring loudly. But all their fortifications were still in place – barricades, walls of sandbags, miles of barbed wire. Even if they could negotiate every obstacle in turn, they'd run out of time.

'Terminal beep,' Uncle Sid uttered.

They all knew that, rather than censor himself, he had simply called the scene on the bridge 'impenetrable', because that was the word that had occurred to each of them.

But Uncle Jasper had taken this into account. He crossed the road, beckoning the others to follow. Four shallow flights of stairs later, they were on the embankment, gazing across the Thames at the Houses of Parliament. Doubling back around the end of a low wall supporting a lantern took them to a dark, narrow path between the steps and the river. Just before the brick wall that formed the base of the bridge, there was an opening on the right to a tunnel that ran under the steps. But another U-turn to the left brought them to an unlocked gate at the top of another, hidden set of steps that led down to the water itself.

Uncle Jasper pushed the gate open and descended; the others remaining dubiously behind. They watched in bewilderment as, having unscrewed the top, he immersed the lemonade bottle in the river until it was a quarter full. He then held it up, peered at it for a while before nodding his approval.

Carrying his prize, he rushed back up the steps and past his audience, turning and facing them, as they formed a semicircle around him. He held the bottle out.

'Clearer than I would have expected,' commented the captain, 'but no, thanks, all the same.'

With an exasperated shake of the head, Uncle Jasper turned to Holly.

'Clever dame,' he emphasised.

The baron got there before Holly.

'Wise Lady?'

Uncle Jasper pointed at him, as though he'd got the right answer in charades.

'Elastic Average,' he persisted with Holly.

Holly remembered that the Wise Lady had been adamant that this line in the grid was particularly important, but he still had no idea why.

'Flexible Fashion,' the man in the boiler suit tried again.

Holly had to mull this over before the penny dropped. Then he stared at the bottle in amazement.

'You mean Elastic Average is just a synonym for Fluid M…?'

Uncle Jasper held up a hand to interrupt him.

'Inflexible Fashion,' he instructed him.

Holly nodded to show he'd understood.

Uncle Jasper held up three fingers, followed by two, then one, by which time he had started pouring a stream of the water out of the bottle.

Kia was already getting out of the way so as not to get her shoes wet. But she needn't have bothered.

Just before the water hit the pavement, Uncle Jasper

gave the signal that had been counted in, and Holly shouted, 'Solid mode!'

The bottle was now empty. The continuous line of water – over a yard long, slightly curved and sinewy, with the occasional lateral spike, like a rose stem – clattered to the ground with a metallic sound, bouncing several times before coming to rest.

Dumbfounded as they all were, Holly was the first to grasp the implications.

'But if that's Restless Matter,' he whispered, 'then that means…'

He spun round, not imagining for a second that his deduction would be proved right.

But it was.

The Thames had frozen solid.

CHAPTER FORTY-ONE

Wally was chuckling.

'Told you he had a head on him.'

'And to think he nearly brought a short plank instead of that bottle,' the captain added. 'How ironic would that have been?'

Having provided the means for crossing the river, Uncle Jasper ushered everyone down the steps. One person declined.

'No, thank you, my friend,' said Wally. 'I've told you all you need to know about the building and its bells. For anything else, I'd just slow you down. Three hundred and thirty-four steps to the top – not for me, thank you. And this will be the best seat in the house when you get those bells ringing. So, the best of British, and just you make sure you do get them ringing.'

'Chiming – tolling,' Uncle Jasper agreed, making each word sounder grander. 'Resounding – booming!'

They shook hands, and Uncle Jasper went and joined the others at the water's edge.

The steps led straight down into the river. Solid as the water looked, so far only the captain had dared to try his weight on it. He had progressed to jumping up and down on it, as Uncle Jasper reached them.

'Bit slippery,' was the captain's verdict, having to put a hand on it to steady himself. 'And cold, it would seem. But perfectly sound.'

'It's not going to crack when we get halfway across, is it?' asked Kia.

'Well, assuming it's all Restless Matter,' reasoned Holly, 'then, unlike a layer of ice, it should be solid all the way through. That's the theory. But how far that extends in reality, there's really no knowing.'

He looked to Uncle Jasper for confirmation and got it.

'Nevertheless,' Holly continued, 'I do think we should get across and restore things to normal as soon as possible. I can't imagine what the consequences of a solid stretch of river might be.'

The weather being calm, the surface was largely smooth, with a gentle ripple, like a coastal rock formation. Most of the team gingerly struck out on their own.

'No foot shall slide, remember?' the captain announced.

Very much with that in mind, Kia held firmly on to Holly's arm.

'You think it would have been like this if we'd gone to that ice rink at Somerset House?' he asked.

'No,' she replied, through gritted teeth. 'That would have been fun.'

The group skirted the wall until they reached the bridge, then turned and made their way furtively from one support to the next, keeping in the bridge's shadow as much as possible. Anyone wandering along the embankment might not have noticed the lack of movement in the water, but seeing seven people walking on its surface would have attracted considerably more attention.

Despite having urged everyone on, Holly couldn't help bringing himself and Kia to a halt by the third of the bridge's six long, brick supports.

'Look at this view,' he said, waving his free arm. 'The Palace of Westminster, all lit up, Lambeth Bridge over there, the Isle of Dogs and Canary Wharf twinkling away in the distance. And from this unique perspective. When are you going to see this again?'

'I'm sorry,' Kia moaned, burying her face in Holly's sleeve. 'All I can see is that horrible thing up there, and the idea that this may well be the last view we ever get.'

'All the more reason,' he said, bringing her face gently back out into the open, 'to make the most of it. So that, in the future, we can say "We'll always have that night on the Thames".'

'In the future? That's optimistic.'

Holly laughed.

'And quite an achievement, for someone who's spent nearly two decades living in the past. But I'm all about the present, now. And yes, I occasionally allow myself a quick glimpse into the future.'

'And what would a glimpse into the future tell you now?'

'Oh, I don't pretend to be a soothsayer. Not a single prediction I ever made has come true. My predictions for myself would have been as a husband and a parent, but neither of those worked out. All I see now is what I want to see, so it's endless trips to the ice rink, all the way.'

'Sounds good.' Kia smiled. 'Let's go and see if we can give that future a chance.'

'As in…'

'As in Big Ben. Ring any bells?'

He made to set off, but she held him back.

'You're not bad at this pep talk lark, are you?' she said, finally letting go of him and striking out on her own.

She reached the others some way ahead of him. It turned out he had been relying on her to hold him up at least as much as the other way round.

They'd found the corresponding set of steps, which led up to a similar gate, but this one was firmly locked, and the railings here were considerably higher than on the other side.

Just as most of them started scratching their heads, wondering whether they'd made a fruitless journey, Uncle Jasper removed the coil of rope from his shoulder and set about tying one end to the spiky branch of Restless Matter. The others crowded round him to see what he was doing.

'Bowline,' the baron commented on the knot being used. Uncle Jasper had taught him quite a few of the more useful ones.

'Not a clove hitch?' the captain asked, that being the only knot he'd heard of.

'That tends to slip,' the baron advised him, getting a smile from his tutor.

Once satisfied with his work, Uncle Jasper threw his spear over the railing, pulling back on the rope until he got a reliable purchase.

'Holy improvisation, a Bat Rope!' the captain said with approval.

With a leg-up from the baron, Uncle Jasper scrambled to the top of the railing, making his way carefully around the short spikes, before using the baron's hands through the railings as another stepping stone. He then reciprocated for the baron. Uncles Sid and Gordo followed, then the captain. By the time Kia went over, the hands providing stepping stones had multiplied to form an entire human ladder. Holly brought up the rear, bringing the shard of Restless Matter down with him. Uncle Jasper then untied it and returned the rope to his shoulder.

'I suppose we should get this river moving again,' Holly said, still in awe of the surreal sight in front of him. 'That really shouldn't wait.'

'Wait!' Uncle Jasper echoed. 'Delay. Hold your horses.'

He waved the remnant of the river he was holding and pointed over at the base of the bell tower some distance away, before setting off in that direction at some speed. Holly understood that giving the command to restore the Thames to its liquid form would have the same effect on Uncle Jasper's prize possession if it wasn't moved out of range.

He watched the boiler suit recede into the darkness of the wide passage between the Palace of Westminster and the bridge. Being so much lower than the bridge put it in the shadow of all the street lights, and out of the glare of the lights pointing up at the building, making it the darkest spot in the landscape.

After a brief hesitation, Uncles Sid and Gordo decided to follow their colleague, and they too slowly disappeared.

Holly noticed the captain looking around with an air of bewilderment.

'What's the matter?' he asked.

'It's a funny thing,' replied the captain. 'I was kind of hoping to be greeted here by a flock of otter-birds.'

'A flock?' asked the baron.

'Well, what would be a better collective noun for something that weird? A hybrid of otter-birds? An impossibility?'

'Well, they've gone,' sighed Holly. 'So, I guess that makes it an absence of otter-birds.'

Kia nudged Holly, as Uncle Jasper re-emerged into the light by the door to the tower, waving his trophy before ducking round the corner – just to be safe, Holly assumed. Taking a last look at the static river, he needed the reassurance of Kia squeezing his arm to murmur the words that released it from its frozen state. It eagerly set off, the waves jostling with each other in an effort to make up for lost time.

The view having lost some of its magic, Holly passively let Kia herd him and the other two along. Adjusting to the lack of light, Holly could soon make out the path that ran between lengths of well-kept lawn. On the right were the wall and the railing that skirted the road on the bridge a little way above them.

It wasn't long before they reached the point he had encountered the red-headed woman during the eclipse. Not for the first time, he wondered what had become of her, whether adding the words Omega Soya Beans to the grid had released her from her role in the Resistance, along with her agents.

The light ahead revealed a large, slightly raised rectangle of grass with rounded corners, surrounded by short trees, which bore no leaves and had recently been cut back. At first sight, this otherwise idyllic setting resembled the scene of a massacre, bodies lying everywhere, their awkward positions betraying the speed with which they were brought down. Only on closer inspection was it apparent that, as at the other end of the bridge, the soldiers were merely unconscious. There was no sign of anyone of a non-military nature.

Holly and his trio stepped blinking into the light. Making their way round the base of the bell tower, they came across the three uncles, standing in front of an unassuming door, their arms folded impatiently. Holly noticed that Uncle Jasper had been right. His piece of Restless Matter was still very much in solid mode.

A sign in the middle of the door announced the Clock Tower. Holly tried the round handle. The door was unlocked. Holly wasn't sure whether to be relieved. He squinted at the top of the tower.

'I can't hear a Bell Tower Demon,' he said, breezily. 'But I'm sure it will have its own version.'

Kia frowned, thinking this a little flippant, under the circumstances. She was right.

'Ever other!' Uncle Sid hissed, pointing over there at one of the inert bodies, suddenly not quite as inert as it had been. It was the merest twitch of a hand, but soon developed into a movement of the head.

'Pink weather guy!'

It quickly became apparent that all the others were indeed waking up.

'That's our window of opportunity closing,' Kia muttered. 'We need to get inside before they see us.'

Holly pushed the door open. The others all crowded round him and looked inside.

Expecting a dark space, they were surprised when the scene that greeted them was almost radiant, although the source of illumination was hidden. The air was thick and had an eerie glow. It moved in a constant, random slow motion, a malevolent swirl that turned Holly's stomach. He'd seen it before.

'Someone's burnt the toast,' said the captain.

As he spoke, the air started to clear, at least enough to make out a pile of sturdy planks leaning against a wall and a staircase leading upwards at the back. The steps were black. A dark red border ran along the wall above them, and above that the walls were a dingy white.

But it was only clearing around the edges of the room, the smoky air converging on its centre. In a few moments, it had formed a pulsating column, leaving the walls clearly visible, along with the glass-covered light fittings that led up the stairs.

As Holly's dread mounted, the column of smoke slowly developed arms, legs, and a head. Holly became acutely aware that there were six people crowding behind him, preventing him from backing off.

It was only when the head assumed the hazy shape of a skull with glowing yellow eyes that Holly's fear acquired a name.

CHAPTER FORTY-TWO

The skeletal face acquired a blurred hole that Holly associated with a laugh he'd hoped never to hear again. It now mirrored the open-mouthed stares from the crowd in the doorway. Even those of them who hadn't seen the Culprit for themselves had heard enough of a description to be in no doubt as to what was facing them. But each member of that crowd stood their ground, knowing that their only hope of success lay in climbing the stairs behind this deadly apparition.

The laugh Holly was dreading didn't come. Instead, the team watched transfixed as the arms developed hands, which in turn developed fingers. The wispy mouth widened into a sneer, its tendrils of smoke going in and out with the creature's breathing. As it raised its arms, the fingers condensed, the rest of the figure thinning out to provide more raw material, until they reached that hardness of steel that Holly remembered so well.

Holding these lethal weapons to the fore, the figure slowly bent its legs at the knees. The mesmerised onlookers in the doorway flinched, some of them raising their arms to deflect the imminent onslaught.

To their amazement, the only one to advance was Holly.

'As I remember,' he said, having taken two steps nearer,

'you wouldn't miss an opportunity to blow your own trumpet.'

He took two more steps.

'The only thing I recall you showing any affection for,' he continued, 'was the sound of your own voice.'

A few more steps brought him face to face with his old adversary. He had to admit he was impressed by the way that jagged aperture changed so convincingly from sneer to snarl. He raised a hand, leaving his open palm inches in front of the points of those steel cords.

'But you're not you, are you?' he whispered. 'And there is no voice to hear.'

He moved his hand forwards. It passed through the lethal digits as though they weren't there.

'Because you're not here, are you? You're just a mute image. A projection.'

He stood back, surveying the steadfastly silent mass of rage seething in front of him.

'A vision.'

The vision went briefly out of focus. Then it vanished.

The crowd behind him finally allowed themselves to breathe, which most of them did very audibly, but only when they'd come inside and closed the door behind them as quietly as they could, so as not to attract the attention of the slowly reanimating soldiers.

'O, Holly bled!' Uncle Sid was the first to reach Holly, giving him a hefty blow to the shoulder. 'Neural!'

'Unreal, indeed,' Kia agreed.

Holly noticed that, despite her best efforts to conceal it, she was far and away the least relieved after the encounter, still looking nervously around.

'False,' Uncle Jasper amplified. 'Imaginary.'

Uncle Gordo was particularly impressed.

'A-W-L R-I-T-E!' he boomed, attempting an awkward

high five with Holly.

'Fugu's done his homework,' Kia muttered. 'The Culprit and the Cloud. At least he can't come up with anything worse.'

Holly remained silent. He could think of something worse.

'But how did you know he was just blowing smoke in your eyes?' the baron asked.

'Well, it was a risk,' Holly admitted. 'But the real thing couldn't have kept his mouth shut that long if he'd wanted to. And he wouldn't have wanted to.'

This generated a certain amount of laughter. But they all started looking as nervous as Kia when they noticed that the sound of laughter quietly continued after it should have stopped.

'Very good, Mr Holly, you recognised my handiwork,' the deep voice finally said, a voice that everyone except the uncles recognised as the demonic one from the phone lying on the sofa. It seemed to be all around them, coming from an invisible tannoy system. 'But you've still got a long, long journey ahead of you. So many steps. Three hundred and thirty-four is unlikely to become your lucky number.'

'Show yourself, Fugu!' Kia shouted, nervousness changing seamlessly to anger.

But nothing appeared, not even an answer. And Kia instantly regretted having shouted, as voices started to be heard outside. Orders were being barked, all indiscernible apart from the phrases 'Intelligence says they're round here somewhere' and 'Keep looking'.

Then a voice very nearby said 'Check that door'. The three people nearest to it, Uncle Sid, Uncle Gordo, and the captain, immediately put their combined weight against it, Uncle Gordo grasping the handle to prevent it turning.

It rattled ineffectually.

'Locked, sir!' was the report.

'You two – guard it!' came the response. 'Don't let anyone in!'

'So much for intelligence,' the captain whispered.

Following Uncle Jasper's guiding signals, they quietly laid a line of the planks, end to end, from the wall opposite to the door. Adding a couple on their side made it a perfect fit. In the absence of any keys, that would at least carry on the illusion that the door was locked without having to leave their own group of sentries behind. He then had them lay another line, this one ending with a plank at a diagonal angle, wedged under the box that housed the handle. Satisfied that he could do no more with the material at hand, he waved them all towards the stairs.

Holly was ushered in front, followed by Kia, then the baron and the captain, the three uncles bringing up the rear. Holly wasn't happy with this arrangement, and he gestured insistently that Uncle Jasper join him in the vanguard. He could think of nobody better suited, and that included himself, to reacting appropriately to any given situation.

The stairwell was square, as was the space in the middle that Holly was looking up at, watching the steps continue into the darkening distance until they disappeared.

They started their ascent. The continuous right-angle turns made it impossible to keep track of their progress.

As the sound of military activity faded, they became aware of a heavy pounding, far above them. This provoked a few nervous glances and a quickening of pace. Despite not being in any hurry to find out what was causing it, they knew that it probably needed to be stopped as soon as possible.

The first feature of note they stopped at was a door marked 'Prison Room'. It was open, revealing a corridor with framed information posters along one wall.

'That's handy,' said Kia. 'At least we'll have somewhere

to put Mr Yakitori when we've finished with him.'

'Not that easy, I'm afraid,' said the baron. 'Even though the cell itself is in the tower, you can't access it from here, only from the Commons. It's exclusively for errant MPs. And on his Save The Comet ticket, I can't see Fugu keeping his deposit.'

He felt, from the suspicious looks he was getting, that knowing this piece of Westminster information demanded some explanation.

'Wally told me,' he shrugged. 'Shall we?'

They trudged on, the light starting to fade, the pounding getting louder. As Holly listened to it, it became his heartbeat. He tried even harder to ignore it.

Having covered roughly the same distance again, the next welcome distraction was another door, this one marked 'DOOR 7'. More worrying were the words 'DANGER VOID BEHIND THIS DOOR'.

'That's the weight shaft,' said the baron. 'For the weights of the clock mechanism.'

'Don't tell me,' sneered Kia, 'Wally told you.'

'I've always wondered what a void looked like,' said the captain, opening the door before anyone could stop him.

Even the most cautious of them was disappointed by the dark passage that was revealed. Having no light of its own, the first three yards were all that were visible. They could just make out a horizontal bar at waist height at the end of this, bearing the word 'DANGER'.

'Bit nothingy, aren't they, voids?' commented the captain.

Any response was prevented by a short, sharp 'Sh!' from Kia.

They listened, everyone but the bewildered captain realising that it was the absence of sound they were meant to notice. There was silence above them. But it didn't last long.

First came the sound of smashing masonry and the splintering of wood, still distant but approaching fast. Then, as they squinted up into the darkness, something loomed into view.

It was the largest bell any of them had ever seen. It filled the entire stairwell, and it was hurtling down towards them, brushing aside the steps as though they were made of polystyrene.

CHAPTER FORTY-THREE

'Get in!' shouted Holly, pushing them all through the open doorway. He made it inside himself just as several tons of bell metal flew past on its way to the ground.

It was all over in seconds. The only remaining sound was that of dust and fragments of concrete and brickwork lightly cascading past them.

'Everyone all right?' asked Holly, peering into the darkness of the passage.

'I've been better,' came the captain's voice.

As Holly grew more accustomed to the lack of light, it became apparent that the barrier across the passage had served little purpose other than to support its warning, and it had offered no resistance as the captain had been pushed through it in the general panic. He had managed to keep one foot in contact with the floor, the rest of him suspended at a forty-five-degree angle over the void he'd been so avid to see, his disappearance into that void only prevented by Uncle Gordo's grasp on the collar of the captain's jacket. The captain's eyes had also acclimatised, enough to see that the passage ended in a brick wall beyond this pit, and that the darkness beneath him had no end.

'Nice work, big man,' he said, as several hands hauled him back to relative safety. 'I've always wondered what hanging over a void felt like.' His flippancy failed him. 'That was a close one.'

'T-W-O R-I-T-E,' agreed Uncle Gordo, peering down into the gloom.

'It may be darker,' said Kia, standing in the doorway with her back to them. 'But it's no worse than this.'

They managed to crowd into the door frame so that they could all see. What they saw filled them with dismay.

The stairs were all but gone. The stairwell being square, some of the corners still showed some clue as to what had been there before, but between them was nothing. There were even large gouges out of the walls that were still trickling brick dust like tiny waterfalls. The air was starting to clear at ground level. The giant bell was slowly becoming visible, lying on its side, a beached whale.

'His curs jest,' muttered Uncle Sid.

'Bit late to start getting religious now,' commented Kia. 'Although some divine intervention wouldn't go amiss. What are you smiling at?'

Holly cleared his throat in embarrassment.

'Yes, I'm sorry,' he said. 'It just struck me that most people, being stuck on a short ledge between two vertical drops and no means of escape, would be thinking "How on earth are we going to get down?" We, on the other hand, would have no trouble getting down. I could instantly get us to the other side of the bridge, or take us all home, if needs be. But what we actually need to do is go up, and either of those options would take us back to ground level and make it impossible to reach where we need to be in time.'

'Right,' Kia summed up, still not sure it was a smiling matter. 'So there's no point going down, and no means of going up. Stalemate. We're stuck. That sounds familiar.'

'Well, at least that's ringing a bell,' said the captain. 'Even if we aren't.'

‘Ringing,’ echoed Uncle Jasper. ‘Chiming. Tolling. Resounding.’ He was shaking his head as he spoke, looking puzzled. ‘Booming.’

‘Yes, yes,’ snapped Kia. ‘They’re all things we’re not doing.’

‘No, Uncle Jasper’s got a point,’ the baron said. ‘They’re all things that bell didn’t do either.’

Getting a vehement nod from Uncle Jasper, he went and stood in the doorway, looking down.

‘Think about it,’ he went on. ‘We’re here, specifically, to ring that bell, yes? But our masked friend should just have done that for us. It should at least have chimed as it hit the ground. And smashing through all those stairs, it should have chimed at least twenty times. But it didn’t.’

‘What does that mean?’ Kia asked.

‘I hope it means… this.’

To everyone’s horror, he took a step out of the door and into the stairwell, then another. Kia squealed and snatched at him, but he was already out of reach. As far as his mortified audience was concerned, he was now suspended in mid-air, a yard from anything that might possibly have taken his weight.

Kia suddenly broke into a huge, wide-eyed grin.

‘No!’ she cried. ‘It can’t be! It’s another vision?’

‘Yes,’ said the baron, holding up a warning finger. ‘But – a vision with a difference. Fugu seems to have learnt from the last one and made sure to provide sound effects this time. I’m guessing he chucked some bricks and planks down the stairs at the same time. A silent bell crashing down wouldn’t have worked. And yet – it *was* a silent bell. He wouldn’t have wanted to replicate that sound, even if he could. That’s what gave it away.’

On his last word, the devastation vanished and the stairs reappeared, including the landing the baron was standing on. The steps showed some recent damage and were indeed strewn with the debris of bricks, a few still intact, most of them having broken up on impact.

Kia and Holly joined the baron, stepping gingerly in case the destruction had been real and it was this restoration that was the illusion.

'It must take a lot of effort to conjure all that up,' Kia murmured. 'I guess that's why it wasn't there a second longer than it had to be.'

They all slowly ventured out of the passage. The captain came out last, and he made a big show of closing the door behind him.

'Best avoided,' he told Uncle Sid, who rolled his eyes.

Kia drove them all upwards with renewed urgency.

'Let's get him before he has time to come up with anything else,' she called out.

A squared circle is still a circle, and they were all getting dizzy by the time they reached the next point of interest. A warm glow was coming from a doorway, all the more noticeable as the light in the stairwell was steadily fading the higher they got. What they saw from the doorway made them gasp.

The passage started out as nondescript as the previous one, but was longer, and had a reassuring doorway at the other end. What really made it stand out was the enormous clock face that formed one of the walls. They immediately recognized the familiar arrangement – the railway track around the outside, then the Gothic-style Roman numerals, finally the opal glass pattern at its heart.

The opposite wall held the huge circle of light bulbs which gave the face its characteristic glow. The lower six feet of this display was protected by framed chicken wire. From the middle of the circle of lights, several yards above the floor, a metal bar ran across the passage to the centre of the clock face.

'That makes the hands turn!' breathed Kia. 'This is actually one of the faces of Big Ben!'

She instantly reined in her enthusiasm.

'If it's real,' she added.

Uncles Sid and Gordo had no such qualms, and they barged past the others like kids determined not to miss out on the last two ice creams. Once inside, there was a litany of 'Oohs' and 'Aahs' as the two men bounced ecstatically off the walls and each other.

'Ten oxen!'

Uncle Sid had made it as far as the other doorway, and was pointing through it at the next clock face, his own face showing even more excitement. They both rushed off to investigate and disappeared, their appreciation still audible.

'Er, guys?' Holly called after them.

'Don't worry,' said Kia. 'They'll catch up. And I don't think we've got far to go now. If that bar turns the hands of that clock, then the mechanism must be at the other end of it.'

She was right about that. Just one more circuit of the stairs took them to a door that was slightly ajar. 'DOOR 9 – CLOCK ROOM', it announced. But she was wrong about the stragglers catching up. The team was now down to five.

This time it was Uncle Jasper who couldn't contain himself. He launched himself through the door, taking the two steps down in one stride. But then he stopped dead, causing the others to concertina into a muttering melee until they saw what had caused him to pull up so suddenly.

In the middle of the room, surrounded by a barrier, the clock mechanism, all five yards of it, sat in a frame, supported at either end by a wide, brick pillar which raised it three feet off the floor. Beneath it, there was a hole for the weights, a hole that would soon become the void that the captain had briefly been so eager to see. Just beyond and perpendicular to this, two large iron girders ran next to each other from wall to wall, taking the weight of another set of wheels and gears. And there should have been connections to the floor above, judging by the array of small, rectangular gaps in the ceiling.

But the girders were the only things to have survived. Everything else was smashed, bent, displaced, or missing. The example of scientific precision that Uncle Jasper had so looked forward to seeing now resembled a piece of experimental art. The floor inside the barrier was strewn with pieces of cogs, rivets, chains, and cast iron.

The team slowly shuffled along the wall, trying not to imagine the frenzy that must have caused such vandalism.

'That accounts for the noise, then,' said Kia, bitterly. 'Maybe if we'd got here earlier...'

'Then we'd be in bits, as well,' finished Holly.

'I am in bits, frankly,' moaned Kia. 'Without all this, we have no hope of getting those bells ringing.'

The baron surveyed the carnage with a look of disbelief.

'Even the flies are gone,' he lamented.

'What's that – like rats deserting a sinking ship?' asked the captain.

'No,' said the baron. 'The flies, or fly fans, are two large, two-bladed fans that spin noisily around to slow down the chiming. They should be up there, beneath those holes.'

Kia managed a hollow laugh.

'Wally told you a lot, didn't he?'

'Did he tell you what could have done this?' the captain asked, bending down and peering at the shards of twisted metal just beyond the barrier.

'It was an axe,' said the baron.

'You sound very confident,' said Kia. 'Seen this sort of thing before? Got a particular model of axe in mind?'

'Yes,' said the baron, quietly. 'That one.'

He pointed back at the doorway, where the weapon of choice was indeed to be seen. Holding it was someone in a motorcycle suit, head encased in a mask, eyes blazing.

CHAPTER FORTY-FOUR

All attention was on the masked figure and the mesmerising movement of the axe. Its wielder was tapping the axe head into the free, gloved hand, making a slow, regular ticking noise, the only sound to be heard.

Holly was desperately hoping this would turn out to be Olivier again, despite her group of Resistance fighters having been disbanded. The red-haired woman would have been infinitely preferable to her counterpart, Maniac-in-chief Fugu Yakitori. Despite this train of thought, or maybe because of it, Holly was the first to break free of his trance, and he did so with a frown.

'I've done way too many crosswords not to know misdirection when I see it,' he said.

This statement did nothing to calm the nerves of his companions – in fact, it may have unsettled them even more.

'Or hear it,' he went on, regardless. 'I can also remember something Wally said. He said that, surprisingly, the only sound this mechanism makes is a slow ticking.'

'That's right,' the baron joined in. 'Every two seconds. Thirty a minute.'

He nodded at the metronomic axe head.

'That sounds about right.'

'Precisely,' said Holly. 'But from where I'm standing, that ticking is actually coming from…'

He pointed at the mangled apparatus on the platform.

'…over there.'

'Another sound effect?' queried Kia. 'This time, to mask a sound that is there, rather than one that isn't?'

'I knew it all along,' claimed the captain, strutting towards the armed figure who was still tapping away impassively. 'It's all a fake. Especially our friend here. No way he's real.'

'Er, genuine – authentic,' Uncle Jasper warned, following the captain. 'Physical.'

'Nonsense,' decided the captain. 'Our visionary is imaginary. As is everything else. I'm not even sure I'm real any more.'

He placed his confident smile right in the face of the masked figure, Uncle Jasper still in close attendance. Then the smile wavered.

'Should I be able to smell a vision's breath?' he asked.

With a grunt that was all too audible, and way too low to allow any more doubt as to identity, Fugu suddenly pulled his axe back as far as it would go and swung it at the captain's head. Unable to move, the captain could only shut his eyes.

Inches from its target, the weapon suddenly encountered far more resistance than it had expected. Uncle Jasper had found another use for his petrified bit of the Thames, blocking the shaft of the axe before it could cause any injury to his petrified companion. The ensuing stand-off was evenly matched, both men straining not to give any ground to the other.

The captain opened his eyes to see what the delay was. Seeing the axe head hovering in front of his nose, still not entirely convinced of its reality, he tapped the side of it with his knuckles.

'Oh,' he said.

Distressing though this sight was for the three remaining spectators, it did bring some unexpected relief. The effort the struggle was costing the masked man meant he could no longer maintain his control over what he was making them see. The scene of mechanical carnage was gradually transformed into one of fully functional clockwork ingenuity, and with it their despair into some semblance of hope. The giant cogs were slowly turning, the fly fans reappeared above them, and steel cables ran reassuringly through their appropriate openings in the ceiling.

Roaring with disappointment at yet another failure, Fugu made one last lunge. Even inflicting a bloody nose would have been something to show for all his efforts. But the captain had seen it coming, and he was at last supplying reinforcement to the branch of Restless Matter. With a final snarl, the visionary disengaged and stood panting in front of them.

Then, to everyone's amazement, as he struggled to regain his breath, he momentarily disappeared from view. For just a split second, then another, his image flickered.

Seemingly embarrassed by these temporary lapses in existence, he fled through the open door, slamming it behind him.

'What was that?' the baron demanded. 'Was he just a vision after all?'

'Oh, no. He was definitely flesh and blood,' said the captain, giving Uncle Jasper a grateful slap on the shoulder.

But the handyman had only just noticed the fully restored clock mechanism and was beyond communication. Without having to get any closer, his eyes darted about, identifying every function, occasionally lingering over a particularly impressive feat of engineering, at which he would nod in appreciation.

'I suppose,' the captain said, jerking his thumb in the direction of the door, 'we should… follow him?'

His face betrayed that this was the last thing he wanted to do.

Indignant at being pointed at, the door's blank surface instantly became a malevolent face, its mouth contorting as though uttering silent curses, a large, hairy wart appearing where the round door handle had been.

The captain started backwards, knocking into Uncle Jasper, bringing his period of contemplative devotion to an abrupt end.

'There's your answer,' said Kia, taking the lead. 'If someone goes to such lengths to discourage you from doing something, it must be worth doing.'

She grabbed the wart and gave it a hefty twist, as the giant face writhed first in fury and pain, then in surprise, at its inability to prevent the door from opening.

Once back on the dark landing, Kia's first thought was to look down over the railing.

'What on earth has happened to Uncle…' was as far as she got.

A bright light shone in her face from one of the tall, narrow windows that punctuated two of the four walls of the stairwell – a light that moved, illuminating all their faces in succession.

'We know you're in there,' announced a voice through a megaphone. 'Give yourselves up.'

'It's the army,' the baron uttered – in a whisper, although he wasn't sure why. 'That's a helicopter.'

'They must have acquired some intelligence at last,' the captain whispered back. 'Maybe I should go and give myself up. They may think I'm working alone.'

'All seven of you,' came the amplified reply. 'You

have five minutes to make your way down and vacate the building. After that, we're coming in.'

'OK!' declared Kia, wearing a huge, forced smile. 'We step things up.'

Her enthusiasm wavered slightly at the return, above them, of the pounding noise that hadn't been the destruction of the clock mechanism after all.

Still two men down, but without the time to worry about that, the quintet hurried up the steps, away from the threat of military intervention, towards the only remaining patch of light in the darkness that was now almost complete.

They reached this light in no time. The first thing it revealed was that they had reached the top, the final landing running into a brick wall. The second was that it was coming out of a slightly open doorway on the left just before this wall, a door with a small, square window at head height, and that the door was marked 'DOOR 10 – BELFRY'. As well as the light, this was also the source of the noise.

Before they could decide what to do next, they jumped as another beam of light danced around on the wall. There was some tutting, as it turned out not to be another helicopter but Uncle Jasper's torch.

'Connection Chamber,' he was mumbling. 'Bridge Hall. Link Room.'

With a suppressed cry of triumph, he found what he was looking for. A yard out from the railing, along the last few steps, they saw a small doorway, not much more than a hatch.

Pausing only to transfer his coil of rope from around his neck to a surprised Holly's, Uncle Jasper climbed over the railing, pushed the door open and shone his torch around inside. Satisfied with what he saw, he stepped over the gap.

'Leaving, hit, ring,' he muttered to himself, recognised by the others as his version of the Going, Strike, and Chime trains of the clock mechanism as Wally had described.

Then he scrambled in and shut the door behind him, leaving a bewildered quartet wondering how to face their masked opponent.

CHAPTER FORTY-FIVE

Obviously, the first thing the four of them would have to do would be to open the door. The trouble was, for three of them, it no longer was a door.

For Holly, it was a beckoning finger, an invitation for an appointment with an arch-Maniac of largely unknown capability who stood between them and their mission of getting these bells ringing and stopping life on earth being annihilated. Oh, and keeping his wife alive.

For the baron, it represented an ending, signalling what was likely to be the last excursion of its kind, and for all he knew, the last time he'd be of any use to Kia.

For Kia, it was a portal to the possibility of a whole new way of life, an unimaginable yet tantalising existence free of the constraints of dictatorial crossword clues.

But for the captain, luckily, it was just a door, so after a quizzical look at his paralysed companions, he pushed it open and marched through, followed reluctantly by the others.

The first thing they noticed was that the light wasn't coming from the room itself, but from outside.

The space they found themselves in was square. Each of the sides consisted of seven tall arches which were open to the elements, as was obvious from the breeze that cut across from their right, strong enough to make them blink, cold enough to make their eyes water. It was these arches that admitted the light, the orange glow of the city below. Quite how far below now became apparent.

Along the arches to their right, an open, metal staircase continued upwards. Ahead of them, a few metal steps led up to a gantry that ran across to the corner diagonally opposite to where they were standing, identical steps then coming back down.

Halfway to the first steps, they saw a hole in the floor, roughly the size of a shoebox. This allowed the free passage of a steel cable, presumably coming from the Link Room where Uncle Jasper was following Wally's instructions in an effort to make the room's title a reality. A natural curiosity made their eyes follow the cable upwards. What they saw there would have rendered them speechless, had they been saying anything.

Hanging in the corners, like four giant bats sleeping peacefully with their wings wrapped round them, were bells the entire team would have sworn were the largest they had ever seen, even taking into account the one that had just missed them on its destructive way down the stairwell. They were suspended by a bewildering, sinewy arrangement of curved iron girders, their endless rows of rivets glowing in the artificial light. A hinged hammer on the nearest one was connected, via a couple of pulleys, to that steel cable from the room below.

But these bells turned out to be the runts of the litter compared to the one at their centre for which they were forming a guard of honour.

'Big Ben,' murmured Holly.

Impressive as it would have been by day, the random patches of illumination, merely suggesting its shape and size, increased the historic bell's majesty and gave it an added menace. The new arrivals could do nothing but stand in silent reverence, Holly's mixed with a heartfelt sympathy for his comrades. He was acutely aware that he was the only one to have experienced its magnificent sound, and he suddenly felt their deprivation intolerable.

Before he could issue a suitable rallying cry, or at least an imploring whisper, a movement caught their eye. It came from beyond and to one side of the giant bell.

Their eyes having adjusted slightly to the dark conditions, they could just make out the rapid descent of an axe head before they heard the now familiar loud thud, which at least cleared up one mystery.

Big Ben was closely surrounded by a square enclosure with what looked like a dark, raised floor. A path led most of the way round it, passing under the four smaller bells. The door through which they had entered was set in a brick wall which went on to form one side of this square. The other sides consisted of metal railings, roughly four-feet high, showing a wire design of open squares, with a thicker balustrade and occasional uprights, giving it the appearance of a series of panels. The railing on the side opposite the brick wall ran for the full length of the enclosure, while the two other sides each had an opening the size of one of these panels for access.

But the railings had all been bent outwards, wrenched aside by some elemental force, and now resembled the petals of a huge flower.

The axe fell three times, accompanied by grunts testifying to the effort they cost. There followed a loud groan, soon accompanied by a deafening splintering sound that went on far too long for comfort, and when that mercifully ended, a pause, then a series of irregular thumps that got quieter, commas that ended in a final, assertive full stop. The only sound left was some heavy panting.

‘You’re – too – late.’ The low, inhuman voice struggled to articulate. ‘I’ve – passed – the test.’

‘What test?’ Holly asked, trying to draw the figure out of the darkness. ‘You’ve done all this, just to prove something?’

A quiet, macabre laugh danced around them.

‘You must have – figured that out.’

He inhaled deeply, and finally regained his breath. He moved slightly to his left, allowing a shaft of light to fall on his mask.

‘You were given a team. I was given a team. Whatever threat appeared, you were given the means – even if only the vaguest chance – to overcome that threat. You set out to do that, and I’m here to thwart you. Thesis and antithesis.’

Even in the gloom, Holly could make out that Kia, the baron, and the captain were all frowning, struggling with the idea that they were all pawns in some predetermined game. He knew there was still a fight ahead, and he couldn’t allow that doubt to set in.

‘Well,’ he argued, ‘if thesis and antithesis have already been set out, why can’t we play it laterally – step outside these preordained paths and resolve our differences for the common good? What are the chances of some sort of synthesis?’

That laugh again.

‘He doesn’t do synthesis.’

Holly took a step forward.

‘Who doesn’t?’ he demanded.

‘And anyway,’ the demonic voice continued, ‘I’ve already won. These preordained paths, as you call them. In the first place, they’re not preordained. Even my self-confidence still allows for the possibility that things could have turned out very differently. And there is no “common good”. It’s not as though the outcome would be mutual destruction. I can assure you the destruction will be very one-sided.’

‘But if we…’ Holly persisted.

‘And there’s another thing you’re wrong about, Mr Solver.’

Having his title thrown at him brought Holly up sharply.

‘You think,’ Fugu acquired a mocking tone, ‘that you’re the only one to have heard this bell ringing out. But you’re not. Most of them have. I have.’

He moved towards them. They managed to stand their ground.

‘The difference between them and me? They’ve forgotten. Which makes them the lucky ones.’

He stretched his arm out in front of him, pointing the glinting axe head at the baron.

‘Be careful what you wish for.’

The baron started.

‘You mean – I was right?’ he cried. ‘We have had past lives? But how…?’

‘That’s irrelevant now,’ Fugu declared, letting his arm fall by his side, the conversational tone strangely at odds with the chilling voice. ‘It’s over. You can count your blessings you’ll never remember. I’ve won.’

Holly could tell by the look on the baron’s face that these words were having the desired, devastating effect, but he refused to treat them as anything other than disinformation.

‘What do you mean?’ he demanded, again. ‘How can it be over?’

‘That’s right,’ Kia chipped in. ‘The bells are still here. They’re all in one piece. All we have to do is get them working.’

This seemed to cheer the masked man up again.

‘The bells,’ he intoned, the voice back in ominous form, ‘may not be all they’re… cracked up to be.’

He pointed his axe at Big Ben.

‘It may be a good idea,’ he advised Holly, ‘to have a closer look.’

Holly was reluctant to comply, as it would admit that the sowing of doubt had been successful. But curiosity got the better of him.

He walked over to the gap in the twisted railing with as much nonchalance as he could manage, knowing full well that the darkness would make it a meaningless gesture. One step on to the platform would be enough to take him within striking distance of the huge bell. After a brief hesitation, keeping his peripheral vision firmly on the blade in his opponent’s hand, he lifted his foot.

A blast of cold light hit them from behind. The light had a voice, and it was coming from a megaphone.

‘Your time’s up,’ it announced. ‘We are entering the building. Please stand clear of any entrances, for your own safety.’

The helicopter hovered at their height for a moment, as though making sure the message had been received. Then it began its slow descent, taking its light with it.

But the light had done its work. It had revealed that the platform under the bell didn’t have a dark surface, as they had assumed. In fact, it had no surface at all. It was just a hole, an opening to a bottomless cavern.

Also revealed was the cause of the noises they had heard on the way up.

There had clearly been a row of sleepers, laid across the opening to take the weight of the massive bell in the event of its coming free from its mooring. All that remained of these beams were short, frayed stumps. The maniacal axe had been busy. Superhumanly busy, to Holly’s mind.

But his mind was currently more concerned with keeping his balance, the helicopter spotlight having appeared just in time to stop him putting his weight on the nothing that was under his foot. After some frantic flailing, during which he was convinced he would lose the fight, he felt a hand close around his arm, as the captain pulled him back.

Their relief was short-lived.

'Aargh! Enough!' roared Fugu, at another plan that had been diverted.

He dropped his axe, initially a relief to all present, particularly Kia, who was now the nearest to him. But that changed as he reached her in a split second, grabbing her and pinning her arms by her side. Before the others had a chance to react, he threw her effortlessly out through the open archway, directly above the swirling helicopter blades.

CHAPTER FORTY-SIX

The scene was playing out in slow motion. Holly, the baron, and the captain had inhaled sharply, the air too scared to come back out.

Kia had locked eyes with Holly as she fell. Holly was glad she couldn't see what was behind her. Despite this being the very worst scenario he could imagine, he was still dreading the reappearance of the scream that would echo the one that had given him sleepless nights for the past few weeks.

But the expected cry of anguish, when it did come, didn't come from Kia. It came from Fugu Yakitori.

The grotesque figure gave an unearthly groan and lurched across their view of the archway, sinking to his knees and clutching his head. Behind him, axe in hand, stood Kia.

'Don't you – *dare* – pull that one!' she managed to shout through gritted teeth. 'Not when he's already seen it for real.'

The three men registered a mixture of intense relief and a certain amount of embarrassment, knowing that they had been completely taken in by yet another one of Fugu's fictions. To these, the baron and the captain managed to add a dash of confusion. They had still been on Claire's cloud when Holly had told Kia about having witnessed her fall from Polarity Avenue, so they had no idea what her last remark meant. Neither man felt it was the time or the place to question it.

These emotions soon gave way to one of alarm at the sight of the axe in Kia's hands.

'What?' she said in response to this silent challenge. 'I only hit him with the blunt side.'

'Well,' Holly said with a pained expression, 'I wouldn't normally condone that, but under the circumstances, just… make sure he stays there until Uncle Jasper gets it all fixed.'

'Fixed!' came the muffled cry through the hole in the floor, followed by a fist with the thumb extended. 'Sorted!'

'He's only gone and made the connections,' said the captain.

'Nice one, Uncle Jasper!' cried Holly, making his way to the source of the voice.

'Now all we have to do,' Kia said, 'is wait a few minutes for the mechanism to do its thing.'

But in turning to address Holly, she had taken her eye off her captive. Fugu grabbed the opportunity with both hands, wrapping them around the handle of the axe she was holding. She tried to pull it free, but to no avail.

Standing up, he easily spun her round, dislodging her with a final yank and sending her careering into the baron. His axe back in one hand, he waved it slowly up and down, his malevolent gaze alternating between Holly on one side and the remainder of the team on the other.

'Not enough time for plan A,' he almost whispered. 'That monster would take more than a few minutes to dislodge. But more than enough time to find a weak spot – cables, obviously. And that's my work done. Leaving a whole hour to see to each one of you – for purely recreational purposes.'

He raised the axe, pausing to turn his head to both sides, making sure to show them it could be intended for any one of them, before starting to bring it sharply across to the vertical steel cable coming out of the hole in the floor.

But before it had a chance to make contact, its wielder vanished momentarily, just as he had done in the Clock Room. By the time he reappeared, he had finished his swing, but the axe had clattered harmlessly to the floor behind him.

He stared at his gloved hands.

'No, no, no,' he protested. 'No! Not yet!'

Holly made a grab for the axe, but came second in reaction time and found himself in retreat.

'I'm unarmed,' he declared, aware of how redundant that statement was – almost as redundant as his show of empty hands.

'Armed!' came Uncle Jasper's disembodied voice. 'Dangerous!'

Out of the hole shot his branch of Restless Matter. It cleared the floor and hovered briefly in the air, ready for Holly to take hold of it. Unfortunately, he lost that race as well. The Maniac now had a weapon in each hand.

'Way to go, Uncle Jasper,' muttered the captain.

But the man in the boiler suit had clearly done something right. A whirring noise, followed by the slow sound of a ratchet, could be heard coming from the room below. The steel cable twitched.

As did Fugu Yakitori.

'Time to go,' he declared, turning his back on Holly. 'For you three, that is.'

Using his deadly implements as extensions of his arms, he herded the trio swiftly through the open doorway and back on to the stairs. Slamming the door on them, he then buried the axe head diagonally into the architrave, making the door impossible to open, as immediately demonstrated by Kia.

'I won't be needing that any more,' he said. He waved

Uncle Jasper's prized possession in the air. 'This should do just nicely.'

After wiggling his fingers at Kia through the small window to wind her up even more, he turned back to the only other person left in the room and pointed at the great bell.

'Hammer,' he said, simply.

Holly noticed, for the first time, the hammer mechanism on Big Ben. A huge grey arm, attached to the top of the bell, followed its curved contour down, ending in a black block – rubber, Holly guessed – the size and shape of a packing chest. Just above this hammer head, a perpendicular section tapered away from the bell, eventually connecting to a steel cable that ran down to another hole in the floor.

The masked figure then moved his arm until his finger was pointing at Holly.

'Muffler,' he said.

Holly really didn't like the sound of that. He was very keen to put some distance between them but, in his haste, ended up flat on his face instead, having caught his foot on a girder. Before he had a chance to move, Fugu had his knee in his back.

'If that hammer is going to strike that bell,' he explained, in case his two-word description hadn't painted a sufficiently graphic picture, 'then I'm going to have to introduce something in between them that will deaden its sound. Of course, it may deaden that object as well, so to speak. But, for the purpose of this experiment, it makes no difference whether you are alive or not.'

So saying, he raised the shard of Restless Matter and brought it down sharply, to muffled shrieks of consternation from the other side of the door.

Holly remembered hearing that, when struck a mortal blow, it is not uncommon to feel no pain immediately. The absence of agony therefore brought him no comfort. It was only when he tried to move that he realised the shard had only gone through the collar of his jacket, pinning him to the floor.

'But there's no point having to drag a dead weight about, is there?' Fugu whispered in his ear. 'Oh! Look at that.'

He dragged Uncle Jasper's coil of rope from around Holly's neck.

'He really is a handy man, isn't he? And there was me wondering how I was going to get you all the way up there.'

Leaving his makeshift spear in place, he forced Holly's arms behind his back and quickly bound his wrists together with the end of the rope.

He was interrupted by the sound of breaking glass. Kia's elbow had lost patience with the window in the door.

'You touch him again,' she screamed, her face framed by the jagged shards, 'and you're dead!'

Fugu shook his head.

'Well, that's an empty threat,' he said calmly, in an even deeper voice than before. 'In the first place, you are in no position to carry it out. And in the second – I'm already on borrowed time. In fact, I think I may have exceeded my overdraft limit.'

He sprang to his feet, pulling Holly upright in front of him, holding the rope taut above his head. The pain in Holly's shoulders was excruciating, as was evident from his expression. He tried to force his wrists down, so that his arms could take some of the strain.

'What do you think of my puppet show?' Fugu asked Kia.

But Kia struggled to find a suitable reply, and more mechanical noises from below prevented him from waiting for one.

'Time for the final number,' he said, jostling his

marionette in the direction of the bell. 'I'm afraid the star's performance may end up a little… two-dimensional.'

He pushed Holly through the gap in the twisted railing that surrounded the great bell, right up to the edge of the featureless chasm below it.

'Bit anonymous, that drop, isn't it?' Fugu said. 'Pity it's dark, or you might have been able to appreciate the full horror of it.'

As if on cue, the entire scene was suddenly bathed in a bright, warm light from above. Holly winced, lamenting even more not having a free hand to shield his eyes.

Fugu just laughed.

'Of course, the Ayrton Light,' he confirmed. 'Parliament must be in emergency session. Global threat – but we mustn't forget to turn our little light on. Well, that's convenient. Who knew politicians could actually be useful?'

Holly didn't share this enthusiasm. Having adjusted to the light, he could now make out, all too clearly, the timber at ground level – timber that would have provided him with a sturdy surface to walk on, but was now a pile of oversized splinters a dizzyingly long way down.

'Don't worry about them,' the puppet master advised, following his gaze. 'In the first place, you would have died of a heart attack long you before you reached them. And in the second…'

He pointed at the bell's giant hammer mechanism, which twitched obligingly.

'…you have an appointment with that. I'm sure we can fit you in.'

He quickly scanned the area and the equipment available. Then he laughed again.

'So far,' he mused, 'everything has pivoted on your Mr Fixit. So let's continue that trend.'

Using his free hand, he climbed on to the railing,

keeping the tension on the rope a foot above Holly's head. The contortion in the railing allowed him to maintain his balance. He then tied that part of the rope securely to one end of the branch of Restless Matter, between two of its lateral spikes, and took hold of the other end.

A dull thud that shook the building made him stop and look over at the door.

'It's the army,' came the captain's voice. 'It looks like they've blown the bloody doors off.'

'And they'll break this door down,' Kia said, her face still in the window. 'And that'll be the end of your plan.'

The Maniac shook his head.

'They won't make it in time.'

With a loud grunt, he leapt to the top of the bell, grabbing the hammer arm. He issued a louder groan as he heaved the barbed stick on to the wide, flat surface around the bell's connection to its support, Holly still hanging from it like a prize catch on a fishing rod.

The loudest moan came from Holly, as he spun in mid-air and crashed against the side of the bell, still desperately trying to push his wrists down to take some of the pressure off his shoulders.

Fugu had no trouble making the slight adjustment that slid Holly into the small gap between the bell and the huge block of its hammer. Satisfied with his handiwork, he let go of the hammer arm, swinging contentedly from the other end of the shard, forming a pendulum.

'Perfect symmetry,' he announced. 'The balance of power, you might say. And all thanks to the generosity of the man in the boiler suit. The saviour. How ironic.'

But Holly's attention had a new focus, one even more compelling than the extreme pain in his shoulders.

The slow retraction of the hammer had started, in preparation for the strike.

CHAPTER FORTY-SEVEN

'Holly! Move! Get out of the way!'

Holly hardly needed any encouragement from Kia to remove himself from the hammer's firing line, but the only things he could move were his feet, and the heels of his shoes refused to get any purchase on the surface of the bell.

'Uncle Jasper!' shouted Kia, seeing Holly's inability to get out of harm's way. 'Stop the mechanism! Shut it down!'

'No!' Holly countermanded. 'Keep it going! You have to keep it going!'

In gratitude at being able to continue, the machinery below seemed to go into overdrive. The majority of the noise came from the rotation of the fly fans that suddenly sprang into action.

'Here we go!' shouted the masked man, swinging happily from his restless fulcrum. 'First the quarter bells, playing Handel's tune from "I know that my Redeemer liveth" – which is very apt, because I do, and he does!'

All five of the bells' hammers were now in motion. Holly made a last desperate effort to move sideways towards relative safety, but to no avail.

'All through this hour!' Fugu chanted.

'Turn it off!' Kia shouted again.

But Uncle Jasper, despite being hidden away, had

assimilated the Maniac's remarks and had correctly visualised the scene. Being a practical man, he offered the only solution he could.

'Wind style!' he bellowed through the hole in the floor.

Holly had no idea what that meant and grimaced even more. He was losing the power of his arms, and the pain was increasing.

Fugu was oblivious.

'Lord be my guide!' he went on.

Uncle Jasper was not to be deterred.

'Flatulence fashion!'

A demonic laugh came from Holly's counterweight.

But not from Holly, who suddenly realised what he was being told to do. And with that realisation came an even deeper appreciation of the team's synonym provider, a man who could always be relied upon to see what needed to be done and had the courage to carry it out, no matter how unpleasant. A saviour, indeed.

'That by thy power!' Fugu cackled, providing the third line of the inscription.

Holly was determined not to give his opponent the opportunity of completing it. He gave Kia an apologetic look. He could see that she still hadn't figured it out, and he was pleased. He knew that, for her and the others to survive, it was imperative that Big Ben be allowed to ring out. He also knew that she wouldn't see it that way.

'Gas mode,' he said.

'Holly, no!'

The branch of Restless Matter, the only thing that was keeping the two men aloft, instantly vaporised.

The giant hammer had moved quite a way, but as Holly slid down the side of the bell, he managed to raise a foot high enough to get the barest toehold on the huge, rubber block and check his descent. The Maniac was not so lucky.

Arms still in the air, he roared his frustration as both his support and his imminent victory evaporated. He had time to make a desperate swipe at the warped railings as they flashed by, but he came nowhere close.

Just as he was about to leave Kia's line of sight, she saw his image flicker, twice. This time, after the second, he did not reappear.

From the opposite side of the bell, Holly had no way of seeing this, but guessed as much from the sound, which followed the same pattern as the vision. The roar was briefly and sharply interrupted, before suddenly being silenced.

Holly felt the atmosphere change immediately with the absence of this malevolent spirit. But that relief was instantly snatched away. The hammer took another step towards striking distance, and it let go of Holly's foot.

As he slid towards the rim of the bell, Holly closed his eyes. He could already hear an inarticulate shriek coming from the other side of the door, and he didn't want that image of her face to be the last thing he saw.

He pictured her and Anna, and how happy they had looked back at the house. The idea that they would both now be safe was more than enough to reconcile himself to the course of action he knew was the only one he could have taken. He wouldn't have been able to stay with them anyway, so looking at it practically, this would make very little difference.

In fact, he could relax. He was no longer in charge, he wouldn't be called upon to solve any more clues, he would no longer have to make any more life-or-death decisions – in short, he could relinquish responsibility. That thought brought him a calmness he wasn't sure he had ever experienced before.

He was so focused on this image that he failed to hear the frantic footsteps that had been fast approaching, and with them, the return of that responsibility. He was, therefore, all the more surprised when he felt a pair of hands grab each of his arms.

Opening his eyes, he found himself still dangling over an abyss, confronted by two beaming faces.

'Handle is lost, fool,' said Uncle Sid, completing the inscription in his own way, as they pulled him to safety and untied the rope around his wrists.

'C-I-T-E F-O-U-R S-A-W A-Y-E-S,' added Uncle Gordo.

Holly smiled, weakly.

'No foot shall slide,' he croaked. 'Well said.'

'Notary!' declared the anagram expert, pointing upwards, from which Holly deduced that the two reprobates had found the backstairs to the Ayrton Light above and made their timely intervention from there.

'Holly!' came the baron's voice. 'I'm assuming you're OK, as Kia won't let us anywhere near the window, but the soldiers are just a few levels down and closing fast. You need to get as many of us out as you can.'

Happy after all to be back in problem-solving mode, Holly could see that, with the window in the door broken, it would be no trouble transporting Kia's trio and his own two rescuers, but that left an omission, one too big to contemplate.

'Uncle Jasper!' he shouted. 'Thumbs up!'

The handyman obligingly stuck his hand through the hole in the floor, making the appropriate gesture. But that hole was a long way from the door.

'Grab that hand,' Holly ordered Uncle Sid, pointing at the floor, as he made his own way to the door, casting a wary eye on the hammer of the nearest quarter bell, which didn't look like it had any further to retract.

'Grab his ankle,' he instructed Uncle Gordo, indicating

the already prostrate Uncle Sid.

Uncle Gordo similarly obliged. The combined length of the two men lying on their stomachs meant that Uncle Gordo only had to bend his leg at the knee to reach Holly's hand – the hand Kia wasn't holding in a vice-like grip through the small, shattered window.

'You've got the other two?' he asked her.

'Ow!' cried the baron.

Kia nodded.

The machinery built to a final crescendo. As Holly whispered the words that would take them away, he was curious how this disjointed human chain would appear when transposed to a different setting.

But that setting would not be home. Holly didn't feel that retreating to the safety of his own house, however keen he was to get back to Anna, was appropriate. He needed to see and hear for himself whether things would work out as they should – whether all they had been through had been worth it.

So he had used 27 Across again, the Musicians' Motto clue, taking them the short distance across the river to the other side of Westminster Bridge.

In the event, the landscape had allowed for their peculiar layout, the two uncles lying in a line on the pavement, Uncle Sid reaching out over the stairs they had taken down to the water before walking across. A few steps down, Uncle Jasper was crouched, reaching up to hold Uncle Sid's hand. They disengaged, too relieved to allow any embarrassment they might normally have felt.

Indeed, no-one seemed surprised to have landed here rather than at home. The least fazed, standing behind them just where they had left him, was Wally.

'Get on all right?' he asked.

Holly couldn't answer. He was staring into the sky, and

all the dread he had felt before came flooding back.

CHAPTER FORTY-EIGHT

The moon had disappeared. The comet's tail had shown it which way to go, but it had slunk off in the opposite direction in a last show of defiance. The young pretender was now the undisputed ruler.

Its reign looked anything but benign. Its face showed a sickly, blotchy, pale green haze, with a thin, pink frame on the side still visible to the sun that had long set. The circumference was in constant motion and seemed to boil. It might have been taken for an immense lump of jade, but all Holly could see was a giant eye, heavy with glaucoma. And it was glaring straight at him.

By now, the relief of the whole team at having escaped the tower before being put in military custody had been replaced by a stifling horror. Even with over an hour to go before the uninvited visitor redefined gatecrashing, it was clearly growing before their eyes. All they could do was stare into the sky. They remained like this in freeze-frame, listening to the very thing they didn't want to hear, a terrifying silence that seemed to go on for eternity. Holly and the baron were even oblivious to the nails Kia was digging into their arms.

In actual fact, it was less than ten seconds between their arrival on the bridge and the sounding of the first bell.

When it struck, it made them all recoil as though it had personally slapped each one of them squarely on the cheek.

The quarter bells combined to play the four melodies that were so familiar to Holly, the settings of the lines of verse that Fugu had nearly finished reciting. The rest of the team were so mesmerised by the sound that they were no longer gazing above them, but at each other.

Holly lost himself in watching their faces. From initially registering relief that the bells were ringing at all, then a certain satisfaction that every one of them had played some part in that achievement, they moved on to a look of wonder, and finally a curiosity, as though a well-buried memory was stirring. The baron threw a questioning look at the captain, who shook his head dismissively.

Only when the quarter bells finished their contribution did Kia's face cloud over.

'Is that it?' she asked, glancing up and finally letting go of her two companions. The wrecking ball in the sky had only got bigger.

Holly allowed himself a faint smile, signalled to her to be patient, and closed his eyes, ready to submerge himself completely in Big Ben's first strike.

When it came, reassuring though that was, it was far from the gentle wash of sound he was expecting. It hit him full in the stomach, setting every one of his atoms in violent motion. He gasped and opened his eyes wide. Kia's nails returned with a vengeance. Everyone else was registering the same shock.

Everyone except Wally. He was standing rigidly to attention, like an old soldier hearing the national anthem, staring at the top of the clock tower, a tear rolling down one side of his smiling face.

The interplay of the bell's harmonics became more complex, as the sound of the first strike slowly died away.

Holly had never noticed before how the individual notes in the chord danced languidly around each other. He got so lost in this choreography that the second strike took him completely by surprise, making him flinch again.

They listened, mesmerised by this musical performance that brought relief and exhilaration in equal measure. It wasn't until the fourth strike that a certain unease started to set in.

'Shouldn't it be…?' began the captain, before being hushed from all sides.

By now, they all had their eyes fixed on the diseased orb in the sky. Far from diminishing in any way, it was clearly still increasing in size, a fact that the captain could only wait until the seventh strike to bring to everyone's notice.

'Yes, but isn't it still…?'

This time it was a flurry of waved hands that silenced him. But their expressions betrayed similar misgivings. Feet were beginning to shuffle restlessly. Kia had removed her nails from Holly's arm so that she could wring her hands more feverishly with every strike.

Exchanged looks also revealed that they had noticed the appearance of a sizzling, crackling noise, the distant sound of a hundred approaching Catherine wheels going off simultaneously. By the time the tenth chime was diminishing, it was too prominent to leave any doubt.

'Isn't this bell actually making things…?'

This time the captain was cut off by the eleventh and final strike, the implication of which made it impossible even for him to carry on talking.

Nothing had changed. The eye in the sky was still growing, its attention now unbearably oppressive. As the sound of the bell slowly faded, so did everyone's optimism. They had all been counting and knew there would be no more. The last dancing harmonics waded into the turbulent wash of this new, fizzing background noise and disappeared.

Uncle Jasper looked mystified. The other two uncles were giving him a consoling pat on the shoulder. The baron wore an expression of resignation. Holly felt that his heart was going through a shredder, seeing the empty look Kia was giving him. Only Wally seemed impervious to this mood of desolation, still lost in the magical sound that had vindicated his entire life's work.

The captain opened his mouth to be the first, as always, to put their shared feelings into words, but he was interrupted before any of those words had a chance to appear.

There was a blinding flash that seemed to come from everywhere at once. The whitest sheet imaginable was momentarily thrown over everything, and then immediately whisked away, leaving them blinking in the light of the suddenly inadequate lanterns along the embankment, peering and trying to focus on objects as their vision slowly returned.

But it was the sound, or rather the collective realisation that the crackling noise had stopped, that made them all look up simultaneously.

The stars gradually became visible, aligning themselves in their familiar constellations, uninterrupted from horizon to horizon.

The comet was gone.

CHAPTER FORTY-NINE

'Move out!'

Everyone turned to Kia, despite the voice being a full octave too low. Laughing, she looked up at the railing. Beyond it, unseen, the army was obviously reassembling and making a strategic withdrawal.

By now, they were all laughing. Wally was vigorously shaking Uncle Jasper's hand while the other uncles danced about. Kia and Holly were hugging and spinning round at the same time.

The captain slapped the baron on the back. They were doubly relieved, not just to see the demise of the comet, but also to have survived the reset function of the great bell. Consequently, they were the first to swap the general euphoria for more sober reflection.

'Looks like we're still here, then,' declared the captain.

'Of course we are,' agreed the baron, shaking his head in disbelief. 'Where else would we be?'

'You don't suppose the Steed will be open, do you, what with everyone wanting to celebrate the world not having blown up?'

'Unlikely. But you know how Uncle Jasper always seems to know what's going to happen beforehand? Well, I did see him carry three cases of Bentley's home yesterday.'

'Did you now? Then, why are we still here?'

This question had occurred to everyone simultaneously. The uncles were missing their home comforts, and Holly didn't want to waste any more time getting back to a certain someone, especially if he had less than an hour before the new day returned him to solitary confinement.

Despite this, the general consensus was that the bridge above them was still worth a quick detour. They rushed up the steps, to be greeted by the last thing they had expected to see.

There was nothing to betray the visit of one army, let alone two, not even a stray rucksack. Cars were cruising in both directions. There were sporadic groups of people strolling along. It was normality. Like an extravagant birthday request, it may have been top of their wish list, but nobody really expected to see it.

One couple walked past them, giving them a contented smile, which only wavered slightly when they caught sight of the man in the boiler suit.

'They may have remembered Camille's description of you from the news,' suggested Kia when the couple had passed.

'Maybe they think you were on *Crimewatch*,' the captain added.

'Right, well, before they summon a member of the constabulary,' Holly decided, 'I think our work here is done.'

He turned to the Keeper of the Great Clock.

'Thank you, Wally,' he said. 'We couldn't have done this without you.'

He shook the man's hand, as everyone crowded round to take their leave.

'Are you all right getting back from here?' Holly asked.

'Oh, I'm not going anywhere,' the happy man replied. 'I'm here for the midnight show. Twelve strikes! And then

I'll probably stick around for one o'clock, just one mighty, solitary chime. I may never go home again!'

Giving him a final pat on the shoulder, Holly shepherded his flock down a few steps and into a dark corner, where their sudden disappearance wouldn't be noticed. Wally already had his back turned to them. Miraculous as their mode of transportation was, it wasn't the miracle he was there for.

So accustomed was the population to being confronted with mortal danger only to have it magically whisked away that, a mere fifteen minutes after the event, the disappearance of the comet had already been relegated to the third headline on the news channel.

Anna had watched it avidly, clapped her hands in jubilation when the cameras showed the night sky with only its usual inhabitants, and had then got busy. By the time the team materialised in the front room, the table was full of cans, bottles, and food.

'Triangular sandwiches,' Holly marvelled with his mouth full, when he had finally put Anna down. 'I haven't had these since…'

'Since that last, awful sports day at school,' laughed Anna. 'When Mr Collins got drunk and tried to do the limbo. We had to call an ambulance.'

Holly stopped in mid sandwich and gazed at his wife.

'I can't believe you've been here all this time,' he muttered, the muffled tone reminding him to carry on chewing.

She hugged his arm.

'I thought Zoso was going to give me away when you saw her in Lady's garden on your first visit.'

His eyes widened.

'That's it! That's where I knew that cat's name from. The symbols on that album.'

'*Led Zeppelin IV*,' she nodded. 'My favourite.'

'Of course. You were always singing that song…'

' "Going to California". Yes.'

'Well,' he said with satisfaction. 'I suppose that's another Teeny Mystery solved.'

Then he frowned.

'A cat?' he queried. 'Not a dog, after all those arguments?'

She shrugged with a smile, and he sighed.

'I never did get round to taking you to California,' he said.

'OK, people,' Kia announced. 'I think we need to see the fruits of our considerable labours first-hand. So, grab what you need and follow me outside. Move out!'

Holly made a show of struggling to decide between Anna and another sandwich, before settling on the former, receiving a punch to the shoulder for his troubles.

He was initially surprised that Kia led them out through the front door, rather than into the kitchen and then the garden. But once there, he had to admit that they had a considerably more expansive view of the sky, and that the constant flow of pedestrians walking past, smiling and nodding, leant a more communal feel to the occasion. It was quiet, the only sound being the serenade of an unseen blackbird.

A few minutes were spent in appreciation of that expansive view, revelling in its cometlessness. The clouds were considerately ruining the event for someone else far away, and the stars were treating the light pollution in the street with disdain, twinkling furiously. Their efforts were not in vain, judging by the neck ache everyone was clearly willing to endure.

'It wasn't a ball of fire after all, was it?' Kia murmured.

Holly put the arm that wasn't already holding Anna around Kia's shoulder.

'You'll always be a Moomin to me,' he said. 'And there's no shame in that.'

Standing in the middle of this trio, there was no longer any room in his mind for comets, temples, armies or bells. This group was all he needed. Knowing his time with them was limited, he didn't dare close his eyes. Instead, he looked down at three pairs of footwear, the only way he could get them all in the same view. They comprised a pair of black, patent leather, Victorian-style, laced ankle boots – Anna's favourites, Holly remembered – his own shoes, still sporting Uncle Jasper's repair work, to Holly's shame, and a pair of trainers of which Kia would undoubtedly have been very proud when they were new, a very long time ago.

This became the new tableau, seven heads craning up at the sky, one hanging forward, equally spellbound.

'A toast,' Kia suggested, bringing them all gently back to earth. 'Absent friends.'

'Too right,' agreed the captain, the first to raise his beer. 'I miss those otter-birds. Whose bright idea was it to get rid of them?'

Kia shook her head.

'Not really who I had in mind,' she said.

'You mean Faceless Taurus and Fireproof Aries?' the captain persisted. 'Creepy. Strange choice, but if you're sure…'

'No, not them, either. And not Camille,' Kia hurried on, to anticipate the captain's next suggestion.

'Ah, fair enough,' he conceded. 'That just leaves our French beans. I was going to get around to them eventually. I always leave the beans until last.'

'Resistance fighters. First. Always.'

The mournful tone carried an authority that cast a shadow over them all. It was also testament to the kind of day they'd had that no-one found it at all weird that the voice came from a gaunt, old man wearing pyjamas and slippers outdoors on a cold, winter's night. He was standing in the uncles' garden next door, just the other side of the fence. Holly assumed he must have appeared unnoticed while everyone was staring either straight up or straight down.

'Always,' agreed the captain, quietly.

Daunting though Holly found the idea of broaching this subject with this particular individual, his curiosity got the better of him.

'Forgive me,' he said, 'but that sounds personal. Do you have some connection with – that line of work?'

But the man had withdrawn into a different scenario, one that made his eyes dart around over his half-glasses, and he was no longer reachable. Uncle Gordo started making his compassionate way over to him, but Uncle Jasper held him back with a shake of the head.

'K-N-O-W?' Uncle Gordo asked, with a pained look.

'Private,' advised Uncle Jasper. 'Confidential. Personal.'

'No pearls,' echoed Uncle Sid.

'But he's quite right,' asserted Kia. 'Our Gallic friends bore the brunt of it, especially with what happened to Odile. I'm glad we could get them home. That's the least we could have done for them. The Soya Beans.'

The toast went round the group.

'And Claire,' added the baron, to unanimous agreement. 'I hope France lives up to her expectations. I don't envy it if it doesn't.'

'She will be sorely missed,' nodded Kia. 'And not just her invaluable help in solving clues.'

'Speaking of which,' Anna almost whispered to Holly. 'Do you really think this was the last crossword?'

Holly shrugged.

'You'll soon find out,' he said. 'And I'm still not sure it wouldn't be a blessing.'

He stroked Kia's head.

'I can't see being relieved of that responsibility as anything other than a good thing, and a long overdue opportunity to do something else, whatever that turns out to be. Skills have definitely been acquired which can be put to good use, even if those skills don't necessarily include solving cryptic clues.'

Kia pushed his hand away in mock indignation, and then laughed.

'The rest of the world will, of course, carry on regardless,' Holly continued. 'The select few will just have to retrain.'

The captain choked on his beer in his haste to say what had just occurred to him.

'What about Cordelia?' he asked. 'Surely not out of a job. And Nigel? All of them? Anyway, good for another toast.'

Uncle Sid, who had already had at least three times as much to drink as anyone else, raised his can as far as it would go.

'Rail code!' he announced, struggling to remember the anagram he usually used for the librarian. 'Road lice!'

Everyone cheered and raised their drinks.

'Room for another absent friend?' said another voice as the merriment died down.

They all turned in its direction, and saw Robin, standing on the pavement, leaning on the gate.

'Well, I'm not sure,' Kia smirked. 'I'd say you were a little overdue, especially on Valentine's Day.'

Robin could only hold his hands out in his defence.

'It's been a busy day.'

Holly was interested to see the mixed reaction the young man was getting. Anna was smiling, although with some effort, he thought. The captain and the baron were registering nothing one way or the other, and the uncles were mostly tutting like disapproving mother hens.

But the most noteworthy response came from the man in the pyjamas. He had instantly snapped out of his reveries and was staring intently at the new arrival, without blinking.

Kia had evidently decided she was in a forgiving mood, and was sidling slowly towards the gate, when she froze. In fact, everyone – everyone, except for the old man in his slippers – recoiled at the same moment, shocked to the core by what Robin did next.

He flickered.

CHAPTER FIFTY

'Damn. That's let the cat out of the bag sooner than I would have liked.'

'Gorgon,' muttered the old man from the other side of the fence.

Kia still couldn't move, her face a picture of dismay.

'Robin,' she faltered. 'You're not…?'

'Not Robin, as it turns out.'

The object of her affection chuckled, also not moving, still welded to the gate.

'No, that Wise Witch of yours was right, although I'm not sure even she's wise enough to know just how right.'

Uncle Sid had to be restrained at this point from taking the young upstart's head off.

'Despite organising that plot,' the lad continued, rewarding Uncle Sid with a smirk, 'the one that succeeded, where Mr Fawkes failed, until you managed to reverse it – my real name actually is Guy.'

Kia could only shake her head in disbelief.

'But your name has to be Robin,' she protested. 'The words in the grid, when I repealed you, were "Robin Goodfellow".'

'Then you're not up on your English folklore,' Guy explained, as though talking to a six-year-old. 'Robin

Goodfellow is another name for Puck, a nature sprite and mischievous prankster, which is a nickname someone gave me a very long time ago.'

'It can't have been that long ago,' muttered the baron. 'You're not old enough.'

'Oh,' Guy assured him, 'I've been around for quite a while. Even here. And the funny thing is…'

He turned back to Kia, lowering his tone for more impact.

'I didn't need repealing.'

He allowed this bombshell to find its mark, revelling in the intoxicating cocktail of emotions in Kia's face – the hurt at having been deceived, the disappointment that she hadn't even been responsible for his return, and the embarrassment of all this playing out in front of everyone.

'I was already here,' he finally went on. 'So I couldn't be solved, and I couldn't be repealed.'

Again, he left a pause for them to catch up.

'You see, the cloud had to be brought back. That was supposed to do for you all or, at very least, show you up to be failures. That's why your squeaky friend over there was stuck inside it as a statue, incentive for you to go back, although it took the arrival of Mr Sad And Lonely for you to get your collective act together.'

Uncle Gordo and Holly exchanged glances, determined not to make Uncle Sid's mistake of rising to the bait.

'In the meantime,' Guy continued, a little disappointed, 'as an extra insurance policy, we thought it would be a good idea to introduce me as a new character. If I suddenly appeared and worked my magic, only to be cruelly whisked away after a mere twenty-four hours, it would sow the seed, however deeply, of the notion of repealing someone. At the appropriate time, that idea could then be transferred to the Latitude Censor as the only way of bringing back Gordo the

Gopher. Who was so sadly missed. Boohoo.'

Holly checked to see if Kia had reached simmer yet, if not boil. But she still looked nothing but crushed.

'We?' he asked. 'Who's we?'

'So, he stuck Robin Goodfellow in the grid,' Guy went on, ignoring him. 'Which meant I had to remember to look round every time someone said "Robin". That wasn't too demanding. I've always been good at role-playing. I think that's why I was his favourite.'

'Dream on, Guy.'

A female voice floated round the hedge on the right, anticipating the appearance of its owner.

'Livvy? What…?' was all he could manage, as the woman came into view for everyone in the front garden.

She was wearing a dark, full-length coat. Her red hair shone in the street lighting.

'I was his favourite,' she went on, without breaking stride. 'You know that. That's why I get all the best parts. And why you only have a few minutes left.'

She had, by now, walked straight past her tongue-tied associate, who had performed nearly a full turn, keeping her in his sights. She gave the others a warm smile as a parting gift before vanishing behind the wall at the far end of the uncles' garden.

'And I looked better in that biker's gear than you did!' she called back.

Consumed with curiosity as they were, they were too surprised to run on to the pavement to see where she was going. In any case, that would have meant getting perilously close to Guy, who was still clinging to the gate. Nobody felt that brave.

'Oh, come on!' Guy shouted after her, having finally found his voice. 'You were just a… a phase! A dead end! That's what he called you! Aargh!'

He dismissed her and turned back in disgust, his face betraying his struggle with several demons in his head. Then, with a slight jolt, all his cares seemed to vanish.

'She was right about one thing,' he said, to no-one in particular, in his lightest tone yet. 'I am a Nutcase. At least, that's how I've been designated today, so I'll just have to accept that.'

His face clouded over, as did his voice.

'What I can't accept,' he breathed, 'is being downgraded to Mortal. And what I absolutely refuse to allow…'

He aimed his indignation at Holly.

'…is to be solved.'

He opened the gate and advanced slowly. Everyone took a small step backwards, except Kia, whose anguished expression hadn't changed since her Robin had been replaced by this Guy.

'You may have erased my team,' he went on, maintaining his relaxed beeline for Holly, 'which you were given every opportunity to do, incidentally. I even warned you this morning that the maniacs would be coming out of the woodwork, just after I pocketed this handy little thing from your mantelpiece.'

He produced the concave mirror that Uncle Jasper had shown Holly, the companion piece to the branch of Restless Matter.

'The ideal object to concentrate that Scourge Sunbeam across a bridge to spotlight your presence to those idiot soldiers. Just to make sure you missed that opportunity after all.'

He casually tossed the object to its boiler-suited owner, who caught it in one hand without breaking eye contact with the thrower.

'But I can't be dismissed that easily,' Guy continued. 'My… status, if you like, means that I do at least have until the end of the day to see to you.'

That was enough to snap Kia out of her suspended animation. She stepped in front of Holly with an expression as resolute as Guy's.

'Then you don't have long enough,' she glowered.

Guy stopped in front of her and smiled.

'Ah, now,' he said, back in conversational mode. 'I'm glad you brought that up. There's a small matter of a debt I have to call in.'

Kia managed to scowl even more.

'I don't owe you anything.'

'Well, technically, princess, I'm afraid you do.'

Pausing only to enjoy watching Kia bristle at this use of his pet name for her, he went on.

'Getting myself solved and then repealed may not have been strictly necessary, but it did have the unwanted side effect of reducing me to the role of a daily curiosity with all the other mayflies. Being repealed may have given me a year's grace, but suddenly finding myself a part of today's puzzle means the midnight deadline now applies to me. And that's where you come in.'

He waited for Kia's demand for an explanation, but she was biting her lip, denying him the satisfaction. She also knew he didn't have much time to get his point across.

'OK, then,' he sighed. 'The law of the land states, as I'm sure your soon-to-be unemployed librarian could tell you...'

He returned to the easy target of Uncle Sid, and this time he wasn't disappointed.

'...that if you repeal someone, you then owe that person an existence.'

He let that sink in for a moment, before delivering the coup de grâce.

'Even if that's at the expense of your own.'

At this point, everyone started protesting. No voice

was more prominent than any other, so not a single word could be made out. The only ones keeping their silence were Guy, a smug smile on his face, the baron, looking thoughtful and detached, and the old man in the next garden, who was nodding at the baron in encouragement. The baron caught his eye, looked surprised, and nodded back.

'Enough!' he shouted, sufficiently loudly not to have to shout it again.

He waited until there was complete silence, even from the uncles.

'As bombshells go, Guy,' he said, 'out of ten…'

He looked pointedly at Holly.

'…I'd give that an eleven.'

He wandered over and took his place between Holly and Kia, putting his hands on Kia's shoulders.

'Let's get this straight,' he insisted. 'Given that this debt is in place, after midnight, you're still here, and Kia… disappears?'

Guy shrugged.

'Law of the land,' he smirked. 'Incontestable.'

The baron shook his head.

'Not going to happen.'

Unperturbed, Guy struck a theatrical pose and adopted an appropriate voice.

'Indeed? For why, pray?'

The baron smiled.

'Well, in the first place, you may be able to cart off a princess.'

He looked down at Kia.

'But you don't mess with a queen.'

Kia blinked and went through several shades of red.

The baron turned his head, and he got the pat on the shoulder from Holly he was expecting.

'And in the second place,' he concluded, 'Kia's just gone

into receivership and been declared bankrupt.'

Holly waved his copy of the newspaper.

'The last solution,' he explained. 'We never worked out what it meant, so didn't write it in. Until now.'

Everyone leant forward, eyes open, eyebrows up, eager to be reminded of the two words – except Guy, who was squinting at Holly, his smile just a memory.

Holly pointed at the grid. It was now complete, the only missing line – starting at 11 Across, as hinted at by the baron – had been filled in.

'It was "Abandon Arrears",' he explained. 'As in "Whatever you may have owed, is now history".'

He gave the baron a more hefty slap on the back.

'Well done, baron,' he muttered.

The baron shuffled, uncomfortably.

'Game.'

The pronouncement came from the man in his pyjamas, and was aimed at the increasingly mortal nutcase.

'Set.'

Kia dismissively turned her back on Guy and ended up staring into the baron's eyes. Then she put her arms around his neck and kissed him full on the lips.

'Match.'

There was a collective intake of breath from the uncles. Anna squeezed Holly's hand.

'Ha! Well, that's told you,' the captain laughed at Guy. 'And very appropriate. I played you at tennis last week. You were rubbish.'

But the former object of Kia's affection paid no attention to him. He wasn't even looking at Kia or the baron. His eyes were fixed on Holly, eyes that started to glow a dull red. And when he spoke, it was no longer Robin's light voice, but the demonic tones of Fugu Yakitori that they had first heard over the phone and then in Big Ben.

'You think I've lost?' he rasped. 'You think I've lost everything? You don't think there's an escape route? There's always a contingency plan. A life for a life.'

He advanced on Holly. The baron moved Kia behind him, but Guy brushed past both of them. Still holding Anna's hand, Holly took a step back, holding his arm out to make sure she didn't follow him.

'There's just three minutes left,' the Maniac growled. 'And how do I know that?'

He pulled back the sleeve of his leather jacket to reveal a watch. Anna gasped when she saw the familiar, rectangular, silver face.

The baron looked equally shocked.

'Oh, that's my fault,' he said, as though that would bring her any comfort. 'I had to borrow it in St Paul's to get the tempo of that tune, and I dropped it. I can't imagine how he got hold of it.'

'I was there,' the proud wearer said, without turning round. 'I had a ringside view. I saw it fall and thought it might come in handy.'

He saw the perplexed look on Holly's face.

'I knew you'd make it to St Paul's,' he explained. 'I was waiting for you. And yes, despite a better vantage point, I did end up skydiving with the rest of you, and although I didn't make your aerobatic display team, I managed to avoid the land by using my coat as a sail. The North Sea's lovely at this time of year.'

Holly was still backing away towards the open front door, and he finally had to let go of Anna's hand.

'Holly Oak!' she pleaded, as Kia came and held her arm.

'Oh, he's about to be felled,' Guy promised her.

All three uncles had been stealthily approaching behind him, like a game of grandmother's footsteps, and were just about to make a collective pounce when, with a snarl, he made his lunge first, propelling Holly back into the house.

In the ensuing melee, the door was slammed shut and the latch went on, preventing anyone from following. The two men tussled, throwing themselves and each other around the hallway, a flurry of arms and legs.

Holly tried his best to withstand the onslaught, but ended up pinned to the wall by the foot of the stairs, despite holding his assailant by the wrists. It was clear that Guy's hands were not needed to deliver the final blow. The Maniac's eyes were now fully ablaze, and Holly couldn't look away.

'Your time's up, old man!'

Holly could hear the crackling of the flames over the sounds of Kia and Anna, shouting his name, and the pounding of several shoulders on the door.

But all he could see was fire. Fire burning into his soul. Fire stretching out to eternity.

1 F	I	2 N	A	3 L	■	4 C	R	5 O	S	6 S	W	7 O	R	8 D
A	■	U	■	U	■	O	■	M	■	C	■	R	■	R
9 N	O	T	I	C	E	D	■	10 E	X	O	T	I	C	A
T	■	C	■	I	■	E	■	G	■	U	■	G	■	W
11 A	B	A	N	D	O	N	■	12 A	R	R	E	A	R	S
S	■	S	■	L	■	A	■	■	■	G	■	M	■	■
13 T	E	E	N	Y	■	14 M	Y	15 S	T	E	R	I	E	16 S
I	■	■	■	■	■	E	■	O	■	■	■	■	■	U
17 C	A	18 M	E	19 R	A	S	H	Y	■	20 S	C	21 R	A	P
■	■	O	■	O	■	■	■	A	■	U	■	I	■	E
22 D	U	R	A	B	L	23 Y	■	24 B	O	N	J	O	U	R
R	■	T	■	O	■	U	■	E	■	B	■	T	■	H
25 E	L	A	S	T	I	C	■	26 A	V	E	R	A	G	E
A	■	L	■	I	■	C	■	N	■	A	■	C	■	R
27 M	U	S	I	C	I	A	N	S	■	28 M	O	T	T	O

CHAPTER FIFTY-ONE

Holly came to with a jolt.

The first thing he noticed was the silence. There wasn't a single sound to give him a clue as to his location. The fact that he was lying on a carpet brought him back to within a few feet of his front door.

The second thing was the darkness. He remembered the lights in the hallway had been on, so he knew he must be back in his own house.

Moving his left arm, he came across the bottom step of the staircase, giving him confirmation of where he was. With some effort, he dragged himself to his feet, and he felt the wall opposite for the light switch. It was further to the right than he had expected, so his arm was at full stretch when he found it, meaning that when he switched it on, he was surprised to find a face right in front of his.

It took him a moment to realise the face was his own. Peering at his reflection in the mirror, he had to admit there were signs of age he had been in denial about, but no more than there had been twenty-four hours ago.

It would have been so much worse, he knew, if he hadn't picked up on something the new arrival in his nightclothes had said. The old man had described the chief Maniac as a gorgon, no doubt a reference to the deadly power he could wield with his eyes. This had, in turn, triggered a memory in Holly of how Perseus had avoided being turned to stone by only looking at Medusa's eyes in the reflection of his shield – the same technique Fireproof Aries had used in the library, he'd been told.

The mirror on the hallway wall had shielded him nicely. Fortunately, Holly didn't have to deprive Guy of his head, just make him think he was on the verge of victory long enough to distract him from the fact that it wasn't Holly's time that was running out but his own.

He remembered he was holding something in his hand. Checking, it revealed that he could only have been unconscious for three minutes. He hadn't held Guy by the wrists for nothing. Staying alive may have held top spot in his list of priorities, but making damn sure he got his watch back from this loathsome individual came a close second. Anna's expression when she had seen it had settled that.

He put it on and smiled. Anna had said he would always see her face in it, and she was right. Right now, she was telling him that the best Valentine's Day ever was over. Thinking of her made the urge to open the door irresistible. He knew the front garden would be empty, but he had to see for himself.

Opening the door provided more confirmation that he was back home. The latch was off. He had put it on himself, as he was being bundled through the doorway. He'd wanted to make sure no-one could use a key to follow them. No-one else needed to be involved in that fight.

An icy blast of air hit him in the face, far colder than he was expecting. But what made him shiver was noticing that there was someone out there after all. A silhouetted figure was standing by the gate.

Panic was rising. Could Guy have followed him? Could they make that jump as well? How was that possible? He looked frantically around for any other presence, and he couldn't find one. If this was Guy, what had he done with everyone else?

The figure raised a hand and waved. Despite his surprise, Holly felt compelled to respond as courtesy demanded, but his arms had no intention of returning the gesture. Fortunately, that courtesy was fulfilled by another arm, this one appearing out of the window of a black car that chose this moment to drive hurriedly off, tyres squealing.

As the dark shape tottered towards the next gate, Holly saw with relief that it was his octogenarian neighbour, Gus. Holly hoped the uncles had left the place tidy for him, before realising that, despite being the same house, it was, of course, a totally different house.

He emerged on to his doorstep.

'Gus!' he called, surprised at himself that he was happily making so much noise in the middle of the night.

The old man, who had already covered half the distance along the path to his front door, stopped and gave Holly a broad smile.

'Exalted neighbour!' he replied, equally unperturbed by the volume.

He made his way towards the intervening fence, coming to rest in the exact space previously occupied by the man wearing pyjamas.

'You know,' he said, in more restrained tones, 'I really oughtn't to be surprised to see you. Our meetings always seem to punctuate proceedings. And now that my narrative has reached – well, not a full stop, exactly, but certainly a heavy comma – there you are! And, if I may say so, you also have a slight air of finality about you?'

Holly found himself nodding.

'I suppose so,' he said. 'But, as you say, not quite a full stop.'

They stood there for a moment, just smiling and

blinking.

'Well,' said Gus, 'time for a well-earned rest. It looks like we've both been chasing a ghost, and that's tiring work.'

Holly marvelled at how appropriate that was.

'Indeed,' he said. 'Even when you have his name. My ghost had the implausible name of Sly W Smith. But it turns out he doesn't exist.'

Gus had started on his way to his front door, but froze. Then he slowly turned back.

'Oh, but he does,' he murmured.

He looked at his neighbour with curiosity, his head to one side.

'My dear Holly,' he eventually concluded. 'It seems we've been enjoying different sides of the same adventure.'

Before Holly could demand an explanation, let alone question the suitability of the word 'enjoying', Gus had turned his back on him and was scuttling over the grass.

'No early start tomorrow,' he called over his shoulder. 'Come round at eleven, and we'll compare notes. OK? Good.'

The door closed behind him, leaving Holly disconcertingly alone.

Anna's face told him it was 12:15. Comet ground zero. Even though he had seen it disappear with his own eyes, he wouldn't have been surprised if midnight had somehow reinstated it. Even if it hadn't, there was a far more pressing issue.

If yesterday's puzzle had indeed been the final one, could the world that revolved around its presence have decided to make a few redundancies, eradicating those formerly responsible for its solution? Deprived of the reason for its very existence, might the entire contrivance indeed have been snuffed out, bursting silently like a soap bubble? Or had it been strong enough to survive?

He needed reassurance. And for once, he just might

know how to get it.

He walked inside with determination and a rising feeling of nausea. He pushed the front door to, letting it slam shut behind him, as he made his way into the living room.

He marched straight up to the mantelpiece and then stopped. Seeing the little picture frame sitting in its usual place on the corner, he faltered. Perhaps he would prefer to live with the possibility that they had all survived. That constant glimmer of hope might be better than the knowledge that he was now truly, and eternally, alone.

Three months ago, he might have found that scenario more persuasive. Now, that cowardly self-delusion would be intolerable. He reached brusquely for the frame, and then he moved it barely an inch to one side, as carefully as though it was made of the thinnest glass, revealing a small patch on the mantelpiece not covered in dust. Then he watched, not daring to breathe.

As he waited, he realised that any sign he might get would not only depend on his friends' survival, but also Kia successfully gaining access to the house through the kitchen window, no doubt having been helped over the garden fence by Uncle Jasper. Having put the latch on the door, Holly had made any entry at the front of the house impossible. He worried now that Kia may have outgrown that particular manoeuvre, not knowing how long ago her nocturnal returns had been. Or maybe the security of the house had long since been reviewed and strengthened.

He knew he was only clutching at straws, an outside chance that the absence of a sign may have another explanation than the one he was dreading. There was that cowardice, after all.

And then it came. Almost imperceptibly, the frame made a small jolt, followed by another that took it back to its starting point. Kia, at the very least, was there, and Holly had no reason to assume that all the others weren't there as well. Including Anna.

He let out one of Captain Persona's explosive laughs, staring at this miraculous little object. He moved it again, for their benefit, and watched with euphoria as it was immediately pushed back by an invisible hand, to leave the layer of dust once more uninterrupted. He wondered whether he would ever clean that off.

Peering closer at the picture, he also wondered what it was about it that set it apart. It was a tiny, black-and-white photograph, dwarfed by the dark, wooden frame around it. It took him a moment to identify it as the ultrasound image that was taken when Anna was six weeks into her pregnancy. She had excitedly given it pride of place in the room. Coming a mere three months before the car crash that had effectively ended Holly's life as well as hers, it evoked very mixed feelings in him. He couldn't bring himself to put it away, but he had also largely succeeded in blocking the image and its associations.

Considering why Kia might have the power to move this particular object took Holly back to his first meeting with the Wise Lady. Kia had denied Lady was her 'ma'. Lady had then described Holly as 'compartmentalised', which Kia had been quick to dismiss as meaning the hidden word 'mental'. But was she directing him away from another word that was also in there?

Holly remembered yesterday's conversation with Kia in the garden. He reached into his pocket and pulled out the small, dark blue notebook. Her maths work. His subject. She had said it would show her reasoning.

He turned to the inside cover and gasped. Trembling, he could just make out the inscription, the owner's name written in a childish but confident hand.

Kia Holly.

EPILOGUE

NOT IN CLEAR VIEW

BOOK FOUR OF THE CRYPTIC CHRONICLES

will finally give Holly that well-earned rest.
Just when he doesn't want it.

ACHNOWLEDGEMENTS

I'd like not to miss this opportunity to mention the two writers I think have had the most influence on me.

Firstly, Norton Juster. *The Phantom Tollbooth* should be required reading for every child. As an introduction to words and wordplay, it can't be rivalled.

And secondly, Tove Jansson. The gently surreal atmosphere she created in her Moomin stories is a reassuring haven that so-called grown-ups like myself can return to whenever necessary.

Specifically for the appearance of this book, more thanks must go again to Andrea, Gabriel, and Stefan at SpiffingCovers. Such professionalism is an increasingly rare thing and must be appreciated – indeed, shouted from the rooftops.

The last word, as always, goes to, and is, my wife, Carol.

www.ingramcontent.com/pod-product-compliance
Lightning Source LLC
Chambersburg PA
CBHW050925220726
48290CB00018B/1536

* 9 7 8 1 9 9 9 7 3 3 7 8 0 *